第08页：露西走进了老教授家的衣橱里，然后她突然发现自己置身于夜幕笼罩下的树林里，脚下白雪皑皑，头上有雪花簌簌落下。她朝着树林里发出光亮的地方走去，看到了一个路灯。

第16页：露西在树林里遇到了羊怪图姆努斯先生，从他那里知道自己来到了纳尼亚。在羊怪家里，露西吃了很多好吃的食物，并听他讲森林里各种各样有趣的故事。

第31页：到处寂静无声，仿佛这里只有埃德蒙一个人，树上连知更鸟和小松鼠都没有。树林朝四面八方延伸，埃德蒙站在空地里颤抖着。

第39页：虽然埃德蒙不喜欢这样的安排，可他也不敢违背女王的指令。他爬上了雪橇，坐在女王的脚边，女王把毛皮斗篷的一角盖在他身上，并仔细掖好。

第66页：四个孩子站在冬日的阳光下，大眼瞪小眼。身后是挂在衣钩上的大衣，面前是白雪覆盖下的树林。

第81页：海狸拿出羊怪图姆努斯先生给它的信物——一小块白色的东西，露西发现那是她送给羊怪的手绢。

第102页：“埃德蒙……埃德蒙……”孩子们和海狸夫妇喊得嗓子都哑了。但他们的呼喊声似乎都被寂静的大雪淹没了，连一点儿回声都听不到。

第113页：皎洁的月光照在雪地上，把周围的一切都照亮了，只是那些影子看上去很奇怪。如果不是月亮出来了，埃德蒙根本就找不到路。现在，他到达了另一条小河，就是刚到海狸夫妇家的时候，他们从水坝上看到的不远处与大河交汇的那条小河。

第132页：一群驯鹿身上挂着铃铛，拉着雪橇。雪橇上坐着一个人，大家一眼就认出了他——圣诞老人来了。

第156页：快要落山的夕阳照在帐篷上，发出黄色的绸缎般的光芒。帐篷顶立着一杆旗，旗面上绣着一头跃起的红色雄狮。

第171页：一人一狮在湿漉漉的草地上散步，没人能听见他们在说什么。对于埃德蒙来说，这段谈话令他终生难忘。

第193页：阿斯兰身上被捆了无数道绳子，无助地躺在石台的台面上。女巫走到阿斯兰脑袋边，表情扭曲而狰狞。但是，阿斯兰平静地望着天空，没有愤怒也没有害怕，只是显得有些悲伤。

第203页：“哦！是真的！阿斯兰是真的！”露西叫着。两个孩子扑上去，把它亲了个遍。

215页：巨人伦波布芬大步走向大门，抡起手中的大棍子，砰—砰—砰地砸了三下，大门被砸成了碎片。

第227页：在这个华美的大厅里，号角声齐鸣，阿斯兰当着所有朋友的面，庄严地为孩子们加冕，带着他们走上了四个王座。

· 卡内基大奖经典儿童系列 ·

张意妮主编

纳尼亚传奇

狮子女巫和魔衣橱

［英］C.S.路易斯◎著

高妍◎译

天津出版传媒集团

天津人民出版社

图书在版编目（CIP）数据

纳尼亚传奇．狮子女巫和魔衣橱 /（英）C.S.路易斯著；高妍译．-- 天津：天津人民出版社，2019.6
（卡内基大奖经典儿童系列 / 张意妮主编）
ISBN 978-7-201-14539-6

Ⅰ．①纳… Ⅱ．①C… ②高… Ⅲ．①儿童小说－长篇小说－英国－现代 Ⅳ．①I561.84

中国版本图书馆CIP数据核字（2019）第032713号

纳尼亚传奇：狮子女巫和魔衣橱
NANIYA CHUANQI：SHIZI NÜWU HE MOYICHU

出　　版　天津人民出版社
出 版 人　刘　庆
地　　址　天津市和平区西康路35号康岳大厦
邮政编码　300051
邮购电话　（022）23332469
网　　址　http://www.tjrmcbs.com
电子邮箱　tjrmcbs@126.com

责任编辑　陈　烨
策划编辑　鲁礼容
装帧设计　余晓琛

制版印刷　天津旭非印刷有限公司
经　　销　新华书店
开　　本　880×1230毫米　1/32
印　　张　7.75
字　　数　75千字
版次印次　2019年6月第1版　2019年6月第1次印刷
定　　价　32.00元

目录

Contents

CHAPTER ONE LUCY LOOKS INTO A WARDROBE

Once there were four children whose names were Peter, Susan, Edmund and Lucy. This story is about something that happened to them when they were sent away from London during the war because of the air-raids. They were sent to the house of an old Professor who lived in the heart of the country, ten miles from the nearest railway station and two miles from the nearest post office. He had no wife and he lived in a very large house with a housekeeper called Mrs Macready and three servants. (Their names were Ivy, Margaret and Betty, but they do not come into the story much.) He himself was a very old man with shaggy white hair which grew over most of his face as well as on his head, and they liked him almost at once; but on the first evening when he came out to meet them at the front door he was so odd-looking that Lucy (who was the youngest) was a little

第一章 露西探索魔法衣橱

很久很久以前，有四个名为彼得、苏珊、埃德蒙和露西的孩子。这个故事发生在第二次世界大战期间，他们为了躲避空袭逃离了伦敦，被送往一名老教授家。老教授的家地处偏僻的乡村，离最近的火车站有10英里[①]远，离最近的邮局也有2英里远。老教授是个单身汉，与管家麦克雷迪太太和三个仆人（分别是艾薇、玛格丽特和贝蒂，不过她们在这个故事中露面的次数不多）住在一幢大房子里。老教授的年纪很大了，他满头蓬乱的白发，连脸上也长着蓬松的白胡子。孩子们很快就喜欢上了他——但他在门

---

① 1 英里＝1.609344 千米。

afraid of him, and Edmund (who was the next youngest) wanted to laugh and had to keep on pretending he was blowing his nose to hide it.

As soon as they had said good night to the Professor and gone upstairs on the first night, the boys came into the girls' room and they all talked it over.

"We've fallen on our feet and no mistake," said Peter. "This is going to be perfectly splendid. That old chap will let us do anything we like."

"I think he's an old dear," said Susan.

"Oh, come off it!" said Edmund, who was tired and pretending not to be tired, which always made him bad-tempered. "Don't go on talking like that."

"Like what?" said Susan; "and anyway, it's time you were in bed."

"Trying to talk like Mother," said Edmund. "And who are

前迎接孩子们的那个晚上，最小的孩子露西却被他那副古怪的模样吓到了。老三埃德蒙觉得好笑，但是，为了忍住笑意，他一直在假装擤鼻涕。

当天晚上，几个孩子向老教授道了晚安上楼之后，男孩子们跑到女孩子们的房间聊天儿。

“太好了，我们现在安然无恙了，”彼得说，“在这里我们想干什么就干什么，那个老头儿根本不会管我们。”

苏珊说：“我觉得他是个可爱的老爷爷。”

“哦，别瞎说了！”埃德蒙说，他明显已经很累了，可还是装作不累，这让他总是脾气火暴，“别总像那样说话。”

“像哪样说话？”苏珊问，“再说了，你们应该上床睡觉了。”

you to say when I'm to go to bed? Go to bed yourself."

"Hadn't we all better go to bed?" said Lucy. "There's sure to be a row if we're heard talking here."

"No there won't," said Peter. "I tell you this is the sort of house where no one's going to mind what we do. Anyway, they won't hear us. It's about ten minutes' walk from here down to that dining-room, and any amount of stairs and passages in between."

"What's that noise?" said Lucy suddenly. It was a far larger house than she had ever been in before and the thought of all those long passages and rows of doors leading into empty rooms was beginning to make her feel a little creepy.

"It's only a bird, silly," said Edmund.

"It's an owl," said Peter. "This is going to be a wonderful place for birds. I shall go to bed now. I say, let's go and explore tomorrow. You might find anything in a place like this. Did you

"别总像老妈一样说话，"埃德蒙说，"你凭什么管我什么时候去睡觉？要睡你就自己睡去。"

"我们还是都去睡觉吧！"露西说，"要是让人听见我们还在聊天，会挨骂的。"

"不会的，"彼得说，"我跟你们说，在这样的房子里没人会管我们做什么，而且他们不会听见的。从这儿到饭厅要走十多分钟的路呢，中间还有好多楼梯和走廊。"

"那是什么声音？"露西突然问道。她从来没住过这么大的房子。一想到那些长长的走廊，一扇扇房门通往一个个空屋子，她就脊背发凉。

"笨蛋，只是一只鸟而已。"埃德蒙说。

"是只猫头鹰，"彼得说，"这里简直是鸟儿的天堂。我要去睡

see those mountains as we came along? And the woods? There might be eagles. There might be stags. There'll be hawks."

"Badgers!" said Lucy.

"Foxes!" said Edmund.

"Rabbits!" said Susan.

But when next morning came there was a steady rain falling, so thick that when you looked out of the window you could see neither the mountains nor the woods nor even the stream in the garden.

"Of course it would be raining!" said Edmund. They had just finished their breakfast with the Professor and were upstairs in the room he had set apart for them a long, low room with two windows looking out in one direction and two in another.

"Do stop grumbling, Ed," said Susan. "Ten to one it'll clear up in an hour or so. And in the meantime we're pretty well off. There's a wireless and lots of books."

了。我的意思是，明天我们再去探险吧。在这种房子里，什么都可能找到。来的路上你们看见那些大山了吗？还有树林？里面可能有老鹰、牡鹿、秃鹰什么的。"

"有獾！"露西说。

"有狐狸！"埃德蒙说。

"有兔子！"苏珊说。

但是，翌日清晨，外面却大雨滂沱，透过窗户完全看不见大山和树林，甚至连花园里的小溪都无法看见。

"终究还是下雨了。"埃德蒙说。他们和老教授一起吃过早餐后，来到楼上专门为他们准备的一间屋子里——屋子又窄又长，两边各有两扇分别朝内和朝外打开的窗户。

"Not for me" said Peter; "I'm going to explore in the house."

Everyone agreed to this and that was how the adventures began. It was the sort of house that you never seem to come to the end of, and it was full of unexpected places. The first few doors they tried led only into spare bedrooms, as everyone had expected that they would; but soon they came to a very long room full of pictures and there they found a suit of armour; and after that was a room all hung with green, with a harp in one corner; and then came three steps down and five steps up, and then a kind of little upstairs hall and a door that led out on to a balcony, and then a whole series of rooms that led into each other and were lined with books most of them very old books and some bigger than a Bible in a church. And shortly after that they looked into a room that was quite empty except for one big wardrobe; the sort that has a looking-glass in the door. There was

"埃德蒙，别抱怨了，"苏珊说，"没准一个小时以后天就晴了。我们现在也挺好的，有无线电广播，还有好多书。"

"对这些我可没兴趣，"彼得说，"我要在这个大房子里探险。"

大家对此表示赞同，这次探险就这样开始了。这幢房子到处都出人意料，而且似乎没有尽头。他们刚开始闯进去的几间卧室都是空荡荡的，并没有什么特别之处。随后，他们进入到一间长长的屋子，里面摆满了照片，还有一套盔甲。之后，他们又进入了一间挂满翠绿枝叶的房间，角落里还有一架竖琴。接着，他们向下走了三级台阶，又向上爬了五级台阶，来到楼上的一个小门厅，那里有一扇通往阳台的门。然后，他们进入了一串相互连通的屋子，里面堆满了书，大部分书都已经很旧了，有的书比教堂

nothing else in the room at all except a dead blue-bottle on the window-sill.

"Nothing there!" said Peter, and they all trooped out again all except Lucy. She stayed behind because she thought it would be worth while trying the door of the wardrobe, even though she felt almost sure that it would be locked. To her surprise it opened quite easily, and two mothballs dropped out.

Looking into the inside, she saw several coats hanging up mostly long fur coats. There was nothing Lucy liked so much as the smell and feel of fur. She immediately stepped into the wardrobe and got in among the coats and rubbed her face against them, leaving the door open, of course, because she knew that it is very foolish to shut oneself into any wardrobe. Soon she went further in and found that there was a second row of coats hanging up behind the first one. It was almost quite dark in there and she kept her arms stretched out in front of her so as not to bump her

里的《圣经》还要大。没过多久，他们又来到一个空荡荡的房间，里面只有一个大大的衣橱，衣橱的门上镶了一面镜子。除此之外，窗台上还有一盆枯萎了的矢车菊。

“那儿什么都没有！”彼得说。几个大孩子都匆匆地离开了，只有露西还留在屋子里。她觉得应该试一下是否能打开衣橱的门——虽然她觉得门肯定上锁了。出乎意料的是，门竟然很轻松地就打开了，从衣橱里面滚出来两个樟脑球。

往衣橱里看去，里面挂了好多长款的毛皮大衣。露西最喜欢毛皮大衣的味道和手感。于是，她立刻走进衣橱里，让自己置于毛皮大衣中间，脸蛋时不时地在上面蹭两下。当然，她一直把门敞开着，因为她知道一个人把自己关在衣橱里是十分愚蠢的。过了一会

face into the back of the wardrobe. She took a step further in then two or three steps always expecting to feel woodwork against the tips of her fingers. But she could not feel it.

"This must be a simply enormous wardrobe!" thought Lucy, going still further in and pushing the soft folds of the coats aside to make room for her. Then she noticed that there was something crunching under her feet. "I wonder is that more mothballs?" she thought, stooping down to feel it with her hand. But instead of feeling the hard, smooth wood of the floor of the wardrobe, she felt something soft and powdery and extremely cold. "This is very queer," she said, and went on a step or two further.

Next moment she found that what was rubbing against her face and hands was no longer soft fur but something hard and rough and even prickly. "Why, it is just like branches of trees!" exclaimed Lucy. And then she saw that there was a light ahead of her; not a few inches away where the back of the wardrobe ought

儿，她继续向里面探索，发现在后面还挂着一排大衣。衣橱里面黑咕隆咚的，伸手不见五指，露西伸出双手小心翼翼地向前试探，总觉得再往前走两三步就会摸到衣橱后面的木板，但却总是摸不到。

“好大的衣橱啊！”露西一边想着，一边把柔软的大衣推到一边，以便给自己腾出活动的空间。过了一会儿，脚下一阵嘎吱作响的声音引起了她的注意，“难道又是樟脑球？”她觉得很疑惑，蹲下来用手摸了摸。但她摸到的并不是衣橱光滑而坚硬的木质壁板，而是软软的、粉末状的东西，手感冰凉。“好奇怪呀，”露西心想，她又小心翼翼地往前迈了一两步。

接下来的事情变得更加奇怪，露西的脸上和手上感觉到的不再是柔软的毛皮，而是坚硬、粗糙还有些刺人的东西。“难道是树

to have been, but a long way off. Something cold and soft was falling on her. A moment later she found that she was standing in the middle of a wood at night-time with snow under her feet and snowflakes falling through the air.

Lucy felt a little frightened, but she felt very inquisitive and excited as well. She looked back over her shoulder and there, between the dark tree trunks; she could still see the open doorway of the wardrobe and even catch a glimpse of the empty room from which she had set out. (She had, of course, left the door open, for she knew that it is a very silly thing to shut oneself into a wardrobe.) It seemed to be still daylight there. "I can always get back if anything goes wrong," thought Lucy. She began to walk forward, crunch-crunch over the snow and through the wood towards the other light. In about ten minutes she reached it and found it was a lamp-post. As she stood looking at

枝吗？”露西感到十分惊讶。随即，她发现前面有光——前面几英寸[①]的地方本应该是衣橱的后壁，可现在看来并不是的。她感觉到有冰冷而柔软的东西落在身上，不一会儿，她发现自己置身于夜幕笼罩下的树林里，脚下白雪皑皑，头上有雪花簌簌落下。

露西觉得既害怕又兴奋，还非常好奇。她回头看了看身后，在黑漆漆的树林中，衣橱敞开的大门还依稀可见，甚至还能瞥见空荡荡的房间（当然了，她一直开着衣橱的门，只有蠢货才会把自己关在衣橱里）。“那里好像还有光亮。要是有什么事情发生，我可以立即跑回去。”露西心想。她继续朝着树林里发出光亮的地方走去，鞋子踩在雪地里发出“咯吱咯吱”的响声。走了大概10分钟，她来到发出光亮的地方，原来，那是一个路灯。她站在那

① 1英寸=2.54厘米。

it, wondering why there was a lamp-post in the middle of a wood and wondering what to do next, she heard a pitter patter of feet coming towards her. And soon after that a very strange person stepped out from among the trees into the light of the lamp-post.

He was only a little taller than Lucy herself and he carried over his head an umbrella, white with snow. From the waist upwards he was like a man, but his legs were shaped like a goat's (the hair on them was glossy black) and instead of feet he had goat's hoofs. He also had a tail, but Lucy did not notice this at first because it was neatly caught up over the arm that held the umbrella so as to keep it from trailing in the snow. He had a red woollen muffler round his neck and his skin was rather reddish too. He had a strange, but pleasant little face, with a short pointed beard and curly hair, and out of the hair there stuck two horns, one on each side of his forehead. One of his hands, as I have said, held the umbrella: in the other arm he carried

里，正想着为什么树林里会有路灯以及接下来要怎么办的时候，忽然听见“啪嗒啪嗒”的脚步声，并逐渐向她靠近。不一会儿，从树林里走出来一个奇怪的陌生人，径直走到了路灯下。

他比露西稍微高一点，手里撑着伞，上面落满了雪花。奇怪的是，他上半身长得是个男人的样子，下半身却长着山羊腿，腿上的毛黑油油的，脚是山羊蹄。一开始，露西并没有注意到他还长着山羊尾巴，为了防止尾巴耷拉在雪地上，他把尾巴搭在了撑着伞的胳膊上，他脖子上戴着一条红色的羊毛围巾，映衬着他的皮肤也红扑扑的。他虽然长着一张奇怪的小脸，看上去却让人很愉悦。他留着可爱的又短又尖的小胡子，卷卷的头发，额头上对称地长着两只角，没有撑伞的那只手里拿着几个棕色的纸包。看

several brown-paper parcels. What with the parcels and the snow it looked just as if he had been doing his Christmas shopping. He was a Faun. And when he saw Lucy he gave such a start of surprise that he dropped all his parcels.

"Goodness gracious me!" exclaimed the Faun.

上去，他像是为了圣诞节进行了一番大采购。这种半人半羊的生物，人们叫他为“羊怪”。羊怪看见露西时，他似乎吓了一大跳，手里的纸包散落了一地。

“哦，我的天哪！”羊怪惊叫道。

CHAPTER TWO　WHAT LUCY FOUND THERE

“Good evening,” said Lucy. But the Faun was so busy picking up its parcels that at first it did not reply. When it had finished it made her a little bow.

“Good evening, good evening,” said the Faun. “Excuse me I don’t want to be inquisitive but should I be right in thinking that you are a Daughter of Eve?”

“My namc’s Lucy,” said she, not quite understanding him.

“But you are forgive me you are what they call a girl?” said the Faun.

“Of course I’m a girl,” said Lucy.

“You are in fact Human?”

“Of course I’m human,” said Lucy, still a little puzzled.

“To be sure, to be sure,” said the Faun. “How stupid of me! But I’ve never seen a Son of Adam or a Daughter of Eve

第二章　露西的发现

“晚上好！”露西说。但是羊怪只顾着捡地上的纸包，并没有回答她。等他捡完东西，才向露西鞠了一躬。

“晚上好啊，”羊怪说，“恕我冒昧地问一句，你就是传说中的夏娃之女吗？”

露西并不是太理解他的问题，只好回答：“我叫露西。”

“抱歉，我是说，您就是他们口中所谓的小女孩吗？”羊怪问。

“对呀！我就是个小女孩呀！”露西回答说。

“所以……你是个人类？”

“我当然是人类啦！”露西还是搞不懂他想问什么。

“当然是，当然是啦！”羊怪说，“我简直笨死了！不过，我

before. I am delighted. That is to say -" and then it stopped as if it had been going to say something it had not intended but had remembered in time. "Delighted, delighted," it went on. "Allow me to introduce myself. My name is Tumnus."

"I am very pleased to meet you, Mr Tumnus," said Lucy.

"And may I ask, O Lucy Daughter of Eve," said Mr Tumnus, "how you have come into Narnia?"

"Narnia? What's that?" said Lucy.

"This is the land of Narnia," said the Faun, "where we are now; all that lies between the lamp-post and the great castle of Cair Paravel on the eastern sea. And you you have come from the wild woods of the west?"

"I I got in through the wardrobe in the spare room," said Lucy.

"Ah!" said Mr Tumnus in a rather melancholy voice, "if only I had worked harder at geography when I was a little Faun,

从来没见过亚当之子和夏娃之女。哎呀，太好了，那就是说……”话到了嘴边，羊怪却停了下来，仿佛说了什么不该说的话。“我很高兴，非常高兴，”羊怪继续道，“请允许我介绍一下自己。我叫图姆努斯。”

“很高兴认识您，图姆努斯先生。”露西说。

“冒昧地问一下，露西——夏娃之女，”羊怪问，“你是如何来到纳尼亚的？”

“纳尼亚？是什么？”露西问道。

“这片土地被人称为纳尼亚。”羊怪回答道，“从这个灯柱到东海边的凯尔·帕拉维尔城堡，都属于这个王国。请问，您是来自西边的树林吗？”

“我……我是从一间空屋子里的衣橱里来的。”露西说。

“唉，”羊怪郁闷地说，“要是我小时候努力学习地理这门课，现

I should no doubt know all about those strange countries. It is too late now."

"But they aren't countries at all," said Lucy, almost laughing. "It's only just back there at least I'm not sure. It is summer there."

"Meanwhile," said Mr Tumnus, "it is winter in Narnia, and has been for ever so long, and we shall both catch cold if we stand here talking in the snow. Daughter of Eve from the far land of Spare Oom where eternal summer reigns around the bright city of War Drobe, how would it be if you came and had tea with me?"

"Thank you very much, Mr Tumnus," said Lucy. "But I was wondering whether I ought to be getting back."

"It's only just round the corner," said the Faun, "and there'll be a roaring fire and toast and sardines and cake."

"Well, it's very kind of you," said Lucy. "But I shan't be

在就应该知道那些稀奇古怪的王国了。不过，现在说这些都晚了。"

"那不是什么王国啦！"露西差点笑了出来。"其实就是后面那里，就是……哎呀我也说不好，那里现在是夏天。"

"不过在这里，"羊怪说，"是纳尼亚的冬天。实际上，这里一年四季都是冬天，而且，如果我们一直站在雪地里这么聊天的话都会感冒的。夏娃之女，来自遥远的空屋之国，有着永恒夏天的明亮城市——衣橱之城，可否随我到家里喝一杯热茶？"

"感谢您的邀请，图姆努斯先生，"露西说，"不过我想我该回去了。"

"就在转角不远处，"羊怪说，"我家有温暖的炉火、烤面包、沙丁鱼和蛋糕。"

"谢谢，您人真好，"露西说，"不过我不能待得太久。"

able to stay long."

"If you will take my arm, Daughter of Eve," said Mr Tumnus, "I shall be able to hold the umbrella over both of us. That's the way. Now off we go."

And so Lucy found herself walking through the wood arm in arm with this strange creature as if they had known one another all their lives.

They had not gone far before they came to a place where the ground became rough and there were rocks all about and little hills up and little hills down. At the bottom of one small valley Mr Tumnus turned suddenly aside as if he were going to walk straight into an unusually large rock, but at the last moment Lucy found he was leading her into the entrance of a cave. As soon as they were inside she found herself blinking in the light of a wood fire. Then Mr Tumnus stooped and took a flaming piece of wood out of the fire with a neat little pair of tongs, and

羊怪说："夏娃之女，请抓住我的胳膊，这样，我们就能共用一把伞了。好的，我们走吧。"

就这样，露西和这个奇怪的生物手挽手地穿过树林，就好像他们是多年的老朋友似的。

没走多远，他们就来到一个地方，这里的道路崎岖不平，到处都是石头，小山丘连绵不断。在一个小山谷的谷底，图姆努斯先生突然向旁边一拐，走向了一块不寻常的大石头。走近一看，露西才明白过来，这是一个山洞的入口。进入山洞后，迎接她的是一堆明亮的篝火。图姆努斯先生蹲下身来，用一只小巧的钳子从火堆里捡出一块燃烧的木头，然后点燃了一盏灯。"马上就好。"他说着，随手把水壶放到了篝火上。

lit a lamp. "Now we shan't be long," he said, and immediately put a kettle on.

Lucy thought she had never been in a nicer place. It was a little, dry, clean cave of reddish stone with a carpet on the floor and two little chairs ("one for me and one for a friend," said Mr Tumnus) and a table and a dresser and a mantelpiece over the fire and above that a picture of an old Faun with a grey beard. In one corner there was a door which Lucy thought must lead to Mr Tumnus's bedroom, and on one wall was a shelf full of books. Lucy looked at these while he was setting out the tea things. They had titles like *The Life and Letters of Silenus* or *Nymphs and Their Ways* or *Men, Monks and Gamekeepers*; *a Study in Popular Legend* or *Is Man a Myth*?

"Now, Daughter of Eve!" said the Faun.

And really it was a wonderful tea. There was a nice brown egg, lightly boiled, for each of them, and then sardines on toast,

露西觉得这儿真是个好地方。山洞虽然小，可是干燥而整洁，到处都是红彤彤的石头，地上铺了地毯，还有两把小椅子。图姆努斯先生说一个是他自己坐，另一个给朋友坐。山洞里还有一张桌子，一个碗橱，篝火上方有个壁炉台，上面挂着一个白胡子老羊怪的照片。角落里有一扇门，露西觉得那里是图姆努斯先生的卧室。另一面墙立着一个架子，上面摆满了书。在羊怪准备茶点的时候，露西随手翻看了一下，这些书都有着奇怪的名字，比如《关于森林之神的知识和生活》《山林水泽的女神及习俗》《人、僧侣及猎场看守》《关于民间传说的研究》以及《神秘的人类》。

“好了，夏娃之女，请享用吧！”羊怪说。

茶点简直太好吃了。先是每人一个煮得很嫩的棕色鸡蛋，然后

and then buttered toast, and then toast with honey, and then a sugar-topped cake. And when Lucy was tired of eating the Faun began to talk. He had wonderful tales to tell of life in the forest. He told about the midnight dances and how the Nymphs who lived in the wells and the Dryads who lived in the trees came out to dance with the Fauns; about long hunting parties after the milk-white stag who could give you wishes if you caught him; about feasting and treasure-seeking with the wild Red Dwarfs in deep mines and caverns far beneath the forest floor; and then about summer when the woods were green and old Silenus on his fat donkey would come to visit them, and sometimes Bacchus himself, and then the streams would run with wine instead of water and the whole forest would give itself up to jollification for weeks on end. "Not that it isn't always winter now," he added gloomily. Then to cheer himself up he took out from its case on the dresser a strange little flute that looked as if it were made of

是沙丁鱼吐司，接着是黄油吐司，然后是蜂蜜拌吐司，然后是甜甜的霜糖蛋糕。当露西再也吃不下去的时候，羊怪就开始和她聊天。他给她讲森林里各种各样有趣的故事。比如：午夜时分，水中的仙女和林中的森林女神会与羊怪一起翩翩起舞；盛大的狩猎派对上如何追逐奶白色的仙鹿，无论是谁抓住了仙鹿，仙鹿都会实现那个人的愿望；红发矮人的宴会，以及与他们一起到距离地面很深的洞穴中寻宝的故事。他还讲到，夏天的时候，树林里郁郁葱葱，年老的森林之神骑着他那头大胖驴来拜访大家，有时，酒神巴库斯也会来，那时候，所有的小溪都变成了醇香浓郁的酒，整个森林接连好几周都会沉浸在狂欢的宴会中。"哪像现在啊，永远都是冬天。"他忧伤地说。为了振奋精神，他从碗橱上面的小箱子里拿出一只笛子

straw and began to play. And the tune he played made Lucy want to cry and laugh and dance and go to sleep all at the same time. It must have been hours later when she shook herself and said:

"Oh, Mr Tumnus I'm so sorry to stop you, and I do love that tune but really, I must go home. I only meant to stay for a few minutes."

"It's no good now, you know," said the Faun, laying down its flute and shaking its head at her very sorrowfully.

"No good?" said Lucy, jumping up and feeling rather frightened. "What do you mean? I've got to go home at once. The others will be wondering what has happened to me." But a moment later she asked, "Mr Tumnus! Whatever is the matter?" for the Faun's brown eyes had filled with tears and then the tears began trickling down its cheeks, and soon they were running off the end of its nose; and at last it covered its face with its hands and began to howl.

吹了起来。笛子看起来很奇怪，好像是稻草做的。羊怪吹的曲子让露西又想哭又想笑，一会儿想翩翩起舞，一会儿却又昏昏欲睡。大概过了几个小时之后，露西突然醒了过来，然后对羊怪说：

"图姆努斯先生，很抱歉打断您，我很喜欢这个曲子，不过我真的要回家了。我开始本来只想待几分钟来着。"

"可是，现在不行啊！"羊怪放下了笛子，摇着头悲伤地说。

"为什么不行？"露西被吓得跳了起来，"您说这话是什么意思？我现在要马上回家，其他人会以为我出了什么事呢。"随即，露西又问道："图姆努斯先生，您怎么了？"她看到羊怪棕色的眼睛里充满了泪水，泪水滑过他的脸颊，在鼻尖处滴落下来。随后，他双手捂着脸放声痛哭。

"Mr Tumnus! Mr Tumnus!" said Lucy in great distress. "Don't! Don't! What is the matter? Aren't you well? Dear Mr Tumnus, do tell me what is wrong." But the Faun continued sobbing as if its heart would break. And even when Lucy went over and put her arms round him and lent him her handkerchief, he did not stop. He merely took the handkerchief and kept on using it, wringing it out with both hands whenever it got too wet to be any more use, so that presently Lucy was standing in a damp patch.

"Mr Tumnus!" bawled Lucy in his ear, shaking him. "Do stop. Stop it at once! You ought to be ashamed of yourself, a great big Faun like you. What on earth are you crying about?"

"Oh oh oh!" sobbed Mr Tumnus, "I'm crying because I'm such a bad Faun."

"I don't think you're a bad Faun at all," said Lucy. "I think you are a very good Faun. You are the nicest Faun I've

"图姆努斯先生！图姆努斯先生！"露西觉得很难过，"您别这样！到底怎么了？您还好吗？亲爱的图姆努斯先生，请告诉我到底发生了什么事。"但羊怪还是不停地啜泣，哭得人心都要碎了。露西走了过去，双手环抱着他，并把自己的手绢借给他擦眼泪。但他还是哭个不停，他边哭边用手绢擦眼泪，手绢湿到不能用了就用手拧两下。不一会儿，露西脚边的一小块儿地面就变得湿漉漉的了。

"图姆努斯先生！"露西摇晃着他的身体，在他耳边大喊道，"求您别哭了！像您这么大的羊怪还哭鼻子，羞死了。您到底在哭什么呀？"

"呜，呜，呜，"羊怪抽泣道，"我哭——因为我是个大坏蛋。"

"可我觉得您根本不坏呀，"露西说，"我觉得您是个好羊怪，

ever met."

"Oh oh you wouldn't say that if you knew," replied Mr Tumnus between his sobs. "No, I'm a bad Faun. I don't suppose there ever was a worse Faun since the beginning of the world."

"But what have you done?" asked Lucy.

"My old father, now," said Mr Tumnus; "that's his picture over the mantelpiece. He would never have done a thing like this."

"A thing like what?" said Lucy.

"Like what I've done," said the Faun. "Taken service under the White Witch. That's what I am. I'm in the pay of the White Witch."

"The White Witch? Who is she?"

"Why, it is she that has got all Narnia under her thumb. It's she that makes it always winter. Always winter and never Christmas; think of that!"

是我见过的最好的羊怪。"

"你要是知道真相就不会这么说了。"羊怪一边抽泣一边说，"我是个坏羊怪，可能是从古至今最坏的一个羊怪了。"

"可您到底做了什么坏事呀？"露西问。

"就比如说我年迈的父亲吧，"羊怪说，"墙上的照片里就是他。他是绝对不会做这种事情的。"

"哪种事情啊？"露西问。

"我做的事情。"羊怪回答道，"在白女巫手下做事，这就是我做的事，我为她效劳。"

"白女巫是谁？"

"她控制着整个纳尼亚王国，是她让这里永远是寒冬，却没有圣诞节。想想吧，这是一种怎样的情况啊。"

"How awful!" said Lucy. "But what does she pay you for?"

"That's the worst of it," said Mr Tumnus with a deep groan. "I'm a kidnapper for her, that's what I am. Look at me, Daughter of Eve. Would you believe that I'm the sort of Faun to meet a poor innocent child in the wood, one that had never done me any harm, and pretend to be friendly with it, and invite it home to my cave, all for the sake of lulling it asleep and then handing it over to the White Witch?"

"No," said Lucy. "I'm sure you wouldn't do anything of the sort."

"But I have," said the Faun.

"Well," said Lucy rather slowly (for she wanted to be truthful and yet not be too hard on him), "well, that was pretty bad. But you're so sorry for it that I'm sure you will never do it again."

"Daughter of Eve, don't you understand?" said the Faun.

“简直太可怕了。”露西说，“不过，您到底为她做了些什么？”

“丧尽天良的事，”图姆努斯先生深深地叹了口气，“我为她拐骗小孩子。夏娃之女，你相信吗？我就是这样的一个大坏蛋，在林中遇到一个天真无邪的小孩子，永远都不会伤害我的那种，我假装和她很友好，邀请她来我家做客，只是为了等她睡着了之后把她交给白女巫。”

“不，”露西说，“我相信您不会做出这种事的。”

“可是我做了呀！”羊怪说。

“哦！”露西放慢了语速，她不想说谎，可也不想对他太苛刻。“那确实是很坏。但是，您为此而感到后悔、难过，我相信您以后再也不会做这种事了。”

“哦，夏娃之女，你还不明白吗？”羊怪说，“不是我之前做

"It isn't something I have done. I'm doing it now, this very moment."

"What do you mean?" cried Lucy, turning very white.

"You are the child," said Tumnus. "I had orders from the White Witch that if ever I saw a Son of Adam or a Daughter of Eve in the wood, I was to catch them and hand them over to her. And you are the first I've ever met. And I've pretended to be your friend and asked you to tea, and all the time I've been meaning to wait till you were asleep and then go and tell Her."

"Oh, but you won't, Mr Tumnus," said Lucy. "Yo won't, will you? Indeed, indeed you really mustn't."

"And if I don't," said he, beginning to cry again "she's sure to find out. And she'll have my tail cut off and my horns sawn off, and my beard plucked out, and she'll wave her wand over my beautiful clove hoofs and turn them into horrid solid hoofs like wretched horse's. And if she is extra and specially angry

过，是我现在正在做这样的事。"

"什么意思？"露西尖叫一声，脸色一下子变得煞白。

"你就是那个孩子，"羊怪说，"白女巫下令，要是我在树林中遇到了亚当之子或者夏娃之女，我要抓到他们并献给她。你是我遇见的第一个。我假装和你交朋友，并邀请你来家里喝茶，就是想等你睡着了之后把你交给白女巫。"

"您不会这么做的，图姆努斯先生，"露西说，"您不会这么做的，对吗？您不可以这么做。"

"我要是不把你交出去，"羊怪说着又哭了起来，"她肯定会发现的。到时候，她会割掉我的尾巴，锯掉我的角，拔掉我的胡子。她会挥动魔棒，把我柔软的偶蹄变成像烈马一样可怕而坚硬的单

she'll turn me into stone and I shall be only statue of a Faun in her horrible house until the four thrones at Cair Paravel are filled and goodness knows when that will happen, or whether it will ever happen at all."

"I'm very sorry, Mr Tumnus," said Lucy. "But please let me go home."

"Of course I will," said the Faun. "Of course I've got to. I see that now. I hadn't known what Humans were like before I met you. Of course I can't give you up to the Witch; not now that I know you. But we must be off at once. I'll see you back to the lamp-post. I suppose you can find your own way from there back to Spare Room and War Drobe?"

"I'm sure I can," said Lucy.

"We must go as quietly as we can," said Mr Tumnus. "The whole wood is full of her spies. Even some of the trees are on her side."

蹄。她要是雷霆大怒，就会把我变成石头，变成一座摆在她恐怖房子里的羊怪石像。直到凯尔·帕拉维尔的四个王座被人类拥有，我才会恢复自由。可谁知道这样的事哪天才会发生，或者到底会不会发生呢。"

"我很抱歉，图姆努斯先生，"露西说，"请让我回家吧！"

"当然了，"羊怪说，"我当然会让你回家。直到遇见你，我才知道人类是什么样子。我当然不会把你交给她，因为我知道你是个好孩子。但我们现在必须马上离开。我会把你送回灯柱那里。到了那儿，你就可以找到回衣橱之城、空屋之国的路了，对吗？"

"我相信我能找到的。"露西说。

"我们必须尽快赶到那里。"图姆努斯先生说，"整个树林都遍布了她的眼线。甚至有些树木都站在她那边。"

They both got up and left the tea things on the table, and Mr Tumnus once more put up his umbrella and gave Lucy his arm, and they went out into the snow. The journey back was not at all like the journey to the Faun's cave; they stole along as quickly as they could, without speaking a word, and Mr Tumnus kept to the darkest places. Lucy was relieved when they reached the lamp-post again.

"Do you know your way from here, Daughter o Eve?" said Tumnus.

Lucy looked very hard between the trees and could just see in the distance a patch of light that looked like daylight. "Yes," she said, "I can see the wardrobe door."

"Then be off home as quick as you can," said the Faun, "and c-can you ever forgive me for what meant to do?"

"Why, of course I can," said Lucy, shaking him heartily by the hand. "And I do hope you won't get into dreadful trouble on

他们匆匆起身，连茶点都没有收拾就离开了。就像来时一样，图姆努斯先生让露西挽着他的胳膊，二人共撑着一把伞走进了大雪中。回家的路和来时的路完全不同，他们默不作声，匆匆地沿着黑暗的林间小路向前小跑着。等他们好不容易到了灯柱那里，露西才算松了一口气。

"夏娃之女，你认得回家的路吗？"羊怪问。

露西仔细地看向远处的树林，看到不远处有一片光亮。她回答道："认得，我可以看见衣橱的门。"

"那么快回家吧，"羊怪说，"同时……你能原谅我之前做的事吗？"

"我当然原谅您！"露西诚恳地握着他的手说，"希望您不会因为我而遭遇不测。"

my account."

"Farewell, Daughter of Eve," said he. "Perhaps I may keep the handkerchief?"

"Rather!" said Lucy, and then ran towards the far off patch of daylight as quickly as her legs would carry her. And presently instead of rough branch brushing past her she felt coats, and instead of crunching snow under her feet she felt wooden board and all at once she found herself jumping out of the wardrobe into the same empty room from which the whole adventure had started. She shut the wardrobe door tightly behind her and looked around, panting for breath. It was still raining and she could hear the voices of the others in the passage.

"I'm here," she shouted. "I'm here. I've come back I'm all right."

"再见了，夏娃之女。"羊怪说，"我可以留着这条手绢吗？"

"当然啦！"露西说完，扭头以最快的速度奔向了那片光亮。不一会儿，她感到擦在脸上的不再是粗糙的树枝，而是柔软的大衣；当脚下不再是"咯吱咯吱"响的雪地，而是木地板时，她发现自己已经出了衣橱，站在原来那间空屋子里，也即这次奇妙探险的起点。她紧紧地关上了衣橱的门，气喘吁吁地望向周围。窗外的雨还在不停地下着，她还可以听见其他几个孩子在走廊里说话的声音。

"我在这里，"她冲着其他孩子们喊道，"我在这里，我平安回来啦！"

CHAPTER THREE EDMUND AND THE WARDROBE

Lucy ran out of the empty room into the passage and found the other three.

"It's all right," she repeated, "I've come back."

"What on earth are you talking about, Lucy?" asked Susan.

"Why?" said Lucy in amazement, "haven't you all been wondering where I was?"

"So you've been hiding, have you?" said Peter. "Poor old Lu, hiding and nobody noticed! You'll have to hide longer than that if you want people to start looking for you."

"But I've been away for hours and hours," said Lucy.

The others all stared at one another.

"Batty!" said Edmund, tapping his head. "Quite batty."

"What do you mean, Lu?" asked Peter.

第三章 埃德蒙和魔法衣橱

露西跑出了空屋，在走廊里看到了另外三个孩子。

"没事了，没事了，"她不断重复着，"我平安回来了。"

"你到底在说些什么呀，露西？"苏珊问道。

"什么？"露西吃惊地问道，"你们不是都在找我吗？"

"所以你就藏起来了，是吗？"彼得问，"可怜的露，自己藏了起来却没人发现！如果你想让别人找你，那要藏得久一点。"

"可是我已经离开好几个小时了呀！"露西说。

孩子们面面相觑。

"疯了疯了！"埃德蒙拍着脑袋叫道，"肯定是疯了！"

"露，你是什么意思啊？"彼得问。

"What I said," answered Lucy. "It was just after breakfast when I went into the wardrobe, and I've been away for hours and hours, and had tea, and all sorts of things have happened."

"Don't be silly, Lucy," said Susan. "We've only just come out of that room a moment ago, and you were there then."

"She's not being silly at all," said Peter, "she's just making up a story for fun, aren't you, Lu? And why shouldn't she?"

"No, Peter, I'm not," she said. "It's it's a magic wardrobe. There's a wood inside it, and it's snowing, and there's a Faun and a Witch and it's called Narnia, come and see."

The others did not know what to think, but Lucy was so excited that they all went back with her into the room. She rushed ahead of them, flung open the door of the wardrobe and cried, "Now! go in and see for yourselves."

露西回答道："我是说，早饭过后我就进到了衣橱里面，在里面待了好几个小时，还喝了茶，发生了好多事情。"

"别傻了，露西。"苏珊说，"我们刚刚从那个空屋子里出来，然后你就跟过来了。"

"她可不傻，"彼得说，"她只不过是编了个故事逗我们开心而已。是不是，露？不然她为什么这么说？"

"我没有编故事，彼得。"露西说，"那是，那是个魔法衣橱，里面的世界叫纳尼亚，那里有一大片树林，还一直在下雪，里面还有一个羊怪和一个女巫。快过来看！"

听她这么一说，大家更觉得莫名其妙了。但露西看上去超级兴奋，所以大家都跟着她回到了那间屋子。露西冲在最前面，"唰"地一下拉开了衣橱的门，然后冲大家叫道："你们自己进去看看！"

"Why, you goose," said Susan, putting her head inside and pulling the fur coats apart, "it's just an ordinary wardrobe; look! there's the back of it."

Then everyone looked in and pulled the coats apart; and they all saw Lucy herself saw a perfectly ordinary wardrobe. There was no wood and no snow, only the back of the wardrobe, with hooks on it. Peter went in and rapped his knuckles on it to make sure that it was solid.

"A jolly good hoax, Lu," he said as he came out again; "you have really taken us in, I must admit. We half believed you."

"But it wasn't a hoax at all," said Lucy, "really and truly. It was all different a moment ago. Honestly it was. I promise."

"Come, Lu," said Peter, "that's going a bit far. You've had your joke. Hadn't you better drop it now?"

"你真是个大笨蛋，"苏珊说着，把头伸进衣橱，推开里面挂着的毛皮大衣，"就只是个衣橱而已，看，那是衣橱的后壁。"

大家纷纷把毛皮大衣推到一边，朝里看去。所有人——包括露西自己——只看到了一个普普通通的衣橱，里面没有什么树林或者雪，只有衣橱后壁上的几个挂钩而已。彼得钻进了衣橱，用手敲了敲衣橱的后壁，确保真的只是木板。

"你可真是把大家骗得团团转啊，露，"彼得爬出衣橱说，"我必须承认，你真把我们骗到了。我们差点信了你的话。"

"我没有骗你们，"露西说，"我说的都是真的，刚才里面真的不是这个样子。我发誓，我没有说谎。"

"行了，露，"彼得说，"你可有点过了，说了谎，总是要承认的。"

Lucy grew very red in the face and tried to say something, though she hardly knew what she was trying to say, and burst into tears.

For the next few days she was very miserable. She could have made it up with the others quite easily at any moment if she could have brought herself to say that the whole thing was only a story made up for fun. But Lucy was a very truthful girl and she knew that she was really in the right; and she could not bring herself to say this. The others who thought she was telling a lie, and a silly lie too, made her very unhappy. The two elder ones did this without meaning to do it, but Edmund could be spiteful, and on this occasion he was spiteful. He sneered and jeered at Lucy and kept on asking her if she'd found any other new countries in other cupboards all over the house. What made it worse was that these days ought to have been delightful. The weather was fine and they were out of doors from morning to

露西急得满脸通红，还想要继续解释，可她也不知道要怎么解释才好，只能“哇”的一声哭了起来。

接下来的几天，露西过得悲惨极了。其实，她只要谎称自己确实只是编了故事骗大家开心，这件事也就这么过去了。但是，露西是个诚实的小女孩，她知道自己说的都是真话，她也不会因为这件事和大家说谎。不过，其他几个孩子都觉得她撒了一个特别愚蠢的谎，这让她闷闷不乐。两个大一点的孩子批评她说谎，也不是故意奚落她，但埃德蒙却针对这件事故意找茬。他好像抓住了把柄一样，总是对露西冷嘲热讽，问她有没有在这幢房子里的其他碗橱里找到新世界。本来，这几天本该高高兴兴的——天公作美，他们可以在屋子外尽情地从早玩到晚：游泳啦，钓鱼啦，爬树啦，躺在石南花丛里小憩啦。可露西却无论如何也高兴不起

night, bathing, fishing, climbing trees, and lying in the heather. But Lucy could not properly enjoy any of it. And so things went on until the next wet day.

That day, when it came to the afternoon and there was still no sign of a break in the weather, they decided to play hide-and-seek. Susan was "It" and as soon as the others scattered to hide, Lucy went to the room where the wardrobe was. She did not mean to hide in the wardrobe, because she knew that would only set the others talking again about the whole wretched business. But she did want to have one more look inside it; for by this time she was beginning to wonder herself whether Narnia and the Faun had not been a dream. The house was so large and complicated and full of hiding-places that she thought she would have time to have one look into the wardrobe and then hide somewhere else. But as soon as she reached it she heard steps in the passage outside, and then there was nothing for it but to jump

来。这样的情况一直持续到下一个阴雨天。

那天，直到下午，雨还没有要停的迹象，所以，孩子们决定在屋子里玩捉迷藏。苏珊负责“捉”，其他三个孩子负责“藏”。露西又来到了有神奇衣橱的那间屋子。她本来不想藏在衣橱里，不然，其他几个人又要开始讲起那件令她难堪的事情来。然而，她确实还想再看一眼，因为她自己都怀疑关于纳尼亚和羊怪的一切都只是个梦。这幢房子这么大，里面的结构错综复杂，肯定有很多适合躲藏的地方，她只是进去衣橱看一眼就出来，肯定还有时间藏到别的地方去。没想到，她一走到衣橱前，就听到了走廊里传来脚步声。她想都没想就躲进了衣橱里，把门轻轻掩上。她并没有将门完全关上——只有傻子才会把自己关进衣橱里，即便那就是个普通的衣橱。原来，来人是埃德蒙。他刚跑进了屋子，

into the wardrobe and hold the door closed behind her. She did not shut it properly because she knew that it is very silly to shut oneself into a wardrobe, even if it is not a magic one.

Now the steps she had heard were those of Edmund; and he came into the room just in time to see Lucy vanishing into the wardrobe. He at once decided to get into it himself not because he thought it a particularly good place to hide but because he wanted to go on teasing her about her imaginary country. He opened the door. There were the coats hanging up as usual, and a smell of mothballs, and darkness and silence, and no sign of Lucy. "She thinks I'm Susan come to catch her," said Edmund to himself, "and so she's keeping very quiet in at the back." He jumped in and shut the door, forgetting what a very foolish thing this is to do. Then he began feeling about for Lucy in the dark. He had expected to find her in a few seconds and was very surprised when he did not. He decided to open the door again and let in some light. But he could not find the door either. He

就看到露西消失在衣橱里。他立刻决定也要钻进这个衣橱，并不是因为这是个绝佳的躲藏地点，而是他还想继续嘲笑露西和她想象出来的那个世界。

埃德蒙打开衣橱的门，看到毛皮大衣还像上次那样挂在那里，还有樟脑球的味道，里面一片漆黑，寂静无声，也不见露西的踪影。“她肯定以为我是苏珊，来抓她呢，”埃德蒙自言自语道，“所以，她躲在衣橱里一言不发。”他迈进了衣橱，随手关上了门，并没有意识到把自己关在衣橱里是件多么愚蠢的事。他在黑暗中四处摸索，本以为几秒钟就可以抓到露西，却惊讶地发现并没有摸到她。他想去开门，这样就有光亮照进来，可怎么也找不到衣橱的门。埃德蒙一点儿也不喜欢这样，他在黑暗中到处乱摸，气得大喊

didn't like this at all and began groping wildly in every direction; he even shouted out, "Lucy! Lu! Where are you? I know you're here."

There was no answer and Edmund noticed that his own voice had a curious sound not the sound you expect in a cupboard, but a kind of open-air sound. He also noticed that he was unexpectedly cold; and then he saw a light.

"Thank goodness," said Edmund, "the door must have swung open of its own accord." He forgot all about Lucy and went towards the light, which he thought was the open door of the wardrobe. But instead of finding himself stepping out into the spare room he found himself stepping out from the shadow of some thick dark fir trees into an open place in the middle of a wood.

There was crisp, dry snow under his feet and more snow lying on the branches of the trees. Overhead there was pale blue sky, the sort of sky one sees on a fine winter day in the

大叫："露西！露！你在哪儿？别藏了，我知道你在这儿！"

没有人回答他，埃德蒙发现，自己叫喊的声音听起来很奇怪，不像在橱子里，而更像是在一片旷野。同时，他觉得出奇的冷，随后就看见眼前的光亮。

"谢天谢地，"埃德蒙说，"肯定是衣橱的门自己开了。"他把要找露西的事忘得一干二净，径直朝着光亮走去。他本以为那是衣橱的门，出去就是那间空屋子，但实际上他从一片浓郁的冷杉树荫里走了出来，到了林中的一片空地上。

脚下的雪又白又软，树枝上也挂满了厚厚的雪。头上是蔚蓝的天空——那种冬日清晨清透的天空，又红又亮的大太阳在他面前的树干中间缓缓升起。到处寂静无声，仿佛这里只有他一个人，

morning. Straight ahead of him he saw between the tree-trunks the sun, just rising, very red and clear. Everything was perfectly still, as if he were the only living creature in that country. There was not even a robin or a squirrel among the trees, and the wood stretched as far as he could see in every direction. He shivered.

He now remembered that he had been looking for Lucy; and also how unpleasant he had been to her about her "imaginary country" which now turned out not to have been imaginary at all. He thought that she must be somewhere quite close and so he shouted, "Lucy! Lucy! I'm here too-Edmund."

There was no answer.

"She's angry about all the things I've been saying lately," thought Edmund. And though he did not like to admit that he had been wrong, he also did not much like being alone in this strange, cold, quiet place; so he shouted again.

"I say, Lu! I'm sorry I didn't believe you. I see now you

树上连知更鸟和小松鼠都没有。树林朝四面八方延伸，埃德蒙站在空地里颤抖着。

现在，他才想起，自己进到衣橱里本来是想找露西。之前，他嘲笑过的露西“想象中的世界”，现在却真实地呈现在自己眼前。埃德蒙觉得露西肯定就在不远处，所以他叫喊道：“露西！露西！我是埃德蒙！我也在这儿！”

还是没人回答。

“她肯定是因为我最近错怪了她生气了。”埃德蒙想。虽然他不想承认自己的错误，可也不想孤零零一个人待在这样又冷又安静的奇怪地方。

所以，他继续叫喊：“露，是我！对不起，我错怪你了。我现

were right all along. Do come out. Make it Pax."

Still there was no answer.

"Just like a girl," said Edmund to himself, "sulking somewhere, and won't accept an apology." He looked round him again and decided he did not much like this place, and had almost made up his mind to go home, when he heard, very far off in the wood, a sound of bells. He listened and the sound came nearer and nearer and at last there swept into sight a sledge drawn by two reindeer.

The reindeer were about the size of Shetland ponies and their hair was so white that even the snow hardly looked white compared with them; their branching horns were gilded and shone like something on fire when the sunrise caught them. Their harness was of scarlet leather and covered with bells. On the sledge, driving the reindeer, sat a fat dwarf who would have been about three feet high if he had been standing. He was dressed in polar bear's fur and on his head he wore a red hood with a long

在知道你说的都对。别藏了，快出来吧，咱们和好吧。"

依旧没人回答。

"真是女孩子气，"埃德蒙自言自语，"不知道跑去哪里生闷气了，还不接受我的道歉。"他环顾四周，感觉一点儿都不喜欢这里，他想回家了。就在这时，埃德蒙听见从树林深处传来铃铛的声音。铃声越来越近，最后，他看见两头驯鹿拉着雪橇疾驰而来。

驯鹿看上去和谢德兰群岛的矮种马差不多大，浑身的毛竟然比雪还要白，开衩的鹿角在朝阳的映衬下红得发亮。身上的鞍具由猩红的皮革制成，上面还绑着铃铛。坐在雪橇上的马夫是个胖胖的矮人，站起来估计也就3英尺[1]高。他穿着北极熊皮做的大

① 1英尺=0.3048米。

gold tassel hanging down from its point; his huge beard covered his knees and served him instead of a rug. But behind him, on a much higher seat in the middle of the sledge sat a very different person a great lady, taller than any woman that Edmund had ever seen. She also was covered in white fur up to her throat and held a long straight golden wand in her right hand and wore a golden crown on her head. Her face was white not merely pale, but white like snow or paper or icing-sugar, except for her very red mouth. It was a beautiful face in other respects, but proud and cold and stern.

The sledge was a fine sight as it came sweeping towards Edmund with the bells jingling and the dwarf cracking his whip and the snow flying up on each side of it.

"Stop!" said the Lady, and the dwarf pulled the reindeer up so sharp that they almost sat down. Then they recovered themselves and stood champing their bits and blowing. In the

衣，头戴红色帽子，从帽尖处坠下一条长长的金色流苏，长长的胡子盖住了膝盖，看上去像是盖了条小毯子。但是，在他身后，雪橇中间高高的座椅上却坐着一个与他截然不同的女人，她比埃德蒙见过的任何女人都要高。她穿着高领的雪白大衣，右手握着一根笔直的金色魔棒，头上戴着金色皇冠。红红的嘴唇，她的脸像雪，或者说是像白纸和糖霜那样白——那是一张美丽却骄傲、冰冷又坚毅的脸庞。

精致的雪橇伴着叮当的铃声和矮人挥舞鞭子的声音朝着埃德蒙疾驰而来。雪橇经过的地方雪花飞溅，甚是好看。

“停！”那位女士喊道。矮人立刻用力地拉住驯鹿的缰绳，驯鹿差点坐到了地上。不过很快它们就恢复了过来，站在那“咯吱咯吱”地咬着嚼子，不停地喘着粗气。寒冷的空气使得驯鹿呼出

frosty air the breath coming out of their nostrils looked like smoke.

"And what, pray, are you?" said the Lady, looking hard at Edmund.

"I'm-I'm-my name's Edmund," said Edmund rather awkwardly. He did not like the way she looked at him.

The Lady frowned, "Is that how you address a Queen?" she asked, looking sterner than ever.

"I beg your pardon, your Majesty, I didn't know," said Edmund:

"Not know the Queen of Narnia?" cried she. "Ha! You shall know us better hereafter. But I repeat-what are you?"

"Please, your Majesty," said Edmund, "I don't know what you mean. I'm at school at least I was it's the holidays now."

的热气像烟雾一样。

"你是什么人？"那个女人问，目光咄咄地看着埃德蒙。

"我——呃，我——我叫埃德蒙。"埃德蒙尴尬地说。他一点儿也不喜欢这个女人看他的样子。

那个女人皱了皱眉头，"你就是这样和女王说话的吗？"她更加严厉地问。

"女王，请原谅我，我并不知道您是女王。"埃德蒙回答道。

"竟然不认识纳尼亚的女王？"她提高了声调，"之后你会认识的。现在，回答我的问题，你是什么人？"

"尊敬的女王陛下，"埃德蒙说，"我不太理解您的意思。我还在上学，不过现在放假了。"

CHAPTER FOUR TURKISH DELIGHT

"But what are you?" said the Queen again. "Are you a great overgrown dwarf that has cut off its beard?"

"No, your Majesty," said Edmund, "I never had a beard, I'm a boy."

"A boy!" said she. "Do you mean you are a Son of Adam?"

Edmund stood still, saying nothing. He was too confused by this time to understand what the question meant.

"I see you are an idiot, whatever else you may be," said the Queen. "Answer me, once and for all, or I shall lose my patience. Are you human?"

"Yes, your Majesty," said Edmund.

"And how, pray, did you come to enter my dominions?"

第四章 土耳其软糖

"回答我，你到底是什么？"女王再次问道，"你是一个剃了胡子，过度生长的矮人吗？"

"不是，陛下。"埃德蒙回答，"我就是个小男孩，从来没长过胡子。"

"小男孩！"她说，"你是亚当之子吗？"

埃德蒙愣在那，不知道怎么回答，他实在搞不懂女王到底想问什么。

"我明白了，无论是什么，你就是个白痴。"女王说，"在我失去耐心之前，我再问你一次，你是人类吗？"

"是的，陛下。"埃德蒙回答。

"那么我问你，你是如何进入我的领地的？"

"Please, your Majesty, I came in through a wardrobe."

"A wardrobe? What do you mean?"

"I I opened a door and just found myself here, your Majesty," said Edmund.

"Ha!" said the Queen, speaking more to herself than to him. "A door. A door from the world of men! I have heard of such things. This may wreck all. But he is only one, and he is easily dealt with." As she spoke these words she rose from her seat and looked Edmund full in the face, her eyes flaming; at the same moment she raised her wand. Edmund felt sure that she was going to do something dreadful but he seemed unable to move. Then, just as he gave himself up for lost, she appeared to change her mind.

"My poor child," she said in quite a different voice, "how cold you look! Come and sit with me here on the sledge and I will put my mantle round you and we will talk."

"回女王陛下，我是从一个衣橱里进来的。"

"衣橱？什么意思？"

"陛下，我——我就是打开了衣橱的门，进来之后就发现自己在这儿了。"埃德蒙说。

"原来如此！"女王像是在自言自语，"一扇门，一扇通向人类世界的大门！我以前听说过这事，这下可糟糕了。不过没关系，他孤身一人，很容易对付。"说着，女王站了起来，死死地盯着埃德蒙，眼中放出恶狠狠的光芒，并举起了魔杖。埃德蒙觉得她肯定要做一些可怕的事情，他被吓得定住了，动弹不得。就在他觉得自己要死的时候，女王一下子改变了主意。

"哦！我可怜的孩子，"她的语气180度大转弯，"瞧你冻得！快过来和我一起坐在雪橇上，你可以盖着我的斗篷取暖，我们聊

Edmund did not like this arrangement at all but he dared not disobey; he stepped on to the sledge and sat at her feet, and she put a fold of her fur mantle round him and tucked it well in.

"Perhaps something hot to drink?" said the Queen. "Should you like that?"

"Yes please, your Majesty," said Edmund, whose teeth were chattering.

The Queen took from somewhere among her wrappings a very small bottle which looked as if it were made of copper. Then, holding out her arm, she let one drop fall from it on the snow beside the sledge. Edmund saw the drop for a second in mid-air, shining like a diamond. But the moment it touched the snow there was a hissing sound and there stood a jewelled cup full of something that steamed. The dwarf immediately took this and handed it to Edmund with a bow and a smile; not a very nice smile. Edmund felt much better as he began to sip the hot drink.

聊天。"

虽然埃德蒙不喜欢这样的安排，可他也不敢违背女王的指令。他爬上了雪橇，坐在女王的脚边，女王把毛皮斗篷的一角盖在他身上，并仔细掖好。

"要不要来点热饮？"女王问，"你喜欢热饮吗？"

"喜欢，女王陛下。"埃德蒙冻得牙齿打战。

女王不知道从哪里掏出一个小小的瓶子，看上去像是铜制的。然后，她伸出手臂，从小瓶子里倒出一滴液体，滴在了雪橇旁边的雪地上。埃德蒙发现，这滴液体在落地之前像钻石一样闪闪发亮，落在地上发出"滋滋"的响声，随后变成了一个宝石茶杯，里面装满了热气腾腾的饮料。驾驶雪橇的矮人马上把杯子递给了埃德蒙，还一脸谄媚地给他鞠了个躬。埃德蒙嘬了一口，瞬间感

It was something he had never tasted before, very sweet and foamy and creamy, and it warmed him right down to his toes.

"It is dull, Son of Adam, to drink without eating," said the Queen presently. "What would you like best to eat?"

"Turkish Delight, please, your Majesty," said Edmund.

The Queen let another drop fall from her bottle on to the snow, and instantly there appeared a round box, tied with green silk ribbon, which, when opened, turned out to contain several pounds of the best Turkish Delight. Each piece was sweet and light to the very centre and Edmund had never tasted anything more delicious. He was quite warm now, and very comfortable.

While he was eating the Queen kept asking him questions. At first Edmund tried to remember that it is rude to speak with one's mouth full, but soon he forgot about this and thought only of trying to shovel down as much Turkish Delight as he could, and the more he ate the more he wanted to eat, and he never

觉好多了。他从来没尝过这种饮料，甜甜腻腻的，泡沫特别多，顿时觉得从头到脚都暖和起来。

"只喝热饮未免太单调了，亚当之子，"女王和蔼地说，"你最喜欢吃什么？"

"土耳其软糖，女王陛下。"埃德蒙说。

女王又从小瓶子里倒出来一滴液体，滴在雪地上后瞬间变成了一个圆盒子，上面还系着绿丝带。打开盒子，里面装着好几磅[①]最好的土耳其软糖。每一颗都柔软香甜，埃德蒙从没吃过这么好吃的软糖。他现在感觉非常暖和，也非常舒适。

埃德蒙一边吃，女王一边问他问题。刚开始的时候，他觉得嘴里塞满东西讲话非常不礼貌。可是不一会儿，他就忘得一干二

① 1 磅 = 0.4536 千克。

asked himself why the Queen should be so inquisitive. She got him to tell her that he had one brother and two sisters, and that one of his sisters had already been in Narnia and had met a Faun there, and that no one except himself and his brother and his sisters knew anything about Narnia. She seemed especially interested in the fact that there were four of them, and kept on coming back to it. "You are sure there are just four of you?" she asked. "Two Sons of Adam and two Daughters of Eve, neither more nor less?" and Edmund, with his mouth full of Turkish Delight, kept on saying, "Yes, I told you that before," and forgetting to call her "Your Majesty", but she didn't seem to mind now.

At last the Turkish Delight was all finished and Edmund was looking very hard at the empty box and wishing that she would ask him whether he would like some more. Probably the Queen knew quite well what he was thinking; for she knew,

净，只想着多吃些土耳其软糖。他越吃越停不下来，却从来没有想过为什么女王要问这么多问题。最后，他把一切都告诉了女王，比如，他们兄弟姐妹一共四人，他有一个妹妹，一个哥哥和一个姐姐。妹妹之前来过一次纳尼亚，还认识了一只羊怪，而且只有他们四个孩子知道纳尼亚的事情。女王对这四个兄弟姐妹非常感兴趣，还不停地问："你确定只有你们四个？两名亚当之子，两名夏娃之女？不多不少就四个？"埃德蒙嘴里塞满了糖，回答道："当然，都跟你说过了。"他并没有称呼其为"女王陛下"，但她似乎一点儿也不在意。

最后，埃德蒙把盒子里所有的土耳其软糖都吃光了，可还是眼巴巴地看着空盒子，希望女王能再给他一些。女王似乎十分了

though Edmund did not, that this was enchanted Turkish Delight and that anyone who had once tasted it would want more and more of it, and would even, if they were allowed, go on eating it till they killed themselves.

But she did not offer him any more. Instead, she said to him, "Son of Adam, I should so much like to see your brother and your two sisters. Will you bring them to see me?"

"I'll try," said Edmund, still looking at the empty box.

"Because, if you did come again bringing them with you of course I'd be able to give you some more Turkish Delight. I can't do it now, the magic will only work once. In my own house it would be another matter."

"Why can't we go to your house now?" said Edmund. When he had first got on to the sledge he had been afraid that she might drive away with him to some unknown place from which he would not be able to get back; but he had forgotten about that

解他在想什么，虽然埃德蒙不知道，但她很清楚这些土耳其软糖被施了魔法，他只要吃了一块就再也停不下来了，甚至到最后会被活活撑死。

但是，女王并没有给他更多的软糖，而是说："亚当之子，我非常希望认识你的几个兄弟姐妹。你可以带他们来见我吗？"

"我试试吧！"埃德蒙一边说，一边望着空空如也的盒子。

"如果你下次再来，把他们也一起带来，我会给你更多的土耳其软糖。可我现在给不了你，这种魔法只能使用一次。不过，在我家里的话情况就不一样了。"

"为什么现在不去你家呢？"埃德蒙问。刚坐上雪橇的时候，他特别害怕女王会把他带到陌生的地方，永远都回不去了。可现

fear now.

"It is a lovely place, my house," said the Queen. "I am sure you would like it. There are whole rooms full of Turkish Delight, and what's more, I have no children of my own. I want a nice boy whom I could bring up as a Prince and who would be King of Narnia when I am gone. While he was Prince he would wear a gold crown and eat Turkish Delight all day long; and you are much the cleverest and handsomest young man I've ever met. I think I would like to make you the Prince some day, when you bring the others to visit me."

"Why not now?" said Edmund. His face had become very red and his mouth and fingers were sticky. He did not look either clever or handsome, whatever the Queen might say.

"Oh, but if I took you there now," said she, "I shouldn't see your brother and your sisters. I very much want to know your charming relations. You are to be the Prince and later

在，他一点儿也不害怕。

"我住在一幢美丽的房子里，"女王说，"你肯定会喜欢。屋子里堆满了土耳其软糖。我自己没有孩子，可我一直想要一个可爱的小男孩，把他当成王子抚养成人，在我仙逝后他可以继承王位，成为纳尼亚的国王。作为王子，他会头戴金色王冠，每天都可以吃土耳其软糖。你是我见过最聪明，最漂亮的小男子汉，我想让你成为王子。你把他们带来的时候，就是你成为王子的时候。"

"为什么不是现在？"埃德蒙问。他的小脸通红，嘴上和手指上都黏糊糊的。无论女王如何夸他，事实上，他可绝对不聪明，也不漂亮。

"如果我现在带你回家，"女王说，"我就见不到你的兄弟姐妹

on the King; that is understood. But you must have courtiers and nobles. I will make your brother a Duke and your sisters Duchesses."

"There's nothing special about them," said Edmund, "and, anyway, I could always bring them some other time."

"Ah, but once you were in my house," said the Queen, "you might forget all about them. You would be enjoying yourself so much that you wouldn't want the bother of going to fetch them. No. You must go back to your own country now and come to me another day, with them, you understand. It is no good coming without them."

"But I don't even know the way back to my own country," pleaded Edmund. "That's easy," answered the Queen. "Do you see that lamp?" She pointed with her wand and Edmund turned and saw the same lamp-post under which Lucy had met the Faun. "Straight on, beyond that, is the way to the World of Men.

了。我非常想了解你的家庭。你会成为王子——未来的国王，同时你手下也要有大臣和贵族。我会册封他们为公爵和公爵夫人。"

"可他们也没什么特别的，"埃德蒙说，"无论怎样，我以后可以随时带他们来。"

"可是，一旦到了我家，"女王说，"你很有可能会把他们都忘掉。到时，你过上了无忧无虑的生活，就不想再回去带他们过来见我。所以，不行，你现在必须回到你的国家去，过几天，带着你的兄弟姐妹来找我。记住，你自己一个人来可不行！"

"可我根本就不知道回家的路。"埃德蒙开始找借口。这时，女王说，"这很简单，你看见那盏灯了吗？"女王用魔杖指向不远处，埃德蒙回头便看见了那根灯柱，就是之前露西和羊怪见面的地方。"一直走，过了那根灯柱，就是通往人类世界的路。你再看

And now look the other way'here she pointed in the opposite direction and tell me if you can see two little hills rising above the trees."

"I think I can," said Edmund.

"Well, my house is between those two hills. So next time you come you have only to find the lamp-post and look for those two hills and walk through the wood till you reach my house. But remember you must bring the others with you. I might have to be very angry with you if you came alone."

"I'll do my best," said Edmund.

"And, by the way," said the Queen, "you needn't tell them about me. It would be fun to keep it a secret between us two, wouldn't it? Make it a surprise for them. Just bring them along to the two hills a clever boy like you will easily think of some excuse for doing that and when you come to my house you could just say "Let's see who lives here" or something like that. I am

另一边，”说着她指向了反方向，“看到树林中耸起的两座小山了吗？”

“看见了。”埃德蒙说。

“我的家就在两座山之间。下次你再来的时候，只要找到那根灯柱，朝着小山的方向穿过树林，就能找到我家。但是，记住，一定要带着其他几个人一起来。不然的话，我会非常生气。”

“我尽力吧。”埃德蒙说。

女王继续说：“还有，不要告诉他们关于我的事情。这算是我们两个之间的小秘密，好吗？到时候，可以吓他们一跳。你要做的就是把他们带到两山之间。像你这么聪明的孩子，应该很容易想到借口。来到我家之后，你可以说‘看看谁住在这里呀’之类的话。我认为这是最好的介绍我出场的方式。如果你的妹妹已经见过一只

sure that would be best. If your sister has met one of the Fauns, she may have heard strange stories about me nasty stories that might make her afraid to come to me. Fauns will say anything, you know, and now -"

"Please, please," said Edmund suddenly, "please couldn't I have just one piece of Turkish Delight to eat on the way home?"

"No, no," said the Queen with a laugh, "you must wait till next time." While she spoke, she signalled to the dwarf to drive on, but as the sledge swept away out of sight, the Queen waved to Edmund, calling out, "Next time! Next time! Don't forget. Come soon."

Edmund was still staring after the sledge when he heard someone calling his own name, and looking round he saw Lucy coming towards him from another part of the wood.

"Oh, Edmund!" she cried. "So you've got in too! Isn't it wonderful, and now-"

羊怪，她可能会从羊怪那里听到很多关于我的不好的故事，这会让她害怕而不想见我。你要知道，羊怪的话不可信。那么现在——"

"求求你了，"埃德蒙突然插话，"可不可以再给我一块土耳其软糖，我想在回家路上吃？"

"这可不行，"女王大笑着说，"想要吃软糖，要等下次再说。"女王一边说着，一边打手势让矮人继续赶路。雪橇疾驰而去，女王冲埃德蒙挥手喊道："下一次！下一次！别忘了，过几天一定来！"

埃德蒙呆望着雪橇远去的方向，这时，听到有人叫他的名字。他回过头，发现露西从树林的另一个方向朝他跑来。

"埃德蒙！"她叫道，"原来你也在这！这里是不是很棒！现在——"

“All right,” said Edmund, “I see you were right and it is a magic wardrobe after all. I’ll say I’m sorry if you like. But where on earth have you been all this time? I’ve been looking for you everywhere.”

“If I’d known you had got in I’d have waited for you,” said Lucy, who was too happy and excited to notice how snappishly Edmund spoke or how flushed and strange his face was. “I’ve been having lunch with dear Mr Tumnus, the Faun, and he’s very well and the White Witch has done nothing to him for letting me go, so he thinks she can’t have found out and perhaps everything is going to be all right after all.”

“The White Witch?” said Edmund; “who’s she?”

“She is a perfectly terrible person,” said Lucy. “She calls herself the Queen of Narnia though she has no right to be queen at all, and all the Fauns and Dryads and Naiads and Dwarfs and Animals at least all the good ones simply hate her. And she

“好吧，”埃德蒙说，“看来关于魔法衣橱什么的，你说的都是真的。你要是想听的话，对不起喽。可是你刚才到底跑到哪里去了？我一直在到处找你。”

露西现在太高兴、太兴奋了，以至于完全没注意到埃德蒙烦躁的语气、通红的面颊和古怪的表情。她回答道：“我要是知道你也来，肯定会等你的。刚才我和图姆努斯先生一起吃了午饭，就是那只羊怪。他现在好得很，完全没有因为放我走而被白女巫责罚。他觉得白女巫根本没发现，所以，以后他也不会遇到什么麻烦。”

“白女巫？她是谁？”埃德蒙问。

“她是个特别可怕的大坏蛋。”露西说，“她称自己为纳尼亚女王，虽然她根本没资格当女王。所有的那些羊怪、树中的神灵、

can turn people into stone and do all kinds of horrible things. And she has made a magic so that it is always winter in Narnia always winter, but it never gets to Christmas. And she drives about on a sledge, drawn by reindeer, with her wand in her hand and a crown on her head."

Edmund was already feeling uncomfortable from having eaten too many sweets, and when he heard that the Lady he had made friends with was a dangerous witch he felt even more uncomfortable. But he still wanted to taste that Turkish Delight again more than he wanted anything else.

"Who told you all that stuff about the White Witch?" he asked.

"Mr Tumnus, the Faun," said Lucy.

"You can't always believe what Fauns say," said Edmund, trying to sound as if he knew far more about them than Lucy.

"Who said so?" asked Lucy.

水中的仙女、矮人和小动物，凡是好心肠的，都无比憎恨她。她把人们变成石头，并做了很多可怕的事。她在这里施了魔法，把纳尼亚变成永远的冬天，还没有圣诞节。她坐着驯鹿拉着的雪橇，手里拿着魔杖，头上还带着皇冠。"

由于吃了太多甜腻的食物，埃德蒙已经觉得很不舒服了，现在又听说他刚刚交的朋友是个危险的女巫，这让他更加难受。尽管如此，他并不在乎其他事，只想再尝尝那好吃的土耳其软糖。

"是谁告诉你关于白女巫的事？"他问。

"图姆努斯先生，就是羊怪呀！"露西回答。

"羊怪的话可不能全信，"埃德蒙的语气听上去好像比露西更了解羊怪。

"Everyone knows it," said Edmund; "ask anybody you like. But it's pretty poor sport standing here in the snow. Let's go home."

"Yes, let's," said Lucy. "Oh, Edmund, I am glad you've got in too. The others will have to believe in Narnia now that both of us have been there. What fun it will be!"

But Edmund secretly thought that it would not be as good fun for him as for her. He would have to admit that Lucy had been right, before all the others, and he felt sure the others would all be on the side of the Fauns and the animals; but he was already more than half on the side of the Witch. He did not know what he would say, or how he would keep his secret once they were all talking about Narnia.

By this time they had walked a good way. Then suddenly they felt coats around them instead of branches and next moment they were both standing outside the wardrobe in the empty room.

"谁说的？"露西问。

"所有人都知道啊，"埃德蒙回答，"随便问问你认识的人。但是，咱们别站在这冰天雪地里了，还是回家吧！"

"哦，对！回家。"露西说，"埃德蒙，我真高兴你也来了。既然咱们俩都来过纳尼亚，其他人一定会相信这里真的存在。那该多有趣啊！"

可埃德蒙暗自认为，对他来说，纳尼亚并不像露西说的那么有趣。他不得不在大家面前承认，露西说的都对，他敢肯定其他人都会站在羊怪和那些动物一边，但他却站在女巫这边。他也不知道该说些什么，也不知道当大家都开始讨论纳尼亚的时候，自己怎么保守这个秘密。

这次他们走对了路。突然间，当他们觉得拂过脸庞的不再是

"I say," said Lucy, "you do look awful, Edmund. Don't you feel well?"

"I'm all right," said Edmund, but this was not true. He was feeling very sick.

"Come on then," said Lucy, "let's find the others. What a lot we shall have to tell them! And what wonderful adventures we shall have now that we're all in it together."

树枝，而是大衣时，他们已经迈出了衣橱，站在空屋里了。

露西这时问道："埃德蒙，你没事吧？你的脸色看起来好差。"

"我没事。"虽然这么说，可埃德蒙觉得胃里翻江倒海。

"快来，"露西说，"快找到他们几个，我们有许多话要告诉他们！以后我们可以一起去探险啦。"

CHAPTER FIVE BACK ON THIS SIDE OF THE DOOR

Because the game of hide-and-seek was still going on, it took Edmund and Lucy some time to find the others. But when at last they were all together (which happened in the long room, where the suit of armour was) Lucy burst out: "Peter! Susan! It's all true. Edmund has seen it too. There is a country you can get to through the wardrobe. Edmund and I both got in. We met one another in there, in the wood. Go on, Edmund; tell them all about it."

"What's all this about, Ed?" said Peter.

And now we come to one of the nastiest things in this story. Up to that moment Edmund had been feeling sick, and sulky, and annoyed with Lucy for being right, but he hadn't made up his mind what to do. When Peter suddenly asked him the question

第五章 回到衣橱这边的现实世界

其他两个孩子还在玩捉迷藏，露西和埃德蒙花了好久才找到他们。最后，他们终于在那间放着盔甲的长屋子里集齐了所有人，露西忍不住大叫："彼得！苏珊！我说的都是真的！埃德蒙也看见了。穿过衣橱是另外一个世界。埃德蒙和我都去过，我们还在里面的树林里碰见了。埃德蒙，快告诉他们。"

"埃德，这究竟是怎么回事？"彼得问。

接下来这段是整个故事中最令人感到不快的地方——之前埃德蒙就觉得很不舒服，对露西说的那些真实的故事感到闷闷不乐，但当时他还没想好要怎么做。直到彼得突然问他，他决

he decided all at once to do the meanest and most spiteful thing he could think of. He decided to let Lucy down.

"Tell us, Ed," said Susan.

And Edmund gave a very superior look as if he were far older than Lucy (there was really only a year's difference) and then a little snigger and said, "Oh, yes, Lucy and I have been playing pretending that all her story about a country in the wardrobe is true. just for fun, of course. There's nothing there really."

Poor Lucy gave Edmund one look and rushed out of the room.

Edmund, who was becoming a nastier person every minute, thought that he had scored a great success, and went on at once to say, "There she goes again. What's the matter with her? That's the worst of young kids, they always -"

"Look here," said Peter, turning on him savagely, "shut up! You've been perfectly beastly to Lu ever since she started this nonsense about the wardrobe, and now you go playing games

定用最恶毒的方式让露西下不了台。

"快告诉我们吧，埃德。"苏珊说。

埃德蒙表现出很老成的样子，就好像他比露西要大很多，可实际上他只比露西大一岁而已。他扑哧一声笑了出来："对，没错，我和露西一直在玩儿呢，假装她说的衣橱里面的世界是真的，就是个玩笑而已，里面可什么都没有。"

可怜的露西看了埃德蒙一眼，气得跑出了屋子。

埃德蒙却变本加厉，觉得自己特别成功，马上接着说："看，她又去了。这孩子怎么了？简直是胡闹，小孩子就喜欢——"

"你个臭小子，"彼得火冒三丈，"闭嘴！自从露西开始胡言乱语，讲些什么衣橱的故事，你就和她针锋相对。现在，你又和她

with her about it and setting her off again. I believe you did it simply out of spite."

"But it's all nonsense," said Edmund, very taken aback.

"Of course it's all nonsense," said Peter, "that's just the point. Lu was perfectly all right when we left home, but since we've been down here she seems to be either going queer in the head or else turning into a most frightful liar. But whichever it is, what good do you think you'll do by jeering and nagging at her one day and encouraging her the next?"

"I thought I thought," said Edmund; but he couldn't think of anything to say.

"You didn't think anything at all," said Peter; "it's just spite. You've always liked being beastly to anyone smaller than yourself; we've seen that at school before now."

"Do stop it," said Susan; "it won't make things any better having a row between you two. Let's go and find Lucy."

一起玩这个游戏，却回过头来陷害她，你完全是不怀好意。"

"可她就是在胡说八道，"埃德蒙很惊讶——彼得竟然会这么说自己。

"当然是胡说八道。"彼得说，"可问题就出在这儿——我们从家里走的时候，露西还好好的。可自从我们来到这，露西就变得奇奇怪怪、谎话连篇。但无论她怎么样，你都不能一边对她冷嘲热讽，一边还落井下石。"

"我以为——我本来以为——"埃德蒙不知道该说些什么。

"你以为什么？"彼得说，"你就是故意刁难。以前在学校的时候我们就见过，你就喜欢欺凌弱小。"

"行了，别说了，"苏珊劝道，"你们无论怎么吵，对这件事都

It was not surprising that when they found Lucy, a good deal later, everyone could see that she had been crying. Nothing they could say to her made any difference. She stuck to her story and said: "I don't care what you think, and I don't care what you say. You can tell the Professor or you can write to Mother or you can do anything you like. I know I've met a Faun in there and I wish I'd stayed there and you are all beasts, beasts."

It was an unpleasant evening. Lucy was miserable and Edmund was beginning to feel that his plan wasn't working as well as he had expected. The two older ones were really beginning to think that Lucy was out of her mind. They stood in the passage talking about it in whispers long after she had gone to bed.

The result was the next morning they decided that they really would go and tell the whole thing to the Professor. "He'll write to Father if he thinks there is really something wrong with Lu," said Peter; "it's getting beyond us." So they went and knocked at

没什么帮助。我们还是先找到露西再说吧。"

过了好久，他们才找到露西。不出所料，她一直在抹眼泪。不过现在说什么都没有用了。露西还是坚持自己说的话："我不在乎你们怎么想，或者说些什么。你们可以去告诉教授，甚至给妈妈写信告状，或是其他怎么样都行，我就是在那里见到了羊怪。我真希望自己留在那里不回来。你们就会欺负我，你们就会欺负我！"

那真是个令人难过的夜晚。露西一直在啜泣，而埃德蒙开始觉得，计划并不像他想象中的那样顺利。而两个大孩子则认为，露西的脑子出了问题。露西上床睡觉后，他们俩站在走廊里窃窃私语了好久。

第二天一早，两个孩子决定把整件事情告诉教授。"如果教

the study door, and the Professor said "Come in," and got up and found chairs for them and said he was quite at their disposal. Then he sat listening to them with the tips of his fingers pressed together and never interrupting, till they had finished the whole story. After that he said nothing for quite a long time. Then he cleared his throat and said the last thing either of them expected: "How do you know," he asked, "that your sister's story is not true?"

"Oh, but -" began Susan, and then stopped. Anyone could see from the old man's face that he was perfectly serious. Then Susan pulled herself together and said, "But Edmund said they had only been pretending."

"That is a point," said the Professor, "which certainly deserves consideration; very careful consideration. For instance if you will excuse me for asking the question does your experience lead you to regard your brother or your sister as the more reliable? I mean, which is the more truthful?"

授觉得有必要，他可以给爸爸写信。"彼得说，"咱俩已经解决不了这件事了。"于是，他们敲了敲书房的门，教授说了声"请进"，起身给两个孩子搬了两把椅子让他们坐下，并且表示很乐意帮助他们。教授坐在那里，双手合拢，安静地听着两个孩子把整件事从头到尾讲了一遍。听完之后，他沉默了好久。然后教授清了清嗓子，出乎意料地问："你们怎么知道，妹妹说的故事是假的？"

"可是——"苏珊顿住了。看着老人一脸严肃的样子，苏珊鼓起勇气说，"可是埃德蒙说，他们只是假装说着玩儿而已。"

"这就是问题的关键。"教授说，"要好好想，认真想。我问你们，你们觉得谁的话更可信一些？是弟弟的？还是妹妹的？"

"That's just the funny thing about it, sir," said Peter. "Up till now, I'd have said Lucy every time."

"And what do you think, my dear?" said the Professor, turning to Susan.

"Well," said Susan, "in general, I'd say the same as Peter, but this couldn't be true all this about the wood and the Faun."

"That is more than I know," said the Professor, "and a charge of lying against someone whom you have always found truthful is a very serious thing; a very serious thing indeed."

"We were afraid it mightn't even be lying," said Susan; "we thought there might be something wrong with Lucy."

"Madness, you mean?" said the Professor quite coolly. "Oh, you can make your minds easy about that. One has only to look at her and talk to her to see that she is not mad."

"But then," said Susan, and stopped. She had never

"教授，这倒是个有趣的问题。"彼得说，"到现在为止，我觉得露西更可信一些。"

"亲爱的孩子，你觉得呢？"教授转向苏珊。

"我嘛，"苏珊回答，"总的来讲，我同意彼得的看法。可是关于树林啊羊怪啊什么的，怎么可能是真的呢？！"

"是不是真的，我也不清楚。"教授说，"不过，随便指责一个从来不说谎话的人说谎，可是一件很严重的事。"

"我们担心，她的问题不仅仅在于说谎。"苏珊说，"我们觉得，露西的脑子出了问题。"

"你是说，她疯了，是吗？"教授冷静地问道，"这点很容易判断。你们只要仔细地观察，再和她说说话，就知道她到底有没有问题。"

"可是……"苏珊刚想开口又停住了。她完全没有想到，像老

dreamed that a grown-up would talk like the Professor and didn't know what to think.

"Logic!" said the Professor half to himself. "Why don't they teach logic at these schools? There are only three possibilities. Either your sister is telling lies, or she is mad, or she is telling the truth. You know she doesn't tell lies and it is obvious that she is not mad For the moment then and unless any further evidence turns up, we must assume that she is telling the truth."

Susan looked at him very hard and was quite sure from the expression on his face that he was no making fun of them.

"But how could it be true, sir?" said Peter.

"Why do you say that?" asked the Professor.

"Well, for one thing," said Peter, "if it was true why doesn't everyone find this country every time they go to the wardrobe? I mean, there was nothing there when we looked; even Lucy didn't pretend the was."

教授这种大人会说出这样的话，现在她完全糊涂了。

“逻辑啊！”教授对他们说，又像是自言自语，“现在的学校怎么都不教逻辑了呀？目前来看，只有三种可能。第一种，你妹妹撒谎；第二种，她疯了；第三种，她说的都是事实。你们都知道，她从来不说谎，而且很明显，她也没疯。那么，在没有更充分的证据之前，我们必须假设，她说的是真话。”

苏珊紧紧地盯着他，从他严肃的表情来看，不像是在和他们开玩笑。

“可是教授，这怎么可能是真的呢？”彼得问。

“为什么这么说呢？”老教授反问道。

“试想一下，”彼得回答，“如果是真的，为什么别人进到衣橱里的时候都没人发现呢？有一次，我们往里看的时候，真的是什么都没有，连露西也承认——什么都没看见。”

"What has that to do with it?" said the Professor.

"Well, sir, if things are real, they're there all the time."

"Are they?" said the Professor; and Peter didn't know quite what to say.

"But there was no time," said Susan. "Lucy had no time to have gone anywhere, even if there was such a place. She came running after us the very moment we were out of the room. It was less than minute, and she pretended to have been away for hours."

"That is the very thing that makes her story so likely to be true," said the Professor. "If there really a door in this house that leads to some other world (and I should warn you that this is a very strange house, and even I know very little about it) if, I say, she had got into another world, I should not be at a surprised to find that the other world had a separate time of its own; so that however long you stay there it would never take up

"这又有什么关系呢？"教授说。

"如果这是真的，那里的世界应该一直存在啊。"

"真的是这样吗？"教授说。彼得被问得哑口无言。

"可是露西没有时间去那里，"苏珊说，"就算真有那个地方，她也完全没有时间去。当时我们从那间屋子里出来之后，她就立马跟了过来，可她却说自己离开了好几个小时呢！"

"正是因为这样，她的故事才特别真实。"教授说，"或许，在这幢房子里，真的有一扇门通往另一个世界。我还要警告你们，这幢房子非常奇怪，连我都知之甚少。如果露西真的跑到了另外一个世界，那么，那个世界的时间和我们这里不同也是不足为奇的。也就是说，无论你在另一个世界待了多久，都不会对我们这

any of our time. On the other hand, I don't think many girls of her age would invent that idea for themselves. If she had been pretending, she would have hidden for a reasonable time before coming out and telling her story."

"But do you really mean, sir," said Peter, "that there could be other worlds all over the place, just round the corner like that?"

"Nothing is more probable," said the Professor, taking off his spectacles and beginning to polish them, while he muttered to himself, "I wonder what they do teach them at these schools."

"But what are we to do?" said Susan. She felt that the conversation was beginning to get off the point.

"My dear young lady," said the Professor, suddenly looking up with a very sharp expression at both of them, "there is one plan which no one has yet suggested and which is well worth trying."

"What's that?" said Susan.

里的时间造成影响。从另一个方面来讲，我认为，她这个年纪的小女孩是无法编造出这样的故事的。如果她真是想骗你们，或是讲一个荒唐的故事的话，为什么不藏得久一点呢？”

“教授，您真的觉得，就在屋子的一角，存在着另外一个世界？”彼得问。

“当然有可能了。”教授说着，摘下老花镜擦了起来。他嘟囔着，“唉，现在的学校都教了些什么呀！”

“可我们应该怎么做呢？”苏珊问。她觉得大家已经说跑题了。

“我亲爱的孩子，”教授说着，突然抬起头，严厉地看着他们，“有一个计划，之前从没有人提起过，不过值得一试。”

“是什么？”苏珊问。

"We might all try minding our own business," said he. And that was the end of that conversation.

After this things were a good deal better for Lucy. Peter saw to it that Edmund stopped jeering at her, and neither she nor anyone else felt inclined to talk about the wardrobe at all. It had become a rather alarming subject. And so for a time it looked as if all the adventures were coming to an end; but that was not to be.

This house of the Professor's which even he knew so little about was so old and famous that people from all over England used to come and ask permission to see over it. It was the sort of house that is mentioned in guide books and even in histories; and well it might be, for all manner of stories were told about it, some of them even stranger than the one I am telling you now. And when parties of sightseers arrived and asked to see

"我们最好都管好自己的事。"教授说。然后，这场对话就这样结束了。

这件事之后，露西似乎开心了许多。彼得发现，埃德蒙也不再讥讽、取笑她。包括露西自己在内，每个人都不再谈起关于衣橱的事。毕竟，这已经成了大家心头的一根刺。似乎一切的探险活动就这样结束了，可事情并非如此。

虽然老教授也对这栋房子了解不多，可并不影响它的知名度。来自英国各个地方的人们总是慕名而来。这栋房子出现在各种旅游指南上，甚至在历史上都留下了浓墨重彩的一笔。在很多传说故事中，都有这所宅子的身影，甚至有的故事比现在这个故事还要离奇有趣。每当有人前来想要参观时，老教授总是允许他们进

the house, the Professor always gave them permission, and Mrs Macready, the housekeeper, showed them round, telling them about the pictures and the armour, and the rare books in the library. Mrs Macready was not fond of children, and did not like to be interrupted when she was telling visitors all the things she knew. She had said to Susan and Peter almost on the first morning (along with a good many other instructions), "And please remember you're to keep out of the way whenever I'm taking a party over the house."

"Just as if any of us would want to waste half the morning trailing round with a crowd of strange grown-ups!" said Edmund, and the other three thought the same. That was how the adventures began for the second time.

A few mornings later Peter and Edmund were looking at the suit of armour and wondering if they could take it to bits when

来。届时，管家麦格雷迪太太会带着人们四处参观，给他们讲那些照片和盔甲背后的故事，带他们看图书馆里稀有的藏书。不过，麦格雷迪太太不喜欢小孩子，尤其是在她带着游客参观时，一点儿都不希望小孩子来打扰他们。在四个孩子到来的第一个清晨，她就告诉苏珊和彼得这栋房子里有各种各样的规矩，同时还告诉孩子们："你们要记住，在我带着游客参观的时候，你们最好离远点儿。"

"谁稀罕呀！就好像我们喜欢跟在一群陌生人的身后瞎晃悠一样。"埃德蒙说，其他人纷纷表示同意。可谁知，第二次探险就是这样开始的。

过了几天之后，彼得和埃德蒙站在那间屋子里，出神地盯着

the two girls rushed into the room and said, "Look out! Here comes the Macready and a whole gang with her."

"Sharp's the word," said Peter, and all four made off through the door at the far end of the room. But when they had got out into the Green Room and beyond it, into the Library, they suddenly heard voices ahead of them, and realized that Mrs Macready must be bringing her party of sightseers up the back stairs instead of up the front stairs as they had expected. And after that whether it was that they lost their heads, or that Mrs Macready was trying to catch them, or that some magic in the house had come to life and was chasing them into Narnia they seemed to find themselves being followed everywhere, until at last Susan said, "Oh bother those trippers! Here let's get into the Wardrobe Room till they've passed. No one will follow us in there." But the moment they were inside they heard the voices in the passage and then someone fumbling at the door and then

那套盔甲，正想着如何把这玩意儿拆开，只见两个小姑娘慌慌张张地跑了进来，说："不好啦！麦格雷迪太太带着一帮人朝这边来啦！"

"快跑！"彼得急忙说道。四个孩子穿过长长的屋子，来到了另一头。当他们跑过那间装饰着绿色植物的屋子，来到图书馆之后，突然听见前面传来了声音，肯定是麦格雷迪太太带着这帮游客从后面的楼梯上来了。此前，他们通常都会走前面的楼梯——或许孩子们已经跑得晕头转向了，或许是麦格雷迪太太想要抓住他们，抑或是这所房子里的魔法显现了出来，故意把他们赶往纳尼亚，孩子们觉得到处都有人在追他们。最后，苏珊说："这些游客真烦人！去那儿！咱们躲到衣橱里，等他们走了之后再出来。

they saw the handle turning.

"Quick!" said Peter, "there's nowhere else," and flung open the wardrobe. All four of them bundled inside it and sat there, panting, in the dark. Peter held the door closed but did not shut it; for, of course, he remembered, as every sensible person does, that you should never never shut yourself up in a wardrobe.

没人会跟着我们去那间屋子的。”可是他们刚跑进空屋，就听见走廊里传来说话的声音，接着有人摸到了那扇门，他们看见门把手在转动。

“快点！只能躲在这儿了。”彼得说着，“唰”地一下拉开了衣橱的门。四个孩子坐在衣橱里抱成一团，在黑暗中喘着粗气。彼得轻轻地把门掩上，但并没有关严——每个有脑子的人都知道，绝对不要把自己关在衣橱里。

CHAPTER SIX INTO THE FOREST

"I wish the Macready would hurry up and take all these people away," said Susan presently, "I'm getting horribly cramped."

"And what a filthy smell of camphor!" said Edmund.

"I expect the pockets of these coats are full of it," said Susan, "to keep away the moths."

"There's something sticking into my back," said Peter.

"And isn't it cold?" said Susan.

"Now that you mention it, it is cold," said Peter, "and hang it all, it's wet too. What's the matter with this place? I'm sitting on something wet. It's getting wetter every minute." He struggled to his feet.

"Let's get out," said Edmund, "they've gone."

"O-o-oh!" said Susan suddenly, and everyone asked her

第六章 进入森林

"希望麦格雷迪太太赶紧带着他们离开。"苏珊忍不住说，"待在这个狭窄的地方好难受啊。"

"樟脑球的味道实在太难闻了。"埃德蒙抱怨道。

"我觉得这些大衣兜里塞满了樟脑球，"苏珊说，"以防长蛀虫。"

"有东西在戳我的后背。"彼得说。

"你们不觉得冷吗？"苏珊继续问。

"你这么一提，确实挺冷的。"彼得说，"哎呀！还特别湿，这到底是什么地方啊？我觉得我坐在一块湿乎乎的东西上面，而且越来越湿。"说着，彼得挣扎着站了起来。

"我们出去吧，"埃德蒙说，"他们应该走了。"

"啊！"苏珊突然大叫。其他人都问她怎么了。

what was the matter.

"I'm sitting against a tree," said Susan, "and look! It's getting light over there."

"By Jove, you're right," said Peter, "and look there and there. It's trees all round. And this wet stuff is snow. Why, I do believe we've got into Lucy's wood after all."

And now there was no mistaking it and all four children stood blinking in the daylight of a winter day. Behind them were coats hanging on pegs, in front of them were snow-covered trees.

Peter turned at once to Lucy.

"I apologize for not believing you," he said, "I'm sorry. Will you shake hands?"

"Of course," said Lucy, and did.

"And now," said Susan, "what do we do next?"

"Do?" said Peter, "why, go and explore the wood, of course."

“我竟然靠在一棵树上，”苏珊说，“快看！那边有光。”

“天哪！这是真的！”彼得说，“你们看，这里到处都是树，湿乎乎的东西是雪——这里看来就是露西说的那片树林了。”

这下可再没人怀疑了。四个孩子站在冬日的阳光下，大眼瞪小眼。身后是挂在衣钩上的大衣，面前是白雪覆盖下的树林。

彼得转过头来对露西说：

“实在对不起，我之前一直觉得你在撒谎。”彼得说，“真对不起！咱们现在能握手言和吗？”

“当然啦。”露西说着，握了握他的手。

“那么，”苏珊问，“接下来咱们怎么办？”

“怎么办？”彼得回答，“当然是去树林里探险啦！”

"Ugh!" said Susan, stamping her feet, "it's pretty cold. What about putting on some of these coats?"

"They're not ours," said Peter doubtfully.

"I am sure nobody would mind," said Susan; "it isn't as if we wanted to take them out of the house; we shan't take them even out of the wardrobe."

"I never thought of that, Su," said Peter. "Of course, now you put it that way, I see. No one could say you had bagged a coat as long as you leave it in the wardrobe where you found it. And I suppose this whole country is in the wardrobe."

They immediately carried out Susan's very sensible plan. The coats were rather too big for them so that they came down to their heels and looked more like royal robes than coats when they had put them on. But they all felt a good deal warmer and each thought the others looked better in their new get-up and more suitable to the landscape.

"哎呀！"苏珊跺着脚说，"可是这里太冷了。要不咱们穿上这些大衣？"

"可这些不是我们的。"彼得有些犹豫。

"放心吧，不会有人介意的。"苏珊说，"咱们又不会把衣服拿到屋子外面去，甚至都不会拿到衣橱外面的。"

"我怎么就没想到呢，苏珊。"彼得说，"要是这么说的话，我们把在衣橱里找到的大衣留在衣橱里，也不会有人说我们随便拿别人的衣服。而且我觉得，这个世界就是完全在衣橱里面的。"

所有人立马同意了苏珊的计划。可是，这些大衣对于孩子们来说实在太大了，长长的大衣垂到了脚踝，看上去更像是穿了龙袍。不过，穿上之后，身上确实暖和了许多。孩子们你看看我，我看看你，都觉得这身行头配着这里的景色，简直再合适不过了。

"We can pretend we are Arctic explorers," said Lucy.

"This is going to be exciting enough without pretending," said Peter, as he began leading the way forward into the forest. There were heavy darkish clouds overhead and it looked as if there might be more snow before night.

"I say," began Edmund presently, "oughtn't we to be bearing a bit more to the left, that is, if we are aiming for the lamp-post?" He had forgotten for the moment that he must pretend never to have been in the wood before. The moment the words were out of his mouth he realized that he had given himself away. Everyone stopped; everyone stared at him. Peter whistled.

"So you really were here," he said, "that time Lu said she'd met you in here and you made out she was telling lies."

There was a dead silence. "Well, of all the poisonous little beasts -" said Peter, and shrugged his shoulders and said no

"我们可以把自己想象成北极的探险家。"露西说。

"都不用想象，这已经很刺激了。"彼得说着，带领着大家走进了森林。天上乌云密布，看来夜晚来临之前，还会下一场大雪。

"我说，"埃德蒙说，"要是我们想去灯柱那里的话，难道不是往左走吗？"他已经忘了需要假装从来没来过这里。可他刚说完，就意识到自己露馅了。所有人都停下脚步，盯着他看，彼得还揶揄地吹起了口哨："上次露西说在这里遇见过你，你还诬陷她说谎。原来，你果然来过这儿。"接下来，是死一般的沉寂。

彼得随后说："多么讨厌的熊孩子都有。"说完他耸耸肩，就不再说话了。其实，也无须多言。四个孩子继续探险，可埃德蒙悄悄对自己说："你们这几个骄傲自大、自私自利的伪君子，总

more. There seemed, indeed, no more to say, and presently the four resumed their journey; but Edmund was saying to himself, “I’ll pay you all out for this, you pack of stuck-up, selfsatisfied prigs.”

“Where are we going anyway?” said Susan, chiefly for the sake of changing the subject.

“I think Lu ought to be the leader,” said Peter; “goodness knows she deserves it. Where will you take us, Lu?”

“What about going to see Mr Tumnus?” said Lucy. “He’s the nice Faun I told you about.”

Everyone agreed to this and off they went walking briskly and stamping their feet. Lucy proved a good leader. At first she wondered whether she would be able to find the way, but she recognized an oddlooking tree on one place and a stump in another and brought them on to where the ground became uneven and into the little valley and at last to the very door of

有一天我会让你们吃苦头的。”

“我们到底要往哪里走啊？”苏珊试图转移话题。

“我认为，应该让露当向导。”彼得说，“她当仁不让。露，咱们往哪走？”

“要不然，咱们去图姆努斯先生家吧。”露西说，“他就是我之前跟你们说的那个好羊怪。”

大家一致同意后，孩子们跺了跺脚，轻快地向树林中走去。露西果然是个好向导。一开始，她还怕自己找不到路，走着走着，她就认出了一棵长得稀奇古怪的大树，不一会儿又认出了一个树桩。就这样，她把大家带到了那片高低不平的小山谷中。最后，来到了图姆努斯先生住的山洞门口。可迎接他们的却是一片可怕

Mr Tumnus's cave. But there a terrible surprise awaited them.

The door had been wrenched off its hinges and broken to bits. Inside, the cave was dark and cold and had the damp feel and smell of a place that had not been lived in for several days. Snow had drifted in from the doorway and was heaped on the floor, mixed with something black, which turned out to be the charred sticks and ashes from the fire. Someone had apparently flung it about the room and then stamped it out. The crockery lay smashed on the floor and the picture of the Faun's father had been slashed into shreds with a knife.

"This is a pretty good wash-out," said Edmund; "not much good coming here."

"What is this?" said Peter, stooping down. He had just noticed a piece of paper which had been nailed through the carpet to the floor.

"Is there anything written on it?" asked Susan.

"Yes, I think there is," answered Peter, "but I can't read it

的景象。

山洞的门被卸了下来，被砸得七零八落。山洞里面又黑又冷，满是霉味儿，显示着这里已经好几天没人住了。从门廊吹进来的雪花堆满地面，里面还掺杂着一些黑色的渣子，看上去应该是火堆中烧焦的木炭和灰烬。看来，是有人把烧着的柴火扔了进来，然后又踩灭了。碗碟的碎片满地都是，羊怪父亲的画像被人用刀划得稀巴烂。

"这里又脏又乱，"埃德蒙说，"咱们来这里要干吗呢？"

"这是什么？"彼得蹲了下来，在地毯下找到了一张纸。

"上面有字吗？"苏珊问。

"应该有，"彼得回答，"不过这里光线太暗了。咱们去外面看。"

in this light. Let's get out into the open air."

They all went out in the daylight and crowded round Peter as he read out the following words:

The former occupant of these premises, the Faun Tumnus, is under arrest and awaiting his trial on a charge of High Treason against her Imperial Majesty Jadis, Queen of Narnia, Chatelaine of Cair Paravel, Empress of the Lone Islands, etc, also of comforting her said Majesty's enemies, harbouring spies and fraternizing with Humans.

signed MAUGRIM, Captain of the Secret Police, LONG LIVE THE QUEEN

The children stared at each other.

"I don't know that I'm going to like this place after all," said Susan.

"Who is this Queen, Lu?" said Peter. "Do you know anything about her?"

"She isn't a real queen at all," answered Lucy; "she's a

孩子们来到山洞外面，围在彼得身边，听着他读到：

本处原房主羊怪图姆努斯，因背叛纳尼亚女王陛下——凯尔·帕拉维尔城堡的女主人——孤岛女皇简蒂斯，包庇女王的敌人，私藏奸细、结交人类，罪行严重。现已收押在监，即刻听审。

女王万岁！

保安局局长 毛戈林

孩子们面面相觑。

"我也说不好，自己是不是真的喜欢这里。"苏珊说。

"露，这个女王是谁？"彼得问，"你知道她吗？"

"她根本就不是什么女王，"露西回答，"她是个可怕的坏女巫，大家都叫她白女巫。森林里的所有生灵都恨她，她在这个王国里施

horrible witch, the White Witch. Everyone all the wood people hate her. She has made an enchantment over the whole country so that it is always winter here and never Christmas."

"I I wonder if there's any point in going on," said Susan. "I mean, it doesn't seem particularly safe here and it looks as if it won't be much fun either. And it's getting colder every minute, and we've brought nothing to eat. What about just going home?"

"Oh, but we can't, we can't," said Lucy suddenly; "don't you see? We can't just go home, not after this. It is all on my account that the poor Faun has got into this trouble. He hid me from the Witch and showed me the way back. That's what it means by comforting the Queen's enemies and fraternizing with Humans. We simply must try to rescue him."

"A lot we could do!" said Edmund, "when we haven't even got anything to eat!"

"Shut up you!" said Peter, who was still very angry with Edmund. "What do you think, Susan?"

了魔法，把这里变得一年四季都是冬天，而且没有圣诞节。"

"我觉得，再往前走没什么意义。"苏珊说，"这里既不安全，也很无聊。而且我感觉越来越冷，我们还没带吃的来。要不咱们现在回去？"

"不行，我们不能回去。"露西突然说，"发生了这样的事情，我们怎么可以这样就走了呢？都是因为我，可怜的羊怪才遇上麻烦。他为了瞒过女巫，把我藏起来，还送我回家，这就是他们说的——包庇敌人，结交人类。我们必须把他救出来！"

"我们连吃的都没有，怎么救他呀！"埃德蒙说。

"你闭嘴！"彼得还在生埃德蒙的气，"苏珊，你觉得呢？"

"我觉得露说得对，"苏珊回答，"虽然我一点儿也不想再往前

"I've a horrid feeling that Lu is right," said Susan. "I don't want to go a step further and I wish we'd never come. But I think we must try to do something for Mr Whatever-his-name is I mean the Faun."

"That's what I feel too," said Peter. "I'm worried about having no food with us. I'd vote for going back and getting something from the larder, only there doesn't seem to be any certainty of getting into this country again when once you've got out of it. I think we'll havc to go on."

"So do I," said both the girls.

"If only we knew where the poor chap was imprisoned!" said Peter.

They were all still wondering what to do next, when Lucy said, "Look! There's a robin, with such a red breast. It's the first bird I've seen here. I say! I wonder can birds talk in Narnia? It almost looks as if it wanted to say something to us." Then she

走了，也后悔咱们来这儿，可我们必须得为那位图什么先生做点什么——就是那个羊怪。"

"我也这么认为，"彼得说，"不过我也很担心，没有吃的怎么办。本来我想的是，咱们先回去，到厨房拿点吃的东西。不过一旦回去了，恐怕就不能回到这里了。所以我觉得，咱们应该继续往前走。"

"说得没错。"两个女孩子说。

"可是，我们并不知道这个可怜的羊怪被关在哪里。"彼得说。

他们正想着接下来要怎么办，露西突然说："快看！那只鸟胸前的羽毛红红的，是只知更鸟。我还是第一次在这里见到这种鸟。我在想，纳尼亚的鸟可能会说话，看上去那只鸟想告诉咱们什么

turned to the Robin and said, "Please, can you tell us where Tumnus the Faun has been taken to?" As she said this she took a step towards the bird. It at once flew away but only as far as to the next tree. There it perched and looked at them very hard as if it understood all they had been saying. Almost without noticing that they had done so, the four children went a step or two nearer to it. At this the Robin flew away again to the next tree and once more looked at them very hard. (You couldn't have found a robin with a redder chest or a brighter eye.)

"Do you know," said Lucy, "I really believe he means us to follow him."

"I've an idea he does," said Susan. "What do you think, Peter?"

"Well, we might as well try it," answered Peter.

The Robin appeared to understand the matter thoroughly. It kept going from tree to tree, always a few yards ahead of them,

事情。”露西转过头对那只知更鸟说：“你能告诉我们，羊怪图姆努斯先生被带去了哪里吗？”她边说，边往前迈了一步。知更鸟立即飞到了不远处的另一棵树上。它站在枝头盯着孩子们，仿佛可以听懂他们说的话。孩子们想都没想，三步并作两步跑过去，谁知那只鸟又飞到另一棵不远处的树上，继续盯着他们。你肯定没见过羽毛比它还红，眼睛比它还亮的知更鸟。

“我觉得，它想让我们跟着它走。”露西说。

“我也这么觉得，”苏珊说，“你呢？彼得？”

“要不我们试试吧。”彼得说。

知更鸟似乎完全听懂了他们的对话。它不断地从一棵树上飞到另一棵树上，虽然距离孩子们有一定的距离，但是一直在他们

but always so near that they could easily follow it. In this way it led them on, slightly downhill. Wherever the Robin alighted a little shower of snow would fall off the branch. Presently the clouds parted overhead and the winter sun came out and the snow all around them grew dazzlingly bright. They had been travelling in this way for about half an hour, with the two girls in front, when Edmund said to Peter, "if you're not still too high and mighty to talk to me, I've something to say which you'd better listcn to."

"What is it?" asked Peter.

"Hush! Not so loud," said Edmund; "there's no good frightening the girls. But have you realized what we're doing?"

"What?" said Peter, lowering his voice to a whisper.

"We're following a guide we know nothing about. How do we know which side that bird is on? Why shouldn't it be leading us into a trap?"

的视线中。就这样，小鸟带着他们几个往山坡下面走去。知更鸟飞过的地方，积雪从枝头簌簌落下。天上的乌云慢慢散开，冬日的阳光穿过树枝照到雪地上，晃得孩子们睁不开眼。他们就这样走了大概半个小时。两个女孩子走在前面，两个男孩子走在后面。这时，埃德蒙对彼得说："你要是对我没那么生气了的话，有些事情我要告诉你。你最好听我说。"

"什么事？"彼得问。

"嘘！小点声！"埃德蒙说，"别吓到女孩子们。你意识到我们在做什么吗？"

"什么？"彼得小声地问。

"我们现在跟着一只陌生的鸟往前走，我们怎么知道那只鸟是哪边的？万一它把我们带进陷阱怎么办？"

"That's a nasty idea. Still a robin, you know. They're good birds in all the stories I've ever read. I'm sure a robin wouldn't be on the wrong side."

"It if comes to that, which is the right side? How do we know that the Fauns are in the right and the Queen (yes, I know we've been told she's a witch) is in the wrong? We don't really know anything about either."

"The Faun saved Lucy."

"He said he did. But how do we know? And there's another thing too. Has anyone the least idea of the way home from here?"

"Great Scott!" said Peter, "I hadn't thought of that."

"And no chance of dinner either," said Edmund.

"你的想法真荒唐。这是知更鸟，在我读过的所有故事里，知更鸟都是善良的。我觉得它不会站在坏人那边。"

"你要这么说的话，哪一边是好人呢？我们怎么知道，羊怪是好的，女王是坏的？虽然据说女王是个女巫，但我们实际上什么都不知道。"

"羊怪救了露西。"

"他是那么说，但我们怎么知道呢？而且还有一件事，咱们有谁知道回去的路吗？"

"糟糕！"彼得说，"我没想过这个问题啊！"

"看来晚饭也泡汤了。"埃德蒙说。

CHAPTER SEVEN A DAY WITH THE BEAVERS

While the two boys were whispering behind, both the girls suddenly cried "Oh!" and stopped.

"The robin!" cried Lucy, "the robin. It's flown away." And so it had right out of sight.

"And now what are we to do?" said Edmund, giving Peter a look which was as much as to say "What did I tell you?"

"Sh! Look!" said Susan.

"What?" said Peter.

"There's something moving among the trees over there to the left."

They all stared as hard as they could, and no one felt very comfortable.

"There it goes again," said Susan presently.

第七章 与海狸夫妇的一天

正当两个男孩在后面窃窃私语时，走在前面的两个女孩子突然叫了一声，并停下了脚步。

"知更鸟！"露西喊道，"知更鸟飞走了。"说着，那只鸟飞出了视线。

"现在怎么办啊？"埃德蒙问，同时给了彼得一个眼神，仿佛在说，"我说什么来着？"

"嘘！快看！"苏珊说。

"看什么？"彼得问。

"左边的树林中间有什么东西在动。"

所有人都睁大了眼睛使劲看，看得眼睛都酸了。

"看，还在动。"过了一会儿，苏珊说。

“I saw it that time too,” said Peter. “It’s still there. It’s just gone behind that big tree.”

“What is it?” asked Lucy, trying very hard not to sound nervous.

“Whatever it is,” said Peter, “it’s dodging us. It’s something that doesn’t want to be seen.”

“Let’s go home,” said Susan. And then, though nobody said it out loud, everyone suddenly realized the same fact that Edmund had whispered to Peter at the end of the last chapter. They were lost.

“What’s it like?” said Lucy.

“It’s it’s a kind of animal,” said Susan; and then, “Look! Look! Quick! There it is.”

They all saw it this time, a whiskered furry face which had looked out at them from behind a tree. But this time it didn’t immediately draw back. Instead, the animal put its paw against

“我也看见了，”彼得说，“它还在那儿，藏在那棵大树后面。”

“是什么东西？”露西问，尽量让自己的声音显得不那么紧张。

“不管是什么，”彼得说，“它在躲着我们，不想让人看见。”

“咱们回家吧！”苏珊说。这时，虽然没人说，但大家都意识到了之前埃德蒙和彼得悄悄说起的那个问题——他们迷路了。

“那个东西长什么样子？”露西问。

“像是某种动物，”苏珊说着，突然指着林中惊呼，“看！快看！在那儿呢！”

这次大家都看见了，树后面探出来一张长满胡子的毛茸茸的脸。这次，它没有躲避，而是把爪子放在嘴上，就好像人类把食指放在嘴上，示意大家安静一样。然后，它又消失不见了。孩子

its mouth just as humans put their finger on their lips when they are signalling to you to be quiet. Then it disappeared again. The children, all stood holding their breath.

A moment later the stranger came out from behind the tree, glanced all round as if it were afraid someone was watching, said "Hush", made signs to them to join it in the thicker bit of wood where it was standing, and then once more disappeared.

"I know what it is," said Peter; "it's a beaver. I saw the tail."

"It wants us to go to it," said Susan, "and it is warning us not to make a noise."

"I know," said Peter. "The question is, are we to go to it or not? What do you think, Lu?"

"I think it's a nice beaver," said Lucy.

"Yes, but how do we know?" said Edmund.

"Shan't we have to risk it?" said Susan. "I mean, it's no good just standing here and I feel I want some dinner."

们站在那儿，大气儿也不敢喘。

过了一会儿，这个陌生的家伙从树后面探出身来，环顾四周，好像怕别人看见一样。它说了声"快来"，然后打手势，让大家跟着它往密林深处走。然后，它又消失了。

"我知道那是什么了，"彼得说，"是海狸，我看见它的尾巴了。"

"它想让我们跟着它，"苏珊说，"还提醒我们不要出声。"

"我看出来了，"彼得说，"可问题是，我们到底要不要跟着它？露，你觉得呢？"

"我觉得它是一只好海狸。"露西说。

"我们怎么能肯定呢？"埃德蒙说。

"总得冒一次险吧，"苏珊说，"我们站在这儿也没用，而且我想吃晚饭。"

At this moment the Beaver again popped its head out from behind the tree and beckoned earnestly to them.

"Come on," said Peter, "let's give it a try. All keep close together. We ought to be a match for one beaver if it turns out to be an enemy."

So the children all got close together and walked up to the tree and in behind it, and there, sure enough, they found the Beaver; but it still drew back, saying to them in a hoarse throaty whisper, "Further in, come further in. Right in here. We're not safe in the open!"

Only when it had led them into a dark spot where four trees grew so close together that their boughs met and the brown earth and pine needles could be seen underfoot because no snow had been able to fall there, did it begin to talk to them.

"Are you the Sons of Adam and the Daughters of Eve?" it said. "We're some of them," said Peter.

"S-s-s-sh!" said the Beaver, "not so loud please. We're not

这时，海狸又从树后面冒出头，很焦急地喊着他们。

"来吧，"彼得说，"咱们总得试试。大家挨得近一点，万一它是个坏人，咱们以四敌一还能打得过它。"

孩子们紧紧地挨在一起，走向了那棵大树。在树后面，他们发现了那只海狸。海狸还在往后退，并用嘶哑低沉的声音小声说："往里点，再往里点。对，就是这。外面不安全。"

直到海狸引着他们来到一片幽暗的地方，四周围了四棵大树，树枝紧密地搭在一起，以至于雪花都飘不进来，低头能看见棕色的土地和一地的松树针叶。他们到了这儿之后，海狸才开始对他们说话。

"你们是亚当之子和夏娃之女吗？"海狸问。"算是吧。"彼得说。

"嘘！小点声！"海狸说，"我们在这儿也不安全。"

safe even here."

"Why, who are you afraid of?" said Peter. "There's no one here but ourselves."

"There are the trees," said the Beaver. "They're always listening. Most of them are on our side, but there are trees that would betray us to her; you know who I mean," and it nodded its head several times.

"If it comes to talking about sides," said Edmund, "how do we know you're a friend?"

"Not meaning to be rude, Mr Beaver," added Peter, "but you see, we're strangers."

"Quite right, quite right," said the Beaver. "Here is my token." With these words it held up to them a little white object. They all looked at it in surprise, till suddenly Lucy said, "Oh, of course. It's my handkerchief the one I gave to poor Mr Tumnus."

"That's right," said the Beaver. "Poor fellow, he got wind of the arrest before it actually happened and handed this over to me.

"你在怕什么？"彼得问，"这里只有我们几个啊。"

"是那些树，"海狸说，"它们总在偷听——大部分是我们这边的，但是有些树会背叛我们，投靠她。你们知道我在说谁。"说着还点了几下头。

"要是这么说的话，我们怎么知道你是敌是友。"埃德蒙说。

"请您别见怪，海狸先生，"彼得接着说，"我们并不认识你。"

"你说得没错，"海狸说，"这是我的信物。"说着，它递给他们一小块白色的东西。他们正觉得奇怪，露西突然开口说："哎呀！这是我的手绢，是我给图姆努斯先生的那块儿手绢。"

"没错，"海狸说，"这个可怜的家伙，当他听到风声有人要逮捕他，他就把手绢交给了我。还说如果他出了事，我必须来这里

He said that if anything happened to him I must meet you here and take you on to -" Here the Beaver's voice sank into silence and it gave one or two very mysterious nods. Then signalling to the children to stand as close around it as they possibly could, so that their faces were actually tickled by its whiskers, it added in a low whisper -

"They say Aslan is on the move perhaps has already landed."

And now a very curious thing happened. None of the children knew who Aslan was any more than you do; but the moment the Beaver had spoken these words everyone felt quite different. Perhaps it has sometimes happened to you in a dream that someone says something which you don't understand but in the dream it feels as if it had some enormous meaning either a terrifying one which turns the whole dream into a nightmare or else a lovely meaning too lovely to put into words, which makes the dream so beautiful that you remember it all your life

与你们会面，并带你们去——”说到这儿，海狸压低了声音，冲他们神秘地点了点头，并示意孩子们尽量靠近它围在一起，海狸的胡子扎在脸上，他们都感觉到痒痒的。接着它低声说：

“据说阿斯兰正在逼近，或许现在已经来了。”

奇怪的事情发生了。虽然孩子们不知道阿斯兰是谁，但当海狸说出这个名字后，所有人的感觉都不同了。就好像有时你在做梦的时候，有人突然说了什么，虽然你不知道是什么意思，但是在梦里却意义重大——或许因为这个词，会导致一场可怕的噩梦，抑或美好到无法用语言表述，美好到可以记住一辈子，恨不得不停地重温这个美梦。现在，孩子们就是这样。听到阿斯兰这个名字后，每个孩子的感觉都不一样：埃德蒙觉得莫名的恐惧；彼得

and are always wishing you could get into that dream again. It was like that now. At the name of Aslan each one of the children felt something jump in its inside. Edmund felt a sensation of mysterious horror. Peter felt suddenly brave and adventurous. Susan felt as if some delicious smell or some delightful strain of music had just floated by her. And Lucy got the feeling you have when you wake up in the morning and realize that it is the beginning of the holidays or the beginning of summer.

"And what about Mr Tumnus," said Lucy, "where is he?"

"S-s-s-sh," said the Beaver, "not here. I must bring you where we can have a real talk and also dinner."

No one except Edmund felt any difficulty about trusting the beaver now, and everyone, including Edmund, was very glad to hear the word "dinner".

They therefore all hurried along behind their new friend who led them at a surprisingly quick pace, and always in the thickest parts of the forest, for over an hour. Everyone was

突然觉得无所畏惧；苏珊觉得好像闻见了一阵香气，或是听到一段美妙的旋律；露西的感觉是，好像早晨一睁开眼睛突然意识到假期已经开始了，或是夏天已经到来。

“图姆努斯先生呢？”露西问，“他在哪儿？”

“嘘，别在这儿说。”海狸说，“咱们必须到一个能说话还有晚餐吃的地方。”

除了埃德蒙，其他人都相信了海狸。而包括埃德蒙在内，当大家听到“晚餐”这个词时，都欢欣雀跃起来。

就这样，他们跟着这位新朋友急匆匆地走入了森林里。海狸的速度快得令人吃惊，而且总是带他们走那些树林密集的地方。就这样走了一个小时，每个人都累得饥肠辘辘。突然，面前的树林变得

feeling very tired and very hungry when suddenly the trees began to get thinner in front of them and the ground to fall steeply downhill. A minute later they came out under the open sky (the sun was still shining) and found themselves looking down on a fine sight.

They were standing on the edge of a steep, narrow valley at the bottom of which ran at least it would have been running if it hadn't been frozen a fairly large river. Just below them a dam had been built across this river, and when they saw it everyone suddenly remembered that of course beavers are always making dams and felt quite sure that Mr Beaver had made this one. They also noticed that he now had a sort of modest expression on his, face the sort of look people have when you are visiting a garden they've made or reading a story they've written. So it was only common politeness when Susan said, "What a lovely dam!" And Mr Beaver didn't say "Hush" this time but "Merely a trifle! Merely a trifle! And it isn't really finished!"

稀疏起来，地面的坡度也变得陡峭了。没走几步，他们就走出了树林，头上是蔚蓝的天空，阳光依旧耀眼，向下望去，风景十分优美。

他们站在陡坡的边缘，下面是一条狭长的山谷，如果没有结冰的话，谷底肯定是一条奔腾的大河。在他们正下方，一座水坝跨河而建。看到水坝，他们陡然想起来——海狸可是建水坝的高手。他们很确定，这个水坝就是海狸先生造的。同时，他们注意到，海狸脸上的表情变得谦虚起来，就好像你去参观别人建的花园，或是阅读别人写的一本书，园丁和作者脸上常有的那种表情。苏珊说："好漂亮的水坝呀！"海狸先生这次却没让她小点声，而是说："就是个小玩意儿，不值一提，还没竣工呢！"当然，海狸先生这样说只是出于礼貌。

Above the dam there was what ought to have been a deep pool but was now, of course, a level floor of dark green ice. And below the dam, much lower down, was more ice, but instead of being smooth this was all frozen into the foamy and wavy shapes in which the water had been rushing along at the very moment when the frost came. And where the water had been trickling over and spurting through the dam there was now a glittering wall of icicles, as if the side of the dam had been covered all over with flowers and wreaths and festoons of the purest sugar. And out in the middle, and partly on top of the dam was a funny little house shaped rather like an enormous beehive and from a hole in the roof smoke was going up, so that when you saw it (especially if you were hungry) you at once thought of cooking and became hungrier than you were before.

That was what the others chiefly noticed, but Edmund noticed something else. A little lower down the river there was

在水坝上游，本来有一汪深水池，不过，现在看上去就像是一片平坦的深绿色冰池。水坝下游的水面则要低一些，冰面凹凸不平，翻起的浪花被冻成了泡沫似的形状，显现出波浪起伏的样子。看来，河水在经过水坝奔流直下的时候，被瞬间冻成了冰。曾经流过水坝以及溅在水坝上的河水，现在变成了晶莹剔透的冰墙，看上去，整座水坝就像被点缀了洁白的花朵和花环，还有各种垂花的装饰。在水坝的中间，有一座有趣的小屋，形状像蜂巢一样，屋顶上的洞口正冒出缕缕炊烟，当你看到的时候，尤其是肚子正饿得咕咕叫的时候，下意识就会想到——锅里正烹煮着美味的菜肴，这时你就会感到更饿了。

当其他人都在看水坝和中间的房子时，埃德蒙注意到了其他

another small river which came down another small valley to join it. And looking up that valley, Edmund could see two small hills, and he was almost sure they were the two hills which the White Witch had pointed out to him when he parted from her at the lamp-post that other day. And then between them, he thought, must be her palace, only a mile off or less. And he thought about Turkish Delight and about being a King ("And I wonder how Peter will like that?" he asked himself) and horrible ideas came into his head.

"Here we are," said Mr Beaver, "and it looks as if Mrs Beaver is expecting us. I'll lead the way. But be careful and don't slip."

The top of the dam was wide enough to walk on, though not (for humans) a very nice place to walk because it was covered with ice, and though the frozen pool was level with it on one side, there was a nasty drop to the lower river on the other. Along this route Mr Beaver led them in single file right out to

一些东西。在大河的下游，有另一条小河从一个小山谷中延伸出来，汇入大河之中。遥望山谷上方，埃德蒙可以看见两座小山，他很确定，那就是那天白女巫在灯柱旁边和他分开时所指的那两座小山。两座山之间，肯定就是她的宫殿，离这里只有不到1英里远。他随即想到了香甜可口的土耳其软糖，以及自己将成为未来的国王。“真想看看到时候彼得脸上的表情。”他心中暗暗想着，一个可怕的计划逐渐在他脑中产生了。

“我们到了，”海狸先生说，“看来我太太正在等我们。大家跟着我，小心不要滑倒哦。”

虽然水坝很宽，可表面已经结冰，一边是表面平滑的冰冻水池，可另一边的落差却很大，对人类而言一点儿也不好走。大家

the middle where they could look a long way up the river and a long way down it. And when they had reached the middle they were at the door of the house.

"Here we are, Mrs Beaver," said Mr Beaver, "I've found them. Here are the Sons and Daughters of Adam and Eve'and they all went in."

The first thing Lucy noticed as she went in was a burring sound, and the first thing she saw was a kindlooking old she-beaver sitting in the corner with a thread in her mouth working busily at her sewing machine, and it was from it that the sound came. She stopped her work and got up as soon as the children came in.

"So you've come at last!" she said, holding out both her wrinkled old paws. "At last! To think that ever I should live to see this day! The potatoes are on boiling and the kettle's singing and I daresay, Mr Beaver, you'll get us some fish."

排成一竖排，跟着海狸先生来到了水坝中间。这时可以看到，沿着河水向上有一条很长的路，向下也有一条路。现在，他们来到了水坝中间，屋子的门口。

"老婆子，我们回来啦，"海狸先生说，"我找到他们了。这就是亚当之子和夏娃之女。"说着，大家走进了屋子。

露西一进屋就听到了缝纫机的声音，然后，她看见一只面容慈祥的海狸老妈妈坐在屋子一角，嘴里叼着线，正在缝纫机旁忙活着。孩子们进屋后，它立即停止了手上的工作，抬头望向他们。

"你们终于来了！"它说着，随即伸出一双满是皱纹的爪子，"可算是把你们盼来了！真没想到，我竟然活着等到了这一天！锅里正煮着土豆，水已经烧开了。老头子，你去抓些鱼回来。"

"That I will," said Mr Beaver, and he went out of the house (Peter went with him), and across the ice of the deep pool to where he had a little hole in the ice which he kept open every day with his hatchet. They took a pail with them. Mr Beaver sat down quietly at the edge of the hole (he didn't seem to mind it being so chilly), looked hard into it, then suddenly shot in his paw, and before you could say Jack Robinson had whisked out a beautiful trout. Then he did it all over again until they had a fine catch of fish.

Meanwhile the girls were helping Mrs Beaver to fill the kettle and lay the table and cut the bread and put the plates in the oven to heat and draw a huge jug of beer for Mr Beaver from a barrel which stood in one corner of the house, and to put on the frying-pan and get the dripping hot. Lucy thought the Beavers had a very snug little home though it was not at all like Mr Tumnus's cave. There were no books or pictures, and instead

"好嘞，这就去。"说着，海狸先生拎着桶走出了屋子，彼得跟着它一起去抓鱼。他们跨过冻成冰的深水池，来到另一边。在那儿，有一个冰窟窿，海狸先生每天都会拿小斧子砸一砸，以防窟窿被冻住。只见它静悄悄地坐在冰窟窿边上，一点都不怕冰冷刺骨的河水。它目不转睛地盯着河水，突然间把爪子伸进水里，瞬间抓上来一条漂亮的鳟鱼。就这样，他们不一会儿就抓了好多鱼。

就在海狸先生出去抓鱼的时候，两个女孩子帮着海狸夫人将水壶灌满，收拾饭桌，切好面包，热菜。并且，她们还从屋子角落里的一个大桶里为海狸先生舀了一大罐啤酒。最后，他们把平底锅放在炉子上，倒油烧热。露西心想："海狸先生的家虽然很

of beds there were bunks, like on board ship, built into the wall. And there were hams and strings of onions hanging from the roof, and against the walls were gum boots and oilskins and hatchets and pairs of shears and spades and trowels and things for carrying mortar in and fishing-rods and fishing-nets and sacks. And the cloth on the table, though very clean, was very rough.

Just as the frying-pan was nicely hissing Peter and Mr Beaver came in with the fish which Mr Beaver had already opened with his knife and cleaned out in the open air. You can think how good the new-caught fish smelled while they were frying and how the hungry children longed for them to be done and how very much hungrier still they had become before Mr Beaver said, "Now we're nearly ready." Susan drained the potatoes and then put them all back in the empty pot to dry on the side of the range while Lucy was helping Mrs Beaver to dish

小，可是很温暖，和图姆努斯先生住的山洞完全不同。”这里没有书，也没有照片，连床也是上下铺，看上去就像轮船船舱里嵌在墙上的床一样。房顶上挂着火腿和一串串洋葱，墙边放着塑胶靴子、油布雨衣、小斧子、几把剪刀、铁锹、挖泥用的铲子和其他运泥灰的工具，以及钓鱼竿、渔网和鱼篓。饭桌上的桌布很粗糙，但干净而整洁。

就在平底锅嘶嘶作响的时候，海狸先生和彼得满载而归。海狸先生事先在外面用刀清理好了鱼。新鲜的鱼在烧热的平底锅里煎着，飘出阵阵香气，孩子们饿得都快等不及了，海狸先生却说：“再等等，快好了。”这让孩子们觉得更饿了。苏珊把土豆滤干后，放进一口空锅里烤，露西帮着海狸太太把煎好的鱼分别放在盘子

up the trout, so that in a very few minutes everyone was drawing up their stools (it was all three-legged stools in the Beavers' house except for Mrs Beaver's own special rockingchair beside the fire) and preparing to enjoy themselves. There was a jug of creamy milk for the children (Mr Beaver stuck to beer) and a great big lump of deep yellow butter in the middle of the table from which everyone took as much as he wanted to go with his potatoes, and all the children thought and I agree with them that there's nothing to beat good freshwater fish if you eat it when it has been alive half an hour ago and has come out of the pan half a minute ago. And when they had finished the fish Mrs Beaver brought unexpectedly out of the oven a great and gloriously sticky marmalade roll, steaming hot, and at the same time moved the kettle on to the fire, so that when they had finished the marmalade roll the tea was made and ready to be poured out. And when each person had got his (or her) cup of tea, each person shoved back his (or her) stool so as to be able to lean

里。不一会儿，主人就摆好凳子准备开饭了。大家都坐在三条腿的凳子上，只有海狸太太坐在炉火边的摇椅上。孩子们每人分到了一大杯浓浓的牛奶，海狸先生自然是喝着啤酒，桌子中间摆了一大块深黄色的黄油，大家吃土豆的时候可以随意自取。孩子们都觉得，没有比新鲜的煎鱼更好吃的东西了，尤其是半小时前刚刚抓回来的、半分钟前刚出锅的煎鱼。吃完煎鱼，海狸太太出乎意料地从炉子里拿出还冒着热气的香喷喷、黏糊糊的果酱卷，然后把水壶放在火上烧。孩子们吃完果酱卷之后，茶就泡好了。大家人手一杯茶，把椅子向后移了一下靠在墙上，心满意足地舒了一口气。

against the wall and gave a long sigh of contentment.

"And now," said Mr Beaver, pushing away his empty beer mug and pulling his cup of tea towards him, "if you'll just wait till I've got my pipe lit up and going nicely why, now we can get to business. It's snowing again," he added, cocking his eye at the window. "That's all the better, because it means we shan't have any visitors; and if anyone should have been trying to follow you, why he won't find any tracks."

"看来大家都吃饱了，"海狸先生把空空的啤酒杯一推，把茶杯拿到面前说，"大家少安毋躁，等我抽袋烟，然后，我们就该干正事儿了。现在，又开始下雪了。"说着，它看了看窗外，"下雪了更好，这样，就不会有人来找我们了。就算有人想跟踪你们，也发现不了你们的足迹。"

Chapter Eight What Happened after Dinner

"And now," said Lucy, "do please tell us what's happened to Mr Tumnus."

"Ah, that's bad," said Mr Beaver, shaking his head. "That's a very, very bad business. There's no doubt he was taken off by the police. I got that from a bird who saw it done."

"But where's he been taken to?" asked Lucy.

"Well, they were heading northwards when they were last seen and we all know what that means."

"No, we don't," said Susan. Mr Beaver shook his head in a very gloomy fashion.

"I'm afraid it means they were taking him to her House," he said.

第八章 晚餐之后

"那么现在，"露西说，"请告诉我们，图姆努斯先生到底发生了什么事。"

"唉，很糟糕的事，"海狸先生说着，摇了摇头，"非常非常糟糕的事。他的确是被警察带走的。有只鸟目睹了全过程，并告诉了我。"

"他被带到哪儿去了呢？"露西问。

"最后看见他们的时候，他们正在往北去——你们知道这意味着什么。"

"意味着什么？"苏珊问。

海狸先生非常沮丧地摇了摇头："意味着，他被带去了她的城堡。"

"But what'll they do to him, Mr Beaver?" gasped Lucy.

"Well," said Mr Beaver, "you can't exactly say for sure. But there's not many taken in there that ever comes out again. Statues. All full of statues they say it is in the courtyard and up the stairs and in the hall. People she's turned" (he paused and shuddered) "turned into stone."

"But, Mr Beaver," said Lucy, "can't we I mean we must do something to save him. It's too dreadful and it's all on my account."

"I don't doubt you'd save him if you could, dearie," said Mrs Beaver, "but you've no chance of getting into that House against her will and ever coming out alive."

"Couldn't we have some stratagem?" said Peter. "I mean couldn't we dress up as something, or pretend to be oh, pedlars or anything or watch till she was gone out oh, hang it all, there

"他们会拿他怎么样，海狸先生？"露西喘着气问。

"唉，"海狸先生说，"这就难说了。不过，被白女巫抓去的人很少有活着出来的。他们都被变成了石像——在她城堡的院子里、楼梯上和厅堂里，都是石像，她会把人——"说着，海狸先生颤抖了一下，"把人变成石头。"

"但是，海狸先生，"露西说，"我们必须要把他救出来。就是因为我，他才会遇到麻烦的。"

"亲爱的孩子，我知道，只要有一线希望，你都会救他出来。"海狸太太说，"但是，你要是去她的宫殿反抗她，是不可能活着出来的。"

"要不然，咱们想个办法？"彼得说，"比如，咱们乔装打扮一下，或者假装是小贩什么的，或者等到她出门，咱们偷偷地进

must be some way. This Faun saved my sister at his own risk, Mr Beaver. We can't just leave him to be to be to have that done to him."

"It's no good, Son of Adam," said Mr Beaver, "no good your trying, of all people. But now that Aslan is on the move-"

"Oh, yes! Tell us about Aslan!" said several voices at once; for once again that strange feeling like the first signs of spring, like good news, had come over them.

"Who is Aslan?" asked Susan.

"Aslan?" said Mr Beaver. "Why, don't you know? He's the King. He's the Lord of the whole wood, but not often here, you understand. Never in my time or my father's time. But the word has reached us that he has come back. He is in Narnia at this moment. He'll settle the White Queen all right. It is he, not you, that will save Mr Tumnus."

去。总之，肯定有办法。海狸先生，羊怪救了我妹妹，我们不能就这样扔下他不管，必须得为他做点事情。"

"不行啊，亚当之子，"海狸先生说，"你们再想办法也没用。不过，听说阿斯兰回来了。"

"哦对！给我们讲讲阿斯兰吧！"几个孩子异口同声地说。一提到这个名字，那种奇怪的感觉再次袭来，就像是春天到来时的信号，又像是喜讯拨动着他们的心弦。

"阿斯兰是谁？"苏珊问。

"阿斯兰？"海狸先生说，"你们不知道它吗？它是国王，是这里的森林之王。但它不经常在这里，无论是我父亲的时代还是我这个时代，它从没来过。但是，有传闻说，它已经回来了，现在就在纳尼亚。它会对付白女巫，也只有它可以救得了图姆努斯先生。"

"She won't turn him into stone too?" said Edmund.

"Lord love you, Son of Adam, what a simple thing to say!" answered Mr Beaver with a great laugh. "Turn him into stone? If she can stand on her two feet and look him in the face it'll be the most she can do and more than I expect of her. No, no. He'll put all to rights as it says in an old rhyme in these parts:

Wrong will be right, when Aslan comes in sight,
At the sound of his roar, sorrows will be no more,
When he bares his teeth, winter meets its death,
And when he shakes his mane, we shall have spring again.

You'll understand when you see him."

"But shall we see him?" asked Susan.

"Why, Daughter of Eve, that's what I brought you here for. I'm to lead you where you shall meet him," said Mr Beaver.

"Is-is he a man?" asked Lucy.

"她不会把它也变成石头吗？"埃德蒙问。

"哎！亚当之子，你这个问题可真幼稚！"海狸先生大笑着说，"把它变成石头？她要是敢站在阿斯兰的面前，正视它一眼，那她就算厉害了。我肯定，她绝对不敢那么做。阿斯兰会重整河山，就好像那首古老的诗歌里写的：

当阿斯兰到来我们面前，是非颠倒的现象将会改变，它怒吼的声音，将所有悲伤化成云烟，它露出獠牙，漫漫严冬就会消失不见，它抖抖鬃毛，我们会重见春天。等你们看见它，就都明白了。"

"所以，我们要去见他？"苏珊问。

"当然了，夏娃之女，这就是我带你们来这儿的原因。我会带着你们去见它。"海狸先生说。

"他——他是人类吗？"露西问。

"Aslan a man!" said Mr Beaver sternly. "Certainly not. I tell you he is the King of the wood and the son of the great Emperor-beyond-the-Sea. Don't you know who is the King of Beasts? Aslan is a lion the Lion, the great Lion."

"Ooh!" said Susan, "I'd thought he was a man. Is he quite safe? I shall feel rather nervous about meeting a lion."

"That you will, dearie, and no mistake," said Mrs Beaver; "if there's anyone who can appear before Aslan without their knees knocking, they're either braver than most or else just silly."

"Then he isn't safe?" said Lucy.

"Safe?" said Mr Beaver; "don't you hear what Mrs Beaver tells you? Who said anything about safe? 'Course he isn't safe. But he's good. He's the King, I tell you."

"I'm longing to see him," said Peter, "even if I do feel frightened when it comes to the point."

"阿斯兰是人类？！"海狸先生严肃地说，"当然不是。我说了，它是森林之王——大洋彼岸大帝的儿子。你们知道百兽之王吗？阿斯兰是头狮子，一头伟大的狮子。"

"哦！"苏珊说，"我还以为它是人类呢。那它——会伤人吗？我要是见到一头狮子，肯定紧张死了。"

"亲爱的孩子，你当然会紧张了，这倒没什么奇怪的。"海狸太太说，"如果有人站在阿斯兰面前而不双腿打战的话，要不他就是个极其英勇的勇士，要不他就是个傻子。"

"那它很吓人了？"露西问。

"吓人？"海狸先生说，"你没听见我家老婆子说的？它当然令人生畏，不过，它是国王，心肠很好的。"

"我真想见见它，"彼得说，"虽然我看见它的时候，肯定会被

"That's right, Son of Adam," said Mr Beaver, bringing his paw down on the table with a crash that made all the cups and saucers rattle. "And so you shall. Word has been sent that you are to meet him, tomorrow if you can, at the Stone Table."

"Where's that?" said Lucy.

"I'll show you," said Mr Beaver. "It's down the river, a good step from here. I'll take you to it!"

"But meanwhile what about poor Mr Tumnus?" said Lucy.

"The quickest way you can help him is by going to meet Aslan," said Mr Beaver, "once he's with us, then we can begin doing things. Not that we don't need you too. For that's another of the old rhymes:

When Adam's flesh and Adam's bone,
Sits at Cair Paravel in throne,
The evil time will be over and done.

吓得半死。"

"你说得没错，亚当之子。"说着，海狸先生一爪子重重地拍在桌子上，震得碗碟哗哗作响，"你会见到它的。有人给我带话，明天，我带你们去石台那里见它。"

"石台在哪儿？"露西问。

"你来看，"海狸先生说，"就在河的下游，离这里很远。我会带你们去的。"

"可是，图姆努斯先生怎么办？"露西问。

"你们想要救他，最快的方式就是去见阿斯兰。"海狸先生说，"只要和它在一起，我们就有办法。可这并不是说不需要你们的帮忙。还有一首古老的歌谣是这么说的：

一旦亚当的后人，登上凯尔·帕拉维尔城堡的王座，一切邪

So things must be drawing near their end now he's come and you've come. We've heard of Aslan coming into these parts before long ago, nobody can say when. But there's never been any of your race here before."

"That's what I don't understand, Mr Beaver," said Peter, "I mean isn't the Witch herself human?"

"She'd like us to believe it," said Mr Beaver, "and it's on that that she bases her claim to be Queen. But she's no Daughter of Eve. She comes of your father Adam's" (here Mr Beaver bowed) "your father Adam's first wife, her they called Lilith. And she was one of the Jinn. That's what she comes from on one side. And on the other she comes of the giants. No, no, there isn't a drop of real human blood in the Witch."

"That's why she's bad all through, Mr Beaver," said Mrs Beaver.

"True enough, Mrs Beaver," replied he, "there may be

灵将一去不复返。

现在，它回来了，你们也来了，那么这一切也该结束了。我们听说，阿斯兰很久很久以前来过，但是人类却从来没出现过。"

"有一点我不太明白，海狸先生。"彼得说，"那个女巫不是人类吗？"

"她希望我们相信她是人类，"海狸先生说，"只有这样她才能称自己是女王。但她并不是夏娃之女。她是亚当——"说到亚当的时候，海狸先生站起来鞠了一躬，"和第一任妻子莉莉丝之女。莉莉丝是女妖，所以女巫身上既有女妖的血统，也有巨人的血统，却没有一丝真正人类的血统。"

"老头子，这就是她为什么这么坏的原因。"海狸太太说。

"没错，老婆子。"它回答说，"对于人类，普遍有两种看

two views about humans (meaning no offence to the present company). But there's no two views about things that look like humans and aren't."

"I've known good Dwarfs," said Mrs Beaver.

"So've I, now you come to speak of it," said her husband, "but precious few, and they were the ones least like men. But in general, take my advice, when you meet anything that's going to be human and isn't yet, or used to be human once and isn't now, or ought to be human and isn't, you keep your eyes on it and feel for your hatchet. And that's why the Witch is always on the lookout for any humans in Narnia. She's been watching for you this many a year, and if she knew there were four of you she'd be more dangerous still."

"What's that to do with it?" asked Peter.

"Because of another prophecy," said Mr Beaver. "Down at Cair Paravel that's the castle on the sea coast down at the mouth

法——我并没有冒犯在座各位的意思。不过，对于那些看着像人其实不是人的东西，就不存在这两种看法了。"

"我就认识一个很好的矮人。"海狸太太说。

"我也认识，"海狸先生说，"不过，要知道，矮人中善良的很少，而且他们是最不像人类的。总之，我想劝你们，如果你们碰到想变成人类但并没有变成的；或者曾经是人类但现在不是的；或者本应该是人类但现在不是的——都要提高警惕，时刻准备好武器对付他们——这就是女巫为什么害怕人类出现在纳尼亚的原因——她已经提防你们很多年了，如果她知道现在你们四个都在这儿，她会比以往更加危险。"

"那会怎么样？"彼得问。

"有另一个预言，"海狸先生说，"在河流入海口的凯尔·帕拉

of this river which ought to be the capital of the whole country if all was as it should be down at Cair Paravel there are four thrones and it's a saying in Narnia time out of mind that when two Sons of Adam and two Daughters of Eve sit in those four thrones, then it will be the end not only of the White Witch's reign but of her life, and that is why we had to be so cautious as we came along, for if she knew about you four, your lives wouldn't be worth a shake of my whiskers!"

All the children had been attending so hard to what Mr Beaver was telling them that they had noticed nothing else for a long time. Then during the moment of silence that followed his last remark, Lucy suddenly said: "I say-where's Edmund?"

There was a dreadful pause, and then everyone began asking "Who saw him last? How long has he been missing? Is he outside?" and then all rushed to the door and looked out. The snow was falling thickly and steadily, the green ice of the pool

维尔城堡，本应是这片王国的首都，那里有四个王座。在纳尼亚有一个很古老的传说——如果两个亚当之子和两个夏娃之女坐上了四个王座，不仅白女巫的统治会结束，连她的生命都会消失殆尽。这就是为什么在来的路上我们特别小心的缘由——如果她知道了你们的存在，想要害死你们就像我抖抖胡子这么容易！”

孩子们都聚精会神地听着海狸先生讲故事，却没有注意周遭的变化。海狸先生说完后，大家一时寂静无声，这时，露西突然说：“埃德蒙去哪了？”

先是一阵可怕的沉默，继而大家开始互相问：“谁最后看见他了？他到底什么时候不见的？他会不会在外面？”随后大家冲出房门，到外面寻找。外面雪下得很大，那一汪墨绿色的冰池已经

had vanished under a thick white blanket, and from where the little house stood in the centre of the dam you could hardly see either bank. Out they went, plunging well over their ankles into the soft new snow, and went round the house in every direction. "Edmund! Edmund!" they called till they were hoarse. But the silently falling snow seemed to muffle their voices and there was not even an echo in answer.

"How perfectly dreadful!" said Susan as they at last came back in despair. "Oh, how I wish we'd never come."

"What on earth are we to do, Mr Beaver?" said Peter.

"Do?" said Mr Beaver, who was already putting on his snow-boots, "do? We must be off at once. We haven't a moment to spare!"

"We'd better divide into four search parties," said Peter, "and all go in different directions. Whoever finds him must come back here at once and-"

被白雪覆盖了。站在水坝中间的屋子旁，几乎看不见两边的河岸。他们屋前屋后地寻找，双脚深深地陷在刚落下的柔软的雪中。“埃德蒙……埃德蒙……”他们喊得嗓子都哑了。但他们的呼喊声似乎都被寂静的大雪淹没了，连一点儿回声都听不到。

“怎么会这样！”他们回到屋子里，苏珊沮丧地说，“我真希望咱们没来过这里。”

“海狸先生，我们现在该怎么办？”彼得问。

“怎么办？”海狸先生立刻穿上了雪地靴，“我们现在必须马上出发，一刻都不能耽误了。”

“我们最好分成两组去搜寻，”彼得说，“每组走不同的方向。无论谁找到了他，都必须马上回来，然后——”

"Search parties, Son of Adam?" said Mr Beaver; "what for?"

"Why, to look for Edmund, of course!"

"There's no point in looking for him," said Mr Beaver.

"What do you mean?" said Susan. "He can't be far away yet. And we've got to find him. What do you mean when you say there's no use looking for him?"

"The reason there's no use looking," said Mr Beaver, "is that we know already where he's gone!" Everyone stared in amazement. "Don't you understand?" said Mr Beaver. "He's gone to her, to the White Witch. He has betrayed us all."

"Oh, surely-oh, really!" said Susan, "he can't have done that."

"Can't he?" said Mr Beaver, looking very hard at the three children, and everything they wanted to say died on their lips, for each felt suddenly quite certain inside that this was exactly

"分组搜寻？"海狸先生问，"亚当之子，为什么？"

"当然是找埃德蒙啦！"

"我们没必要找他。"海狸先生说。

"您到底什么意思？"苏珊问，"他肯定不会走得太远。我们必须要找到他。您为什么说没有必要呢？"

"我说没有必要，"海狸先生说，"是因为我已经知道他去哪儿了！"大家都疑惑地盯着它。"你们还不明白吗？"海狸先生继续说，"他去投奔白女巫了，他背叛了我们。"

"哦，天哪！怎么可能！"苏珊说，"他不会这么做的。"

"是吗？"海狸先生严肃地注视着三个孩子，孩子们话到嘴边，还是咽了回去。大家瞬间明白了——埃德蒙原来真的做了那样的事。

what Edmund had done.

"But will he know the way?" said Peter.

"Has he been in this country before?" asked Mr Beaver. "Has he ever been here alone?"

"Yes," said Lucy, almost in a whisper. "I'm afraid he has."

"And did he tell you what he'd done or who he'd met?"

"Well, no, he didn't," said Lucy.

"Then mark my words," said Mr Beaver, "he has already met the White Witch and joined her side, and been told where she lives. I didn't like to mention it before (he being your brother and all) but the moment I set eyes on that brother of yours I said to myself 'Treacherous'. He had the look of one who has been with the Witch and eaten her food. You can always tell them if you've lived long in Narnia; something about their eyes."

"All the same," said Peter in a rather choking sort of voice, "we'll still have to go and look for him. He is our brother after

"可是，他知道路吗？"彼得说。

"他之前来过这儿吗？"海狸先生问，"他之前自己一个人来过吗？"

"来过，"露西小声地回答，"他一个人来过。"

"他告诉过你，上次来他干了什么，见了什么人吗？"

"没有，他没跟我说过。"露西说。

"你们听我说，"海狸先生说，"他已经见过白女巫了，也已经投靠了她，并且知道她的城堡在哪里。之前我不想说，毕竟他是你们的兄弟——当我第一眼看见他时，我就知道他有问题。他一看就是和白女巫待过一段时间，并且吃了她给的东西。如果你们在纳尼亚待上一段时间，就能通过眼神看出来。"

"无论怎样，"彼得有些哽咽地说，"我们还是要找到他。虽然

all, even if he is rather a little beast. And he's only a kid."

"Go to the Witch's House?" said Mrs Beaver. "Don't you see that the only chance of saving either him or yourselves is to keep away from her?"

"How do you mean?" said Lucy.

"Why, all she wants is to get all four of you (she's thinking all the time of those four thrones at Cair Paravel). Once you were all four inside her House her job would be done and there'd be four new statues in her collection before you'd had time to speak. But she'll keep him alive as long as he's the only one she's got, because she'll want to use him as a decoy; as bait to catch the rest of you with."

"Oh, can no one help us?" wailed Lucy.

"Only Aslan," said Mr Beaver, "we must go on and meet him. That's our only chance now."

他被女巫蒙骗了，可毕竟还是我们的兄弟——他还是个孩子啊！"

"怎么救？去女巫的城堡？"海狸太太说，"你们还不明白吗，唯一能救他和救你们自己的办法，就是离女巫越远越好。"

"为什么这么说呢？"露西问。

"她肯定想要把你们四个都抓住，因为她一直觊觎凯尔·帕拉维尔城堡的王座。你们四个要是都去了她的城堡，那就相当于帮了她。到时候，你们还来不及说话，她就会直接把你们变成石像。可如果她只抓住了一个，就会保住他的性命，因为女巫想要用他当诱饵，把你们都抓住。"

"难道就没人能帮我们吗？"露西哭着说。

"只有阿斯兰可以帮你们。"海狸先生说，"我们现在必须出发去见它，它是我们唯一的机会了。"

"It seems to me, my dears," said Mrs Beaver, "that it is very important to know just when he slipped away. How much he can tell her depends on how much he heard. For instance, had we started talking of Aslan before he left? If not, then we may do very well, for she won't know that Aslan has come to Narnia, or that we are meeting him, and will be quite off her guard as far as that is concerned."

"I don't remember his being here when we were talking about Aslan -" began Peter, but Lucy interrupted him.

"Oh yes, he was," she said miserably; "don't you remember, it was he who asked whether the Witch couldn't turn Aslan into stone too?"

"So he did, by Jove," said Peter; "just the sort of thing he would say, too!"

"Worse and worse," said Mr Beaver, "and the next thing is this. Was he still here when I told you that the place for meeting

"老头子，有个问题。"海狸太太说，"你们知道他是什么时候溜走的吗？他跟女巫告密了多少事情，取决于他刚才听到了多少。如果他是在我们讲到阿斯兰之前就溜走了，那还好办些，因为女巫不会知道阿斯兰已经回到了纳尼亚，以及我们要见它的事情。这样，我们还能避开她的耳目。"

"我不记得咱们讲到阿斯兰的时候他在不在了……"彼得正说着，露西打断了他。

"他当时还在，"她的语气听起来很沮丧，"你们记不记得？他当时问，女巫难道不会把阿斯兰也变成石头吗？"

"哦，天哪，他确实在，"彼得说，"也就是他会问出这样的问题。"

Aslan was the Stone Table?"

And of course no one knew the answer to this question.

"Because, if he was," continued Mr Beaver, "then she'll simply sledge down in that direction and get between us and the Stone Table and catch us on our way down. In fact we shall be cut off from Aslan."

"But that isn't what she'll do first," said Mrs Beaver, "not if I know her. The moment that Edmund tells her that we're all here she'll set out to catch us this very night, and if he's been gone about half an hour, she'll be here in about another twenty minutes."

"You're right, Mrs Beaver," said her husband, "we must all get away from here. There's not a moment to lose."

"这下可糟了，"海狸先生说，"还有件事，当我们说到要在石台见阿斯兰的时候，他还在吗？"

没人能回答这个问题。

"如果当时他还在的话，"海狸先生继续说，"她就会驾着雪橇，在我们去石台的路上截住我们，这样我们就见不到阿斯兰了。"

"我觉得她不会这么做，"海狸太太说，"据我对她的了解，当埃德蒙告诉她我们都在这儿的时候，她今晚就会来抓我们。要是他已经溜走了半个小时的话，女巫20分钟后就会到。"

"老婆子，你说得太对了，"海狸先生说，"现在，所有人必须全部离开，真的是一分钟都不能耽误了。"

CHAPTER NINE IN THE WITCH'S HOUSE

And now of course you want to know what had happened to Edmund. He had eaten his share of the dinner, but he hadn't really enjoyed it because he was thinking all the time about Turkish Delight and there's nothing that spoils the taste of good ordinary food half so much as the memory of bad magic food. And he had heard the conversation, and hadn't enjoyed it much either, because he kept on thinking that the others were taking no notice of him and trying to give him the cold shoulder. They weren't, but he imagined it. And then he had listened until Mr Beaver told them about Aslan and until he had heard the whole arrangement for meeting Aslan at the Stone Table. It was then that he began very quietly to edge himself under the curtain which hung over the door. For the mention of Aslan gave him a mysterious and horrible feeling just as it gave the others a mysterious and lovely feeling.

Just as Mr Beaver had been repeating the rhyme about

第九章 女巫的房子

现在，你们已经知道埃德蒙发生了什么事。他吃完了自己的那份饭，感觉味同嚼蜡，因为他一直想着土耳其软糖——任何人间美味都无法和记忆中施了魔法的食物相比。埃德蒙听着他们之间的对话，感觉很不是滋味，他觉得其他人都不理他、冷落他。然而，事实并非如此，这一切都是他想象出来的。当他听到海狸先生说了关于阿斯兰的事，以及如何与阿斯兰在石台见面的安排。埃德蒙便悄悄地挪到挂在门旁边的帘子下——他一听到阿斯兰这个名字，就感到莫名的恐惧，就好像其他人感到莫名的开心一样。

就在海狸先生讲到关于亚当后人的那首歌谣时，埃德蒙悄悄

Adam's flesh and Adam's bone Edmund had been very quietly turning the door handle; and just before Mr Beaver had begun telling them that the White Witch wasn't really human at all but half a Jinn and half a giantess, Edmund had got outside into the snow and cautiously closed the door behind him.

You mustn't think that even now Edmund was quite so bad that he actually wanted his brother and sisters to be turned into stone. He did want Turkish Delight and to be a Prince (and later a King) and to pay Peter out for calling him a beast. As for what the Witch would do with the others, he didn't want her to be particularly nice to them certainly not to put them on the same level as himself; but he managed to believe, or to pretend he believed, that she wouldn't do anything very bad to them, "Because," he said to himself, "all these people who say nasty things about her are her enemies and probably half of it isn't true. She was jolly nice to me, anyway, much nicer than they are.

地拧开了门把手；在海狸先生讲到白女巫实际上一半是女妖一半是巨人之前，他悄悄地起身来到屋外，小心地把门关上。

其实，埃德蒙没有大家想象的那么坏，他并不想让女王把他的几个兄弟姐妹都变成石像。然而，他确实非常想吃土耳其软糖，还想成为王子，甚至是未来的国王，而且要给自己出一口恶气——因为彼得曾经叫他"熊孩子"。而对于女巫会怎么对待其他人，他倒是希望不要对他们太好，至少不要和他过得一样好。他让自己试图相信，女巫不会对他们做出可怕的事。他告诉自己："所有说她坏话的人都是她的敌人，也许这些坏话有一半都是假的。无论怎样，她对我很好，比对其他人都好。我认为，她就是名正言顺的女王。而且，她绝对比那个可怕的阿斯兰要好！"反

I expect she is the rightful Queen really. Anyway, she'll be better than that awful Aslan!" At least, that was the excuse he made in his own mind for what he was doing. It wasn't a very good excuse, however, for deep down inside him he really knew that the White Witch was bad and cruel.

The first thing he realized when he got outside and found the snow falling all round him, was that he had left his coat behind in the Beavers' house. And of course there was no chance of going back to get it now. The next thing he realized was that the daylight was almost gone, for it had been nearly three o'clock when they sat down to dinner and the winter days were short. He hadn't reckoned on this; but he had to make the best of it. So he turned up his collar and shuffled across the top of the dam (luckily it wasn't so slippery since the snow had fallen) to the far side of the river.

It was pretty bad when he reached the far side. It was growing darker every minute and what with that and the

正，他就是给自己做的事情在找借口而已。当然，这并不是一个高明的借口。因为在他的内心深处，他其实知道——白女巫又狠毒又凶残。

出门后，他就发现外面在下雪，可他却把大衣落在了海狸夫妇家。现在，他也不可能回去拿了。然后，他意识到，现在天色已晚，他们坐下来吃饭的时候已经是下午三点多了，而在冬天，白天很短。他之前没估计到这一点，不过，现在只能是走一步算一步了。埃德蒙立起衣领，蹒跚地走过水坝——幸亏下了雪，水坝上没有那么滑。然后，他朝着远处的河岸走去。

等他到了河的另一边时，情况就不大妙了。天越来越黑，雪花打着旋儿地从天空落下，他几乎看不见3英尺以外的地方。而

snowflakes swirling all round him he could hardly see three feet ahead. And then too there was no road. He kept slipping into deep drifts of snow, and skidding on frozen puddles, and tripping over fallen tree-trunks, and sliding down steep banks, and barking his shins against rocks, till he was wet and cold and bruised all over. The silence and the loneliness were dreadful. In fact I really think he might have given up the whole plan and gone back and owned up and made friends with the others, if he hadn't happened to say to himself, "When I'm King of Narnia the first thing I shall do will be to make some decent roads." And of course that set him off thinking about being a King and all the other things he would do and this cheered him up a good deal. He had just settled in his mind what sort of palace he would have and how many cars and all about his private cinema and where the principal railways would run and what laws he would make against beavers and dams and was putting the finishing touches to some schemes for keeping Peter in his place, when

且，这地方没有路，他总是踩进深深的雪堆里，滑倒在结冰的水洼上，或是被大树干绊倒，从陡峭的河岸上滑下去，还被岩石划破了皮。他又湿又冷，浑身疼得不行。寂静和孤独是如此可怕，让人都以为他会放弃这个计划，回去认个错，再跟大家和好呢。可是，埃德蒙却一直对自己说："我要是当上了纳尼亚的国王，第一件事就是修几条像样的路。"就这样，他一直想着自己当上国王后要做些什么事，这大大地鼓舞了他的士气。他还想着，自己要修建一座怎么样的皇宫，要有多少台车和私人影院，主要铁路通向哪里，以及针对海狸和水坝要定怎样的法律加以限制，还要制定不许彼得出去乱讲话的制度，等等。他正想着，雪停了，刺骨的狂风刮了起来，埃德蒙感觉更冷了。风把云彩吹走，露出

the weather changed. First the snow stopped. Then a wind sprang up and it became freezing cold. Finally, the clouds rolled away and the moon came out. It was a full moon and, shining on all that snow, it made everything almost as bright as day only the shadows were rather confusing.

He would never have found his way if the moon hadn't come out by the time he got to the other river you remember he had seen (when they first arrived at the Beavers') a smaller river flowing into the great one lower down. He now reached this and turned to follow it up. But the little valley down which it came was much steeper and rockier than the one he had just left and much overgrown with bushes, so that he could not have managed it at all in the dark. Even as it was, he got wet through for he had to stoop under branches and great loads of snow came sliding off on to his back. And every time this happened he thought more and more how he hated Peter just as if all this had been Peter's fault.

But at last he came to a part where it was more level and the

又圆又亮的月亮。皎洁的月光照在雪地上，把周围的一切都照亮了，只是那些影子看上去很奇怪。

如果不是月亮出来了，埃德蒙根本就找不到路。现在，他到达了另一条小河，就是刚到海狸夫妇家的时候，他们从水坝上看到的不远处与大河交汇的那条小河。他沿着小河继续往前走，这个小山谷的地势更加陡峭，岩石众多、灌木丛生。要是在黑暗中的话，他绝对会迷路。即便现在有月光照亮，他还是浑身湿透了，因为他得弯腰走在树枝下，所以，树上的积雪全都落在了他的后背上——越是这样，他越对彼得恨得牙根儿痒痒，好像自己经历的这一切都是彼得的错！

终于，他走到了一片平坦的路上，前面的山谷也开阔了许多。

valley opened out. And there, on the other side of the river, quite close to him, in the middle of a little plain between two hills, he saw what must be the White Witch's House. And the moon was shining brighter than ever. The House was really a small castle. It seemed to be all towers; little towers with long pointed spires on them, sharp as needles. They looked like huge dunce's caps or sorcerer's caps. And they shone in the moonlight and their long shadows looked strange on the snow. Edmund began to be afraid of the House.

But it was too late to think of turning back now.

He crossed the river on the ice and walked up to the House. There was nothing stirring; not the slightest sound anywhere. Even his own feet made no noise on the deep newly fallen snow. He walked on and on, past corner after corner of the House, and past turret after turret to find the door. He had to go right round to the far side before he found it. It was a huge arch but the great iron gates stood wide open.

Edmund crept up to the arch and looked inside into the

这时候，月亮似乎更加明亮了。在离他很近的河的另一边，在两座小山中间的一片平地上，埃德蒙看见了一所房子——那一定就是白女巫的住处了。说是房子，其实更像是一座城堡。整座城堡由很多塔组成，塔顶尖尖的，看上去好像笨学生的帽子，或是巫师帽。在月光的照耀下，塔尖在雪地上留下了长长的、奇怪的影子。埃德蒙有些害怕这个城堡了。

不过，现在他即使想要回头，也已经来不及了。

他走过被冻成冰的小河，来到城堡前。周围寂静无声，就连他踩在深深的雪地里，都没有发出声音。他走啊走啊，走过了每个角落、每个塔楼，就是没看见大门。直到他绕到城堡的另一面，才看见一个敞开的拱形的大铁门。

courtyard, and there he saw a sight that nearly made his heart stop beating. Just inside the gate, with the moonlight shining on it, stood an enormous lion crouched as if it was ready to spring. And Edmund stood in the shadow of the arch, afraid to go on and afraid to go back, with his knees knocking together. He stood there so long that his teeth would have been chattering with cold even if they had not been chattering with fear. How long this really lasted I don't know, but it seemed to Edmund to last for hours.

Then at last he began to wonder why the lion was standing so still for it hadn't moved one inch since he first set eyes on it. Edmund now ventured a little nearer, still keeping in the shadow of the arch as much as he could. He now saw from the way the lion was standing that it couldn't have been looking at him at all. ("But supposing it turns its head?" thought Edmund.) In fact it was staring at something else namely a little: dwarf who

埃德蒙蹑手蹑脚地走向拱门，朝院子里张望。结果，那景象差点把他吓死。借着月光，可以看见，在大门里，有一头巨大的狮子蹲坐在那里，看姿势好像要马上跳起来似的。埃德蒙站在拱门的阴影里，双膝颤抖，进也不是走也不是。他站在那里好长时间，最后牙齿不停地打战——不是怕，而是被冻的。也不知站了多久，埃德蒙觉得至少有几个小时。

最后，他的脑子清醒了些，想知道为什么从他看见那头狮子开始，它就一直一动不动。埃德蒙小心翼翼地靠近了一点，但还是尽量让自己待在拱门的阴影里。而他现在所在的那个地方，狮子根本看不到他。“可万一它突然回头了怎么办？”埃德蒙心想。看上去，那头狮子正盯着什么，在它前方4英尺远的地方，有一

stood with his back to it about four feet away. "Aha!" thought Edmund. "When it springs at the dwarf then will be my chance to escape." But still the lion never moved, nor did the dwarf. And now at last Edmund remembered what the others had said about the White Witch turning people into stone. Perhaps this was only a stone lion. And as soon as he had thought of that he noticed that the lion's back and the top of its head were covered with snow. Of course it must be only a statue! No living animal would have let itself get covered with snow. Then very slowly and with his heart beating as if it would burst, Edmund ventured to go up to the lion. Even now he hardly dared to touch it, but at last he put out his hand, very quickly, and did. It was cold stone. He had been frightened of a mere statue!

The relief which Edmund felt was so great that in spite of the cold he suddenly got warm all over right down to his toes, and at the same time there came into his head what seemed a

个矮人背对着它。"啊，太好了！"埃德蒙想，"等它扑向矮人的时候，我就可以趁机逃跑了。"可狮子还是一动不动，矮人也是一样。终于，埃德蒙想起来，其他人说白女巫会把人变成石头。这么说，这头狮子其实就是块石头！正想着，他注意到，狮子的后背和头顶落满了积雪。没错，那绝对是一尊石像！要是活着的动物，怎么可能身上有这么多积雪呢！埃德蒙慢慢地靠近狮子，心脏扑通扑通跳着，都快跳出胸膛来了。来到近前，他还是不敢去摸。最后，他终于鼓起勇气，伸手快速地摸了一下——果然是冰冷的石头。原来，他害怕了大半天的东西，竟然是石头。

埃德蒙瞬间松了一口气，尽管天那么冷，他突然从头到脚都暖和起来了。这时，他脑中蹦出了一个心满意足的想法："或许，

perfectly lovely idea. “Probably,” he thought, “this is the great Lion Aslan that they were all talking about. She’s caught him already and turned him into stone. So that’s the end of all their fine ideas about him! Pooh! Who’s afraid of Aslan?”

And he stood there gloating over the stone lion, and presently he did something very silly and childish. He took a stump of lead pencil out of his pocket and scribbled a moustache on the lion’s upper lip and then a pair of spectacles on its eyes. Then he said, “Yah! Silly old Aslan! How do you like being a stone? You thought yourself mighty fine, didn’t you?” But in spite of the scribbles on it the face of the great stone beast still looked so terrible, and sad, and noble, staring up in the moonlight, that Edmund didn’t really get any fun out of jeering at it. He turned away and began to cross the courtyard.

As he got into the middle of it he saw that there were dozens of statues all about standing here and there rather as the

这就是他们说的那头伟大的狮子阿斯兰。女巫肯定是抓住了它，然后把它变成石头了。他们竟然还想指望这头狮子！呸！现在谁还怕阿斯兰啊！”

他在那里幸灾乐祸地看着石狮子，然后，做了一件特别孩子气的蠢事。他从口袋里掏出铅笔，在狮子的嘴唇上涂了两撇小胡子，还在狮子的眼睛上画了一副眼镜。画完后，他说：“又笨又蠢的阿斯兰，变成石头的滋味怎么样啊？你以为自己很了不起，是吧？”尽管他在狮子脸上乱涂乱画，可它看起来还是那么吓人——它仰头望着月光，看起来又悲伤、又高贵。结果，埃德蒙并没有因为戏弄狮子而感到很开心。他转过身，穿过院子走了进去。

来到院子中间，埃德蒙看见这里到处都是站立的石像，就好

pieces stand on a chess-board when it is half-way through the game. There were stone satyrs, and stone wolves, and bears and foxes and cat-amountains of stone. There were lovely stone shapes that looked like women but who were really the spirits of trees. There was the great shape of a centaur and a winged horse and a long lithe creature that Edmund took to be a dragon. They all looked so strange standing there perfectly life-like and also perfectly still, in the bright cold moonlight, that it was eerie work crossing the courtyard. Right in the very middle stood a huge shape like a man, but as tall as a tree, with a fierce face and a shaggy beard and a great club in its right hand. Even though he knew that it was only a stone giant and not a live one, Edmund did not like going past it.

He now saw that there was a dim light showing from a doorway on the far side of the courtyard. He went to it; there was a flight of stone steps going up to an open door. Edmund went up them. Across the threshold lay a great wolf.

像一局棋下到一半，摆在棋盘上的棋子似的。这里有森林之神、狼、熊、狐狸和山猫的石像。还有一些很可爱的石像，看上去像是女人——其实是树中的精灵。这里还有一个半人半马的巨大石像，以及一只长着翅膀的石马。另外，还有一条长长的软体动物，埃德蒙觉得那是一条龙。在冰冷的月光下，它们一动不动地站在那里，却又栩栩如生，埃德蒙在穿过院子的时候感觉头皮发麻。在院子的正中间，有一个巨大的人形石像，和树一样高，面相凶残，胡子拉碴，右手还拿了根大棒子。即便知道这只是个石头巨人，不是活的，埃德蒙还是不愿意从他身边走过去。

这时，他看见院子另一头的门口透出一丝昏暗的灯光。埃德蒙走过去，那里有几级通向门口的石台阶。埃德蒙走上去，看见门槛上趴着一只巨狼。

"It's all right, it's all right," he kept saying to himself; "it's only a stone wolf. It can't hurt me", and he raised his leg to step over it. Instantly the huge creature rose, with all the hair bristling along its back, opened a great, red mouth and said in a growling voice: "Who's there? Who's there? Stand still, stranger, and tell me who you are."

"If you please, sir," said Edmund, trembling so that he could hardly speak, "my name is Edmund, and I'm the Son of Adam that Her Majesty met in the wood the other day and I've come to bring her the news that my brothcr and sisters are now in Narnia quite close, in the Beavers' house. She she wanted to see them."

"I will tell Her Majesty," said the Wolf. "Meanwhile, stand still on the threshold, as you value your life." Then it vanished into the house.

Edmund stood and waited, his fingers aching with cold

"没关系，没关系，"他不停地对自己说，"只是一只石头狼，不会伤害我的。"他正要抬腿迈过去，那只巨兽立马站了起来，身上的毛根根竖起，张开血盆大口吼道："你是谁？你是谁？站住，报上名来。"

"这位先生，麻烦您通报一下，"埃德蒙哆哆嗦嗦地，都快说不出话了，"我叫埃德蒙，我是亚当之子，几天前在树林里见过女王陛下。我来想告诉女王，我的兄弟姐妹现在都在纳尼亚，离这里很近，就在海狸夫妇家里。她……她想见他们。"

"我会禀告女王陛下的。"那头狼说，"与此同时，你要是想活命的话，就站在这里别动。"然后，它消失在了城堡里。

埃德蒙站在那里等着，他的手指都冻僵了，心脏怦怦直跳。就

and his heart pounding in his chest, and presently the grey wolf, Maugrim, the Chief of the Witch's Secret Police, came bounding back and said, "Come in! Come in! Fortunate favourite of the Queen or else not so fortunate."

And Edmund went in, taking great care not to tread on the Wolf's paws.

He found himself in a long gloomy hall with many pillars, full, as the courtyard had been, of statues. The one nearest the door was a little faun with a very sad expression on its face, and Edmund couldn't help wondering if this might be Lucy's friend. The only light came from a single lamp and close beside this sat the White Witch.

"I'm come, your Majesty," said Edmund, rushing eagerly forward.

"How dare you come alone?" said the Witch in a terrible voice. "Did I not tell you to bring the others with you?"

在这时，那头大灰狼——女巫手下的秘密警察队长——毛戈林，小跑着回来说："快来吧！女王的幸运宠儿，不然，你就没那么幸运了。"

埃德蒙跟着这只狼走进城堡，一路提心吊胆，生怕踩到狼尾巴。

他来到一间长长的、有很多柱子的阴暗大厅里，里面摆满了和院子里一样的石像。离门最近的石像是一只表情沮丧的小羊怪。埃德蒙忍不住想，这是否就是露西的那个羊怪朋友。大厅里只点了一盏灯，白女巫就坐在这盏灯后面。

"女王陛下，我来了。"埃德蒙赶忙走上前说道。

"你怎敢一人前来？"女王的声音听起来很可怕，"我不是告诉你，要把其他人一起带来吗？"

"Please, your Majesty," said Edmund, "I've done the best I can. I've brought them quite close. They're in the little house on top of the dam just up the river with Mr and Mrs Beaver."

A slow cruel smile came over the Witch's face.

"Is this all your news?" she asked.

"No, your Majesty," said Edmund, and proceeded to tell her all he had heard before leaving the Beavers' house.

"What! Aslan?" cried the Queen, "Aslan! Is this true? If I find you havc licd to mc -"

"Please, I'm only repeating what they said," stammered Edmund.

But the Queen, who was no longer attending to him, clapped her hands. Instantly the same dwarf whom Edmund had seen with her before appeared.

"Make ready our sledge," ordered the Witch, "and use the harness without bells."

"女王陛下，"埃德蒙解释说，"我已经尽力了，他们离这里很近，就在不远处水坝上方海狸夫妇的家里。"

女巫冷笑道："你就只有这些消息吗？"

"不，女王陛下，"埃德蒙说，然后将在海狸夫妇那里听来的事情都告诉了女巫。

"什么？阿斯兰？"女巫叫道，"阿斯兰！这是真的？如果我发现你对我说谎——"

"女王陛下，我只是复述了他们说的话而已。"埃德蒙结结巴巴地说。

然而，女王已经不再对他有兴趣了。她拍了拍手，那个埃德蒙曾经见过的矮人瞬间出现在她面前。

"备好雪橇，"女巫吩咐道，"挽具上不要挂铃铛。"

CHAPTER TEN THE SPELL BEGINS TO BREAK

Now we must go back to Mr and Mrs Beaver and the three other children. As soon as Mr Beaver said, "There's no time to lose," everyone began bundling themselves into coats, except Mrs Beaver, who started picking up sacks and laying them on the table and said: "Now, Mr Beaver, just reach down that ham. And here's a packet of tea, and there's sugar, and some matches. And if someone will get two or three loaves out of the crock over there in the corner."

"What are you doing, Mrs Beaver?" exclaimed Susan.

"Packing a load for each of us, dearie," said Mrs Beaver very coolly. "You didn't think we'd set out on a journey with nothing to eat, did you?"

"But we haven't time!" said Susan, buttoning the collar of her coat. "She may be here any minute."

第十章 魔法解除

话分两头，我们再回到海狸夫妇和另外三个孩子这里。当海狸先生说完“一分钟都不能耽误了”之后，大家纷纷穿上了大衣准备出发——除了海狸太太。它拿出一些小袋子放在桌子上说：“老头子，帮我拿点火腿下来。这是茶包、糖、还有些火柴。谁帮我去屋角的那个罐子里拿两三块面包过来。”

“您在干什么呢，海狸太太？”苏珊惊叫道。

“小宝贝，我要给每个人都收拾个小包裹呀，”海狸太太冷静地说，“你也不想我们在赶路的时候饿肚子，不是吗？”

“可是我们没时间了呀！”苏珊边说边系上了大衣领上的扣子，“女巫随时都会到的。”

"That's what I say," chimed in Mr Beaver.

"Get along with you all," said his wife. "Think it over, Mr Beaver. She can't be here for quarter of an hour at least."

"But don't we want as big a start as we can possibly get," said Peter, "if we're to reach the Stone Table before her?"

"You've got to remember that, Mrs Beaver," said Susan. "As soon as she has looked in here and finds we're gone she'll be off at top speed."

"That she will," said Mrs Beaver. "But we can't get there before her whatever we do, for she'll be on a sledge and we'll be walking."

"Then have we no hope?" said Susan.

"Now don't you get fussing, there's a dear," said Mrs Beaver, "but just get half a dozen clean handkerchiefs out of the drawer. 'Course we've got a hope. We can't get there before her

"说得没错。"海狸先生插嘴说。

"看看你们几个，"海狸太太说，"老头子，你想想，她最快也要一刻钟以后才能到呢！"

"可是我们也要尽量提前走吧，"彼得说，"要是我们比她更早到达石台，岂不是更好？"

"你要知道，海狸太太，"苏珊接着说，"女巫来到这儿发现我们都走了，她会立即快马加鞭赶上我们的。"

"这倒是真的。"海狸太太说，"但是无论如何我们也不可能比她早到。她有雪橇啊，咱们只能步行。"

"那咱们就没希望了吗？"苏珊问。

"好啦好啦，孩子们乖，别大惊小怪了。"海狸太太说，"帮我从抽屉里拿半打儿纸巾。我们还有希望啊，虽然我们没法比她早

but we can keep under cover and go by ways she won't expect and perhaps we'll get through."

"That's true enough, Mrs Beaver," said her husband. "But it's time we were out of this."

"And don't you start fussing either, Mr Beaver," said his wife. "There. That's better. There's five loads and the smallest for the smallest of us: that's you, my dear," she added, looking at Lucy.

"Oh, do please come on," said Lucy.

"Well, I'm nearly ready now," answered Mrs Beaver at last, allowing her husband to help her into; her snow-boots. "I suppose the sewing machine's took heavy to bring?"

"Yes. It is," said Mr Beaver. "A great deal too heavy. And you don't think you'll be able to use it while we're on the run, I suppose?"

到，但是我们可以走隐蔽的小路，这样就可以避开她。说不准，我们真能早到呢。"

"老婆子，你说得都对，"海狸先生说，"不过，咱们是不是该走了？"

"老头子，你也不要毛毛躁躁的。"海狸太太说，"看，这样就好多了。我这里呢，有五个包裹。最小的这个，就给咱们这儿最小的小朋友吧。给你，小宝贝。"海狸太太说着，看向露西。

"哦，拜托！咱们快点吧！"露西说。

"好了好了，我快准备好了。"海狸太太终于让海狸先生帮着它把雪地靴穿上了，"缝纫机是不是太重了，不好带呀？"

"是的，是的，"海狸先生回答，"那东西太重了，没法带。你不会想在逃命的时候还要用吧？"

"I can't abide the thought of that Witch fiddling with it," said Mrs Beaver, "and breaking it or stealing it, as likely as not."

"Oh, please, please, please, do hurry!" said the three children. And so at last they all got outside and Mr Beaver locked the door ("It'll delay her a bit," he said) and they set off, all carrying their loads over their shoulders.

The snow had stopped and the moon had come out when they began their journey. They went in single file first Mr Beaver, then Lucy, then Peter, then Susan, and Mrs Beaver last of all. Mr Beaver led them across the dam and on to the right bank of the river and then along a very rough sort of path among the trees right down by the river-bank. The sides of the valley, shining in the moonlight, towered up far above them on either hand. "Best keep down here as much as possible," he said. "She'll have to keep to the top, for you couldn't bring a sledge down here."

"想到女巫随便乱用我的缝纫机，我就受不了。"海狸太太说，"她八成会把缝纫机砸了或偷走。"

"求求你了，快点吧！"三个孩子焦急地说。最后，他们终于出门了，海狸先生把门锁上，觉着这样还能拖延点时间。随后，大家肩扛着小包出发了。

他们上路后，雪就停了，月亮也出来了。大家排成一排行进，海狸先生打头，紧跟在后面的依次是露西、彼得、苏珊，海狸太太走在最后。海狸先生带着大家穿过水坝，走到了河的右岸，然后走向河岸下方的一条小路。两侧的山谷高耸入云，山谷上的积雪在月光的照耀下闪闪发光。"咱们最好尽量在山谷下面走，"海狸先生说，"女巫坐着雪橇，她只能走上面。"

It would have been a pretty enough scene to look at it through a window from a comfortable armchair; and even as things were, Lucy enjoyed it at first. But as they went on walking and walking and walking and as the sack she was carrying felt heavier and heavier, she began to wonder how she was going to keep up at all. And she stopped looking at the dazzling brightness of the frozen river with all its waterfalls of ice and at the white masses of the tree-tops and the great glaring moon and the countless stars and could only watch the little short legs of Mr Beaver going pad-pad-pad-pad through the snow in front of her as if they were never going to stop. Then the moon disappeared and the snow began to fall once more. And at last Lucy was so tired that she was almost asleep and walking at the same time when suddenly she found that Mr Beaver had turned away from the river-bank to the right and was leading them steeply uphill into the very thickest bushes. And then as she came fully awake

如果是坐在舒适的沙发上，透过窗户看着眼前的景色，那绝对是风景如画。即便现在他们一路急行，露西在最开始的时候也还是很享受的。可是，走啊走啊，她感觉肩上的小包裹越来越重，开始怀疑自己要怎么才能撑下去。河面和瀑布都结了冰，露西不再看着那条耀眼的冰河、头顶树枝上大团大团的积雪和天上明亮的月亮和数不清的星星，只盯着前面的海狸先生，它迈着小短腿在雪地里“啪嗒啪嗒”地走着，仿佛永远都不会停下来。不一会儿，乌云遮住了月亮，天上又开始飘起了雪花。后来，露西实在太累了，她觉得自己都能边走边睡了。正在这时，她突然发现，海狸先生离开了河岸，朝着右边走去。随即它带着大家爬上陡峭的河岸，走进了一片密集的灌木丛中。露西看着海狸先生消失在

she found that Mr Beaver was just vanishing into a little hole in the bank which had been almost hidden under the bushes until you were quite on top of it. In fact, by the time she realized what was happening, only his short flat tail was showing.

Lucy immediately stooped down and crawled in after him. Then she heard noises of scrambling and puffing and panting behind her and in a moment all five of them were inside.

"Wherever is this?" said Peter's voice, sounding tired and pale in the darkness. (I hope you know what I mean by a voice sounding pale.)

"It's an old hiding-place for beavers in bad times," said Mr Beaver, "and a great secret. It's not much of a place but we must get a few hours' sleep."

"If you hadn't all been in such a plaguey fuss when we were starting, I'd have brought some pillows," said Mrs Beaver.

河岸上灌木丛中的一个小洞里，这会儿她一下子就醒了。这个洞被灌木丛覆盖着，非常隐蔽，要不是走到跟前，根本发现不了。等她意识到的时候，她只能看见海狸先生小小的扁尾巴了。

露西马上跟着它爬进了山洞，然后，她听见身后传来攀爬声和气喘吁吁的声音。不一会儿，他们五个都进了山洞。

"这是哪儿啊？"彼得的声音在黑暗中显得疲惫无力（我想，大家应该知道疲惫无力的声音听起来是什么样的）。

"这是海狸遇险时藏身的一个老地方。"海狸先生说，"这里很安全。虽然地方不怎么样，好歹大家可以睡上几个小时。"

"你要是走的时候不那么手忙脚乱的，我还能带几个枕头呢！"海狸太太说。

It wasn't nearly such a nice cave as Mr Tumnus's, Lucy thought just a hole in the ground but dry and earthy. It was very small so that when they all lay down they were all a bundle of clothes together, and what with that and being warmed up by their long walk they were really rather snug. If only the floor of the cave had been a little smoother! Then Mrs Beaver handed round in the dark a little flask out of which everyone drank something it made one cough and splutter a little and stung the throat, but it also made you feel deliciously warm after you'd swallowed it and everyone went straight to sleep.

It seemed to Lucy only the next minute (though really it was hours and hours later) when she woke up feeling a little cold and dreadfully stiff and thinking how she would like a hot bath. Then she felt a set of long whiskers tickling her cheek and saw the cold daylight coming in through the mouth of the cave. But immediately after that she was very wide awake indeed, and

露西想，这里和图姆努斯先生的山洞简直没法比，不过地上还算是干燥。山洞非常小，大家只能紧挨着躺在地上。经过长途跋涉，大家身上也都暖和起来，所以，现在都觉得很舒服。如果这里的地面更平整一些，那就更好了！海狸太太拿出一个小瓶子，在黑暗中，大家互相传递着一人喝了一口。瓶子里的东西特别呛人，喝下去的时候喉咙火辣辣的，但是，喝下去之后让人觉得浑身暖和。随即，大家就睡着了。

虽然睡了好几个小时，不过，露西醒来时，觉得自己才睡了几分钟而已。她感觉有点冷，浑身酸痛，想着如果现在能洗个热水澡该有多好啊。她觉得脸上被胡子扎得痒痒的，然后就看见洞口照进来冷冷的日光。突然，包括露西在内，大家完全清醒了，他们坐了起来，惊讶地瞪着眼睛、张着嘴，仔细听着外面的声音。

so was everyone else. In fact they were all sitting up with their mouths and eyes wide open listening to a sound which was the very sound they'd all been thinking of (and sometimes imagining they heard) during their walk last night. It was a sound of jingling bells.

Mr Beaver was out of the cave like a flash the moment he heard it. Perhaps you think, as Lucy thought for a moment, that this was a very silly thing to do? But it was really a very sensible one. He knew he could scramble to the top of the bank among bushes and brambles without being seen; and he wanted above all things to see which way the Witch's sledge went. The others all sat in the cave waiting and wondering. They waited nearly five minutes. Then they heard something that frightened them very much. They heard voices. "Oh," thought Lucy, "he's been seen. She's caught him!"

Great was their surprise when a little later, they heard Mr

他们昨天赶路的时候，就一直在注意着这种声音，甚至都有些幻听了——那是铃铛的声音。

在听见铃声的那一刻，海狸先生立即起身，迅速地爬出了山洞。这时，你可能会和露西想的一样——这么做岂不是犯傻吗？实际上，这是个很聪明的举动。海狸先生很清楚，它可以躲在河岸顶上的灌木丛中，却不会被人发现——而这样它就可以看见女巫的雪橇往哪个方向走了。其他人都坐在山洞里等着。他们等了大概有五分钟，随后，听见外面有动静。大家都吓得不行，因为他们听见了说话声。"完了完了！"露西心想，"它肯定被发现了，女巫把它抓住了！"

出乎意料的是，不一会儿，海狸先生就出现在洞口，叫他们出去。

Beaver's voice calling to them from just outside the cave.

"It's all right," he was shouting. "Come out, Mrs Beaver. Come out, Sons and Daughters of Adam. It's all right! It isn't Her!" This was bad grammar of course, but that is how beavers talk when they are excited; I mean, in Narnia in our world they usually don't talk at all.

So Mrs Beaver and the children came bundling out of the cave, all blinking in the daylight, and with earth all over them, and looking very frowsty and unbrushed and uncombed and with the sleep in their eyes.

"Come on!" cried Mr Beaver, who was almost dancing with delight. "Come and see! This is a nasty knock for the Witch! It looks as if her power is already crumbling."

"What do you mean, Mr Beaver?" panted Peter as they all scrambled up the steep bank of the valley together.

"没事的，"它大叫，"老婆子，出来吧！亚当和夏娃的儿女们，快出来吧！他不是她！"这话听起来当然有些不通，不过在纳尼亚，当海狸们激动的时候，就是这么说话的。当然啦，在我们的世界里，海狸根本就不会说话。

海狸太太和孩子们爬出了山洞，阳光晃得人睁不开眼睛。他们每个人都灰头土脸，浑身脏兮兮的，完全没有梳洗过，个个都睡眼惺忪。

"快来！"海狸先生喊道。它高兴得就差手舞足蹈了，"快来看呀！女巫要完蛋啦！看来她的权力已经开始瓦解了。"

"海狸先生，您是什么意思啊？"彼得气喘吁吁地问。这时，大家都沿着陡峭的河岸爬到了山谷上面。

"Didn't I tell you," answered Mr Beaver, "that she'd made it always winter and never Christmas? Didn't I tell you? Well, just come and see!"

And then they were all at the top and did see.

It was a sledge, and it was reindeer with bells on their harness. But they were far bigger than the Witch's reindeer, and they were not white but brown. And on the sledge sat a person whom everyone knew the moment they set eyes on him. He was a huge man. in a bright red robe (bright as hollyberries) with a hood that had fur inside it and a great white beard, that fell like a foamy waterfall over his chest.

Everyone knew him because, though you see people of his sort only in Narnia, you see pictures of them and hear them talked about even in our world the world on this side of the wardrobe door. But when you really see them in Narnia it is

"还记得我之前说过吗？"海狸先生回答，"女巫把这里变得永远是冬天，还没有圣诞节？还记得吗？快过来看！"

他们站在山谷顶端，然后看见——

一群驯鹿身上挂着铃铛，拉着雪橇。但这些驯鹿可比女巫的大很多，浑身棕色，女巫的驯鹿是白色的。雪橇上坐着一个人，大家一眼就认出了他——他身材高大，身穿红色袍子，红得好像冬青的红果子，头上的帽子毛茸茸的，白色的大胡子垂到胸前，看上去好像满是泡沫的瀑布一样。

大家都知道他是谁——即便他只会出现在纳尼亚，但在衣橱这边的人类的世界，你总能看见他的照片，总能听见人们在谈论他。然而，在纳尼亚亲眼见过他之后，你就会发现，其实是不一样的——在我们的世界里，有些圣诞老人的照片看上去很搞笑。

rather different. Some of the pictures of Father Christmas in our world make him look only funny and jolly. But now that the children actually stood looking at him they didn't find it quite like that. He was so big, and so glad, and so real, that they all became quite still. They felt very glad, but also solemn.

"I've come at last," said he. "She has kept me out for a long time, but I have got in at last. Aslan is on the move. The Witch's magic is weakening."

And Lucy felt running through her that deep shiver of gladness which you only get if you are being solemn and still.

"And now," said Father Christmas, "for your presents. There is a new and better sewing machine for you, Mrs Beaver. I will drop it in your house as, I pass."

"If you please, sir," said Mrs Beaver, making a curtsey. "It's locked up."

可孩子们现在见到了真人，却发现并不是这样的——他看上去如此高大，如此快乐，如此真实。

大家就这样静静地站在那里，他们感到十分高兴，但也非常严肃。

“哈哈，我可终于回来啦！”他说，“她把我赶走了好多年，不过我又回来啦！阿斯兰正在行动，女巫的魔法正在减弱。”

露西觉得自己从头到脚都在欢欣雀跃，那是一种只有在庄严肃穆的情况下才会有的心情。

“那么现在，”圣诞老人说，“我要给大家发礼物了。海狸太太，给你一台更好、更新的缝纫机。我会在路过你家的时候给你放在屋子里。”

“谢谢您！”海狸太太说着，行了一个屈膝礼，“但是我家的

"Locks and bolts make no difference to me," said Father Christmas. "And as for you, Mr Beaver, when you get home you will find your dam finished and mended and all the leaks stopped and a new sluicegate fitted."

Mr Beaver was so pleased that he opened his mouth very wide and then found he couldn't say anything at all.

"Peter, Adam's Son," said Father Christmas.

"Here, sir," said Peter.

"These are your presents," was the answer, "and they are tools not toys. The time to use them is perhaps near at hand. Bear them well." With these words he handed to Peter a shield and a sword. The shield was the colour of silver and across it there ramped a red lion, as bright as a ripe strawberry at the moment when you pick it. The hilt of the sword was of gold and it had a sheath and a sword belt and everything it needed, and it was just the right size and weight for Peter to use. Peter was silent and

门锁上了。"

"门锁和门闩对我来说没什么关系。"圣诞老人说，"至于你嘛，海狸先生，回家后你会发现，你的水坝已经修缮一新了，所有漏水的缝隙都会被堵住，而且还会有一个新的水闸。"

海狸先生高兴极了，它张开嘴巴，却什么话也说不出来。

"彼得，亚当之子。"圣诞老人说。

"在，先生。"彼得回答。

"这些是你的礼物。"圣诞老人继续说，"它们是武器，可不是玩具。不久后，你就要用到。好好使用它们。"说着，圣诞老人递给彼得一面盾牌，还有一把剑。盾牌是纯银色的，上面有一只跃起的红色雄狮，红得好像熟透的草莓；而剑柄是金铸的，还配有

solemn as he received these gifts, for he felt they were a very serious kind of present.

"Susan, Eve's Daughter," said Father Christmas. "These are for you," and he handed her a bow and a quiver full of arrows and a little ivory horn. "You must use the bow only in great need," he said, "for I do not mean you to fight in the battle. It does not easily miss. And when you put this horn to your lips; and blow it, then, wherever you are, I think help of some kind will come to you."

Last of all he said, "Lucy, Eve's Daughter," and Lucy came forward. He gave her a little bottle of what looked like glass (but people said afterwards that it was made of diamond) and a small dagger. "In this bottle," he said, "there is cordial made of the juice of one of the fireflowers that grow in the mountains of the sun. If you or any of your friends is hurt, a few drops of this restore them. And the dagger is to defend yourself at great need.

剑鞘和可以挂在身上的带子，以及所有用剑必备的东西，剑的尺寸和重量对于彼得来说正合适。彼得接过这些礼物的时候沉默无言、态度严肃，觉得此刻庄严无比。

“苏珊，夏娃之女，”圣诞老人说，“这些是给你的。”他递给苏珊一把弓，一个装满箭的箭袋，以及一个小小的象牙号角。“这把弓只有在紧急时才能使用，”他说，“它百发百中，可我并不想让你去冲锋陷阵。而这个号角，无论你在哪里，只要你吹响它，你就会得到帮助。”

最后，他对露西说：“露西，夏娃之女。”露西走上前去。他给了她一个玻璃瓶子（不过后来人们说那是钻石做的）和一把小匕首。“瓶子里，是用生长在太阳神山里的一种火花提炼出来的灵

For you also are not to be in battle."

"Why, sir?" said Lucy. "I think I don't know but I think I could be brave enough."

"That is not the point," he said. "But battles are ugly when women fight. And now" here he suddenly looked less grave "here is something for the moment for you all!" and he brought out (I suppose from the big bag at his back, but nobody quite saw him do it) a large tray containing five cups and saucers, a bowl of lump sugar, a jug of cream, and a great big teapot all sizzling and piping hot. Then he cried out "Merry Christmas! Long live the true King!" and cracked his whip, and he and the reindeer and the sledge and all were out of sight before anyone realized that they had started.

Peter had just drawn his sword out of its sheath and was showing it to Mr Beaver, when Mrs Beaver said:"Now then, now then! Don't stand talking there till the tea's got cold. Just

丹妙药，如果你或者你的朋友受伤了，只要滴几滴，他们就会康复。这把匕首是用来在紧急时刻防身的，我也不想你去打仗。"

"可是先生，为什么呢？"露西问，"我想——我也不知道要怎么说，不过真的要战斗的话，我也会很勇敢的。"

"这不是重点，"他说，"连女人都要参加的战斗是会非常惨烈的。那么，现在，"他突然看上去没那么严肃了，"我要给你们所有人一个礼物！"他不知从哪（应该是从他背后的大袋子里，但是没人看清楚）拿出来一个大托盘，上面摆了五个茶杯和碟子，还有一碗方糖，一罐奶油，以及一个嘶嘶作响的大茶壶。然后，他一边喊着"圣诞快乐！真王万岁！"一边挥舞着鞭子，大家还没看清楚呢，他就坐着驯鹿拉的雪橇消失不见了。

like men. Come and help to carry the tray down and we'll have breakfast. What a mercy I thought of bringing the bread-knife."

So down the steep bank they went and back to the cave, and Mr Beaver cut some of the bread and ham into sandwiches and Mrs Beaver poured out the tea and everyone enjoyed themselves. But long before they had finished enjoying themselves Mr Beaver said, "Time to be moving on now."

彼得将剑从剑鞘里拔出来，正给海狸先生看的时候，海狸太太说："好了好了，大家别傻站在那里啦，等会儿茶就凉了。像个男子汉一样，帮我把托盘拿下来，我们就可以吃早饭啦。幸亏我想着把切面包的刀也带来了。"

他们走下了陡峭的河岸，回到了山洞里。海狸先生帮着切面包和火腿来做三明治，海狸太太给每个人都倒了杯茶，大家喝得很开心。在他们享用完早餐之后，海狸先生说："好了，咱们得抓紧出发了。"

CHAPTER ELEVEN ASLAN IS NEARER

Edmund meanwhile had been having a most disappointing time. When the dwarf had gone to get the sledge ready he expected that the Witch would start being nice to him, as she had been at their last meeting. But she said nothing at all. And when at last Edmund plucked up his courage to say, "Please, your Majesty, could I have some Turkish Delight? You you said -" she answered, "Silence, fool!" Then she appeared to change her mind and said, as if to herself, a "And yet it will not do to have the brat fainting on the way," and once more clapped her hands. Another, dwarf appeared.

"Bring the human creature food and drink," she said.

The dwarf went away and presently returned bringing an iron bowl with some water in it and an iron plate with a hunk of dry bread on it. He grinned in a repulsive manner as he set them

第十一章 阿斯兰即将到来

在这段时间里，埃德蒙过得很郁闷。当矮人去准备雪橇的时候，他本以为女巫会对他态度好一些，就像他们第一次见面的时候一样。但是，女巫一句话都没说。最后，埃德蒙鼓起勇气说："女王陛下，能给我一些土耳其软糖吗？你——你说过——""闭嘴，笨蛋！"女王大吼。然后，她似乎改变了主意，仿佛自言自语道，"也不能让这个小崽子在半路上饿晕过去。"她拍了拍手，另一个矮人出现了。

"给这个人类拿点吃的喝的。"她说。

小矮人走开了，不一会儿，他拿来了一个铁腕，里面盛着一点儿水，还有一个铁盘子，里面放着一块干面包。他嘴角一咧，

down on the floor beside Edmund and said: “Turkish Delight for the little Prince. Ha! Ha! Ha!”

“Take it away,” said Edmund sulkily. “I don’t want dry bread.” But the Witch suddenly turned on him with such a terrible expression on her face that he, apologized and began to nibble at the bread, though, it was so stale he could hardly get it down.

“You may be glad enough of it before you taste bread again,” said the Witch.

While he was still chewing away the first dwarf came back and announced that the sledge was ready. The White Witch rose and went out, ordering Edmund to go with her. The snow was again falling as they came into the courtyard, but she took no notice of that and made Edmund sit beside her on the sledge. But before they drove off she called Maugrim and he came bounding like an enormous dog to the side of the sledge.

露出让人厌恶的笑容，然后把东西放到埃德蒙旁边的地板上，说：“来喽！王子的土耳其软糖来喽！哈哈哈哈哈！”

“拿走，”埃德蒙生气地说，“我才不吃干面包呢！”这时，女巫“噌”地一下扑到他面前，对他露出凶狠的目光。埃德蒙只好赔了个不是，小口地啃着面包。可是，这块面包实在太硬了，根本无法下咽。

“你应该庆幸，现在还能吃到面包，下次再吃到东西可就不一定是什么时候了。”女巫说。

正当他嚼着面包，第一个矮人回来，禀告说雪橇已经备好。白女巫起身走了出去，并命令埃德蒙跟着她。他们来到院子里的时候，又开始下雪了。但女巫一点儿也不在意。她命令埃德蒙挨

"Take with you the swiftest of your wolves and go at once to the house of the Beavers," said the Witch, "and kill whatever you find there. If they are already gone, then make all speed to the Stone Table, but do not be seen. Wait for me there in hiding. I meanwhile must go many miles to the West before I find a place where I can drive across the river. You may overtake these humans before they reach the Stone Table. You will know what to do if you find them!"

"I hear and obey, O Queen," growled the Wolf, and immediately he shot away into the snow and darkness, as quickly as a horse can gallop. In a few minutes he had called another wolf and was with him down on the dam sniffing at the Beavers' house. But of course they found it empty. It would have been a dreadful thing for the Beavers and the children if the night had remained fine, for the wolves would then have been able to follow their trail and ten to one would have overtaken them before they had got to

着她坐在雪橇上。出发前，她叫来巨狼毛戈林——它像一只大狗一样蹦到了雪橇旁。

"你带上跑得最快的狼，去一趟海狸家。"女巫吩咐道，"无论那里有什么，格杀勿论。如果他们已经走了，你就尽快赶到石台那里，别让人发现。在那里藏好等着我。我要向西走好几英里，才能找到过河的地方。或许你能赶在那几个人类之前到达石台，要是找到了他们几个，你知道该怎么做。"

"遵命，女王陛下！"巨狼吼了一声，像疾驰的骏马一般消失在了大雪和黑暗中。不一会儿，它叫来了另外一只狼。两只狼来到了水坝上，围着海狸家四处嗅来嗅去。当然，它们到的时候，已经人去屋空。如果那晚没下雪的话，海狸夫妇和孩子们就要遭

the cave. But now that the snow had begun again the scent was cold and even the footprints were covered up.

Meanwhile the dwarf whipped up the reindeer, and the Witch and Edmund drove out under the archway and on and away into the darkness and the cold. This was a terrible journey for Edmund, who had no coat. Before they had been going quarter of an hour all the front of him was covered with snow he soon stopped trying to shake it off because, as quickly as he did that, a new lot gathered, and he was so tired. Soon he was wet to the skin. And oh, how miserable he was! It didn't look now as if the Witch intended to make him a King. All the things he had said to make himself believe that she was good and kind and that her side was really the right side sounded to him silly now. He would have given anything to meet the others at this moment even Peter! The only way to comfort himself now was to try to believe that the whole thing was a dream and that he might wake

殃了——狼会循着踪迹，在他们没到藏身的山洞之前就赶上他们。可是，现在，又开始下雪，气味淡了，连脚印都被大雪覆盖了。

与此同时，矮人挥舞着鞭子赶着驯鹿，女巫和埃德蒙坐着雪橇驶出了拱门，驶进了黑暗和寒冷之中。对于埃德蒙来说，这真是一次可怕的旅程——他没有用来保暖的大衣。他们才走了一刻钟，埃德蒙身上就堆满了积雪。他不停地掸掉落在身上的雪花，可雪花却不停地落下来，到后来，他干脆放弃了——这简直就是做无用功。而且，他已经筋疲力尽了。不一会儿，他就全身湿透了。唉，太惨了！看起来，女巫并不想让他当国王了。他之前还不停地劝自己，试图让自己相信女巫是个好人，女巫的那一边才是正义的。而现在，想起之前自己说的种种话，简直愚蠢得要死。现在，他愿意放弃一切去找其他几个人，哪怕是彼得！唯一能安

up at any moment. And as they went on, hour after hour, it did come to seem like a dream.

This lasted longer than I could describe even if I wrote pages and pages about it. But I will skip on to the time when the snow had stopped and the morning had come and they were racing along in the daylight. And still they went on and on, with no sound but the everlasting swish of the snow and the creaking of the reindeer's harness. And then at last the Witch said, "What have we here? Stop!" and they did.

How Edmund hoped she was going to say something about breakfast! But she had stopped for quite a different reason. A little way off at the foot of a tree sat a merry party, a squirrel and his wife with their children and two satyrs and a dwarf and an old fox, all on stools round a table. Edmund couldn't quite see what they were eating, but it smelled lovely and there seemed to be decorations of holly and he wasn't at all sure that he didn't see

慰自己的就是，现在经历的一切都是一场梦，他随时都会从这场梦中醒来。他们就这样走了好几个小时，对于埃德蒙来讲，这段行程真的就像是一场梦。

他们走了好久好久，我都可以写上好几页呢。不过，我不想在这上面浪费时间。后来，雪停了，天也亮了，他们继续前行。他们走啊走啊，谁都不说话，只听见雪橇划过雪地的声音，以及驯鹿身上挽具的摩擦声。最后，女巫终于说："停下！看看这里有些什么。"然后雪橇就停了下来。

埃德蒙多么希望她说——该吃早饭啦！然而，她停下来的理由却出人意料。只见不远处的树下坐着一群快乐的小动物：一对松鼠夫妇带着自己的孩子、两个森林之神、一个矮人和一只老狐狸，他们都围坐在一张桌子旁边。虽然埃德蒙看不清他们在吃什

something like a plum pudding. At the moment when the sledge stopped, the Fox, who was obviously the oldest person present, had just risen to its feet, holding a glass in its right paw as if it was going to say something. But when the whole party saw the sledge stopping and who was in it, all the gaiety went out of their faces. The father squirrel stopped eating with his fork half-way to his mouth and one of the satyrs stopped with its fork actually in its mouth, and the baby squirrels squeaked with terror.

"What is the meaning of this?" asked the Witch Queen. Nobody answered.

"Speak, vermin!" she said again. "Or do you want my dwarf to find you a tongue with his whip? What is the meaning of all this gluttony, this waste, this selfindulgence? Where did you get all these things?"

"Please, your Majesty," said the Fox, "we were given them. And if I might make so bold as to drink your Majesty's very

么，不过闻起来真香啊，看起来食物还用冬青装饰了一番，他都不敢相信看见了葡萄干布丁之类的东西。当雪橇停下来的时候，那只看起来年纪最长的老狐狸刚刚站起来，右爪子里正举着一只玻璃杯，好像要说些什么。然而，当他们看见谁坐在雪橇上之后，脸上的笑容立刻就消失了。松鼠爸爸正举着叉子要往嘴里送食物，一个森林之神嘴里含着叉子就停了下来，松鼠宝宝吓得吱吱叫。

"你们在干什么？"女巫问，但是没人回答。

"说话！你们这群愚蠢的低等动物！"她继续说，"难道你们想要小矮人用鞭子让你们开口吗？你们如此贪吃，铺张浪费，任意妄为，难道不感到羞耻吗？这些东西，你们是从哪里弄来的？"

"哦，尊敬的女王陛下，"那只狐狸说，"这些都是别人给的。

good health."

"Who gave them to you?" said the Witch.

"F-F-F-Father Christmas," stammered the Fox.

"What?" roared the Witch, springing from the sledge and taking a few strides nearer to the terrified animals. "He has not been here! He cannot have been here! How dare you but no. Say you have been lying and you shall even now be forgiven."

At that moment one of the young squirrels lost its head completely. "He has he has he has!" it squeaked, beating its little spoon on the table. Edmund saw the Witch bite her lips so that a drop of blood appeared on her white cheek. Then she raised her wand. "Oh, don't, don't, please don't," shouted Edmund, but even while he was shouting she had waved her wand and instantly where the merry party had been there were only statues of creatures (one with its stone fork fixed forever half-way to its stone mouth) seated round a stone table on which there were

恕我冒昧，让我们为陛下的健康干杯——"

"谁给你们的？"女王问。

"是……是圣……圣诞老人。"狐狸磕磕巴巴地说。

"什么？"女王怒吼道，随即从雪橇上一跃而起，大步走向这群受惊吓的动物们，"他没有来过！他怎么可能来过！你们岂敢——不可能。你们要是现在就承认说了谎，我会饶恕你们。"

那只小松鼠被吓昏了头："他来过！他来过！他就是来过！"他一边吱吱叫着，一边拿小勺敲着桌子。埃德蒙看见女王咬着嘴唇，雪白的脸上沁出一丝血红色。她举起魔杖，埃德蒙大喊道："别！求你了！别！"就在埃德蒙大喊着求情的时候，女巫挥动魔杖，一瞬间将这群原本满怀欢乐的生灵变成了一堆石像，其中一

stone plates and a stone plum pudding.

"As for you," said the Witch, giving Edmund a stunning blow on the face as she re-mounted the sledge, "let that teach you to ask favour for spies and traitors. Drive on!" And Edmund for the first time in this story felt sorry for someone besides himself. It seemed so pitiful to think of those little stone figures sitting there all the silent days and all the dark nights, year after year, till the moss grew on them and at last even their faces crumbled away.

Now they were steadily racing on again. And soon Edmund noticed that the snow which splashed against them as they rushed through it was much wetter than it had been all last night. At the same time he noticed that he was feeling much less cold. It was also becoming foggy. In fact every minute it grew foggier and warmer. And the sledge was not running nearly as well as it had been running up till now. At first he thought this was because the reindeer were tired, but soon he saw that that

只石像手里的叉子还没送到嘴边。连盘子和葡萄干布丁都变成了石头。

"至于你，"女巫回到雪橇上，扇了埃德蒙一巴掌，"这就是你为那些叛徒和奸细们求情的下场。出发！"在这个故事里面，这是埃德蒙第一次为别人感到难过。想想那些可怜的石像，他们就坐在那里，日复一日，年复一年，直到身上长满青苔，最后甚至连脸都坍塌瓦解。

现在，雪橇又继续快速地飞驶。不一会儿，埃德蒙注意到，雪橇溅起的雪花比昨晚湿润多了。同时，他感觉自己没那么冷了。周围雾气缭绕，而且，雾慢慢变浓，天气也越来越暖和，雪橇也不像原来那么快了。开始，他以为拉雪橇的驯鹿跑累了，但是不

couldn't be the real reason. The sledge jerked, and skidded and kept on jolting as if it had struck against stones. And however the dwarf whipped the poor reindeer the sledge went slower and slower. There also seemed to be a curious noise all round them, but the noise of their driving and jolting and the dwarf's shouting at the reindeer prevented Edmund from hearing what it was, until suddenly the sledge stuck so fast that it wouldn't go on at all. When that happened there was a moment's silence. And in that silence Edmund could at last listen to the other noise properly. A strange, sweet, rustling, chattering noise and yet not so strange, for he'd heard it before if only he could remember where! Then all at once he did remember. It was the noise of running water. All round them though out of sight, there were streams, chattering, murmuring, bubbling, splashing and even (in the distance) roaring. And his heart gave a great leap (though he hardly knew why) when he realized that the frost was over. And

久他就发现，这不是真正的原因。雪橇猛地向前一动，然后滑向一边，颠簸得不行，好像撞上了石头似的。虽然小矮人不断地鞭打着可怜的驯鹿，但雪橇却越来越慢。同时，周围还有一种奇怪的声音。这种声音被颠簸的雪橇和小矮人呵斥驯鹿的嘈杂声干扰到，因而，埃德蒙没法听得很清楚。最后，雪橇卡在那里，一动不动了。一时间，四下里一片寂静，埃德蒙可以仔细倾听那个奇怪的声音了。这是一种奇怪的、美好的、沙沙的声音，其实也没什么奇怪的，埃德蒙以前就听过，只是想不起来在哪里听见过罢了。突然，他想起来了，这是流水声！虽然他们看不见，可是，你可以感受到附近的小溪在欢快地流淌，潺潺的流水在噗噗冒泡，远处还有激流咆哮的声音。他的心猛然跳了一下，虽然他也不知

much nearer there was a drip-drip-drip from the branches of all the trees. And then, as he looked at one tree he saw a great load of snow slide off it and for the first time since he had entered Narnia he saw the dark green of a fir tree. But he hadn't time to listen or watch any longer, for the Witch said: Don't sit staring, fool! Get out and help."

And of course Edmund had to obey. He stepped out into the snow but it was really only slush by now and began helping the dwarf to get the sledge out of the muddy hole it had got into. They got it out in the end, and by being very cruel to the reindeer the dwarf managed to get it on the move again, and they drove a little further. And now the snow was really melting in earnest and patches of green grass were beginning to appear in every direction. Unless you have looked at a world of snow as long as Edmund had been looking at it, you will hardly be able to imagine what a relief those green patches were after the endless

道为什么，但他明白，严冬已过。在他们身边，树枝上冰雪融化，"滴答滴答"地落在地上。他看见不远处的一棵大树上，一大片积雪从树上滑落。这是埃德蒙来到纳尼亚后，第一次见到冷杉树的深绿色。他没看多久，就听女巫说："别傻坐在那儿，笨蛋！快去帮忙。"

埃德蒙只好服从命令下了雪橇。他一脚踩到雪地里，雪融化后，地上都是湿漉漉的泥巴。他帮着矮人去拉陷在泥里的雪橇。最后，他们终于把雪橇拉了出来。小矮人非常凶残，硬是让驯鹿又往前拉了一段。现在，冰雪已经完全融化了，到处都可以看到一小块一小块的绿草地。像埃德蒙这样在看了这么久的冰天雪地之后，突然间看到一片片绿地时，那种欢欣雀跃的心情简直是无以言表。这时，雪橇又停了下来。

white. Then the sledge stopped again.

"It's no good, your Majesty," said the dwarf. "We can't sledge in this thaw."

"Then we must walk," said the Witch.

"We shall never overtake them walking," growled the dwarf. "Not with the start they've got."

"Are you my councillor or my slave?" said the Witch. "Do as you're told. Tie the hands of the human creature behind it and keep hold of the end of the rope. And take your whip. And cut the harness of the reindeer; they'll find their own way home."

The dwarf obeyed, and in a few minutes Edmund found himself being forced to walk as fast as he could with his hands tied behind him. He kept on slipping in the slush and mud and wet grass, and every time he slipped the dwarf gave him a curse and sometimes a flick with the whip. The Witch walked behind the dwarf and kept on saying, "Faster! Faster!"

"这可不行啊，女王陛下，"矮人说，"冰雪融化后，就没法乘坐雪橇了。"

"那我们就走路。"女巫说。

"可是，我们就没办法追上他们了，"小矮人嘟囔道，"他们先走一步了。"

"你到底是我的顾问还是我的奴隶？"女巫说，"让你怎么做，你就怎么做。把这个人类的双手绑在身后，你在后面拉着绳子赶他走。把驯鹿身上的行头卸下来，它们认得回家的路。"

矮人服从了命令。不一会儿，埃德蒙的双手就被他绑在身后，被迫着继续赶路。他不停地摔倒在泥泞的土地上和湿滑的草地里。每次他一摔倒，矮人就骂他，有时还给他一鞭子。女巫走在矮人的身后，不停地说："快点！快点！"

Every moment the patches of green grew bigger and the patches of snow grew smaller. Every moment more and more of the trees shook off their robes of snow. Soon, wherever you looked, instead of white shapes you saw the dark green of firs or the black prickly branches of bare oaks and beeches and elms. Then the mist turned from white to gold and presently cleared away altogether. Shafts of delicious sunlight struck down on to the forest floor and overhead you could see a blue sky between the tree tops.

Soon there were more wonderful things happening. Coming suddenly round a corner into a glade of silver birch trees Edmund saw the ground covered in all directions with little yellow flowers celandines. The noise of water grew louder. Presently they actually crossed a stream. Beyond it they found snowdrops growing.

"Mind your own business!" said the dwarf when he saw that Edmund had turned his head to look at them; and he gave the rope a vicious jerk.

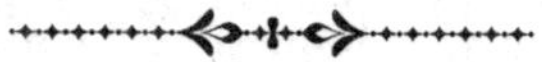

慢慢地，绿地越变越大，雪地越变越小。每一分钟都有大块的积雪从树上掉落。不久后，放眼望去，到处都是深绿色的冷杉树和光秃秃的橡树上黑色带刺的枝干，以及山毛榉和榆树。然后，雾气从白色变为金色，最后慢慢散去。温暖的阳光洒在地面上，抬头望去，可以透过树枝看见蔚蓝的天空。

不久，更奇妙的事情发生了。在转过一个弯后，在银色的白桦树中间的空地上，埃德蒙看见白屈菜的小黄花开得遍地都是。水声越来越大，不一会儿，他们就跨过了一条小溪，在溪边还看见了雪莲花。

"少管闲事！"矮人看见埃德蒙扭头去看那些花花草草，对他呵斥道，并且恶毒地拽了拽绳子。

But of course this didn't prevent Edmund from seeing. Only five minutes later he noticed a dozen crocuses growing round the foot of an old tree gold and purple and white. Then came a sound even more delicious than the sound of the water. Close beside the path they were following a bird suddenly chirped from the branch of a tree. It was answered by the chuckle of another bird a little further off. And then, as if that had been a signal, there was chattering and chirruping in every direction, and then a moment of full song, and within five minutes the whole wood was ringing with birds' music, and wherever Edmund's eyes turned he saw birds alighting on branches, or sailing overhead or chasing one another or having their little quarrels or tidying up their feathers with their beaks.

"Faster! Faster!" said the Witch.

There was no trace of the fog now. The sky became bluer and bluer, and now there were white clouds hurrying across it

当然，这并不能阻止埃德蒙继续欣赏美景。5分钟后，他发现一棵老树下长满了各种颜色的藏红花，有金色的、紫色的还有白色的。接着，又传来一种比流水声更美妙的声音。在他们走的那条小路旁边，一只小鸟突然在树上“叽叽喳喳”地叫了起来。不远处的树上传来另一只鸟的叫声，似乎是在回应。然后，两只鸟好像开启了什么信号，各个方向都传来了鸟叫声，一时间，耳中充满了鸟鸣声。不到5分钟，整个树林里都回荡着鸟儿的歌声。埃德蒙发现，无论他看向哪个方向，都有一只只鸟儿落在枝头，或是叽叽喳喳叫个不停，或是站在树上整理着羽毛。

“快点走！快点走！”女巫说。

雾气已经完全散去，天空越来越蓝，时而飘过朵朵白云。林

from time to time. In the wide glades there were primroses. A light breeze sprang up which scattered drops of moisture from the swaying branches and carried cool, delicious scents against the faces of the travellers. The trees began to come fully alive. The larches and birches were covered with green, the laburnums with gold. Soon the beech trees had put forth their delicate, transparent leaves. As the travellers walked under them the light also became green. A bee buzzed across their path.

"This is no thaw," said the dwarf, suddenly stopping. "This is Spring. What are we to do? Your winter has been destroyed, I tell you! This is Aslan's doing."

"If either of you mention that name again," said the Witch, "he shall instantly be killed."

间空地上开满了迎春花。一阵微风吹过，摇曳的树枝上，露水纷纷洒落，送来阵阵清凉而美妙的香气。树木似乎活了过来，落叶松和白桦树披上了绿装，金莲花在阳光下变得金灿灿的，山毛榉的树枝上长出了晶莹剔透的叶子。走在树下，阳光都变成了绿色。一只蜜蜂“嗡嗡”地飞过他们走的那条小路。

“积雪都融化了。”矮人突然停下来说，“春天来了。我们怎么办？冬天被赶跑了，这是阿斯兰干的！”

“如果我再听到你们任何人提起这个名字，”女巫说，“我就叫他立刻送命！”

CHAPTER TWELVE PETER'S FIRST BATTLE

While the dwarf and the White Witch were saying this, miles away the Beavers and the children were walking on hour after hour into what seemed a delicious dream. Long ago they had left the coats behind them. And by now they had even stopped saying to one another, "Look! there's a kingfisher," or "I say, bluebells!" or "What was that lovely smell?" or "Just listen to that thrush!" They walked on in silence drinking it all in, passing through patches of warm sunlight into cool, green thickets and out again into wide mossy glades where tall elms raised the leafy roof far overhead, and then into dense masses of flowering currant and among hawthorn bushes where the sweet smell was almost overpowering.

They had been just as surprised as Edmund when they saw the winter vanishing and the whole wood passing in a few hours

第十二章　彼得首战告捷

女巫和矮人正在说这些话的时候，好几英里外的孩子们和海狸夫妇已经走了好几个小时，周围的景色让他们恍恍惚惚地进入了美好的梦境。他们早就把大衣脱了。如今，他们不再说什么"看！那里有只翠鸟！"或者"那是风信子！"或者"好香的味道啊！"或者"你听那只画眉在唱歌！"大家静静地走着，沉醉在这醉人的美景之中，从暖和的太阳底下，走进阴凉的、郁郁葱葱的灌木丛中，又走到长满苔藓的林间空地中。高大的榆树枝叶茂密，红醋栗花团锦簇，山楂树飘来馥郁的芬芳。

他们和埃德蒙一样，看见冰雪消融时个个惊讶无比。冬天逝去了，在短短几个小时内，整片树林从1月份变成了5月份。他们

or so from January to May. They hadn't even known for certain (as the Witch did) that this was what would happen when Aslan came to Narnia. But they all knew that it was her spells which had produced the endless winter; and therefore they all knew when this magic spring began that something had gone wrong, and badly wrong, with the Witch's schemes. And after the thaw had been going on for some time they all realized that the Witch would no longer be able to use her sledge. After that they didn't hurry so much and they allowed themselves more rests and longer ones. They were pretty tired by now of course; but not what I'd call bitterly tired only slow and feeling very dreamy and quiet inside as one does when one is coming to the end of a long day in the open. Susan had a slight blister on one heel.

They had left the course of the big river some time ago; for one had to turn a little to the right (that meant a little to the south) to reach the place of the Stone Table. Even if this had not

并不像女巫那样肯定，认为是阿斯兰的到来才让纳尼亚春回大地。但是，他们知道，正是女巫的咒语让这里变成无尽的寒冬，而现在，春天已来临，女巫的阴谋诡计就要失败了，而且是一败涂地。冰雪融化了之后，他们意识到，女巫没办法再乘坐雪橇了。所以，他们也没有急匆匆地赶路，而是经常停下来休息一段时间。现在，大家都很累了，不过不是那种筋疲力尽的累，就好像人们在外面忙碌了一天之后那种有些无精打采的累。苏珊的一只后脚跟磨出了小水泡。

他们早就离开了那条大河，为了到达石台，他们需要稍向右转，也就是向南走。就算不是该走的路，他们也不可能再继续沿着河谷走了。随着冰雪的融化，河水逐渐高涨，不久就形成了咆

been their way they couldn't have kept to the river valley once the thaw began, for with all that melting snow the river was soon in flood a wonderful, roaring, thundering yellow flood and their path would have been under water.

And now the sun got low and the light got redder and the shadows got longer and the flowers began to think about closing.

"Not long now," said Mr Beaver, and began leading them uphill across some very deep, springy moss (it felt nice under their tired feet) in a place where only tall trees grew, very wide apart. The climb, coming at the end of the long day, madc them all pant and blow. And just as Lucy was wondering whether she could really get to the top without another long rest, suddenly they were at the top. And this is what they saw.

They were on a green open space from which you could look down on the forest spreading as far as one could see in every direction except right ahead. There, far to the East, was

哮轰鸣的浑浊洪水，他们走的那条路会被洪水淹没。

这会儿，太阳就要下山了，阳光变得红彤彤的，地上的影子也拉长了，花瓣儿慢慢开始收拢。

“不远了，”海狸先生说。它带着大家爬上山坡，穿过一片柔软的青苔，疲累的双脚踩在上面很舒服。那里地势开阔，稀稀拉拉地长着几棵大树。经过漫长的跋涉之后还要爬山，大家都累得气喘吁吁的。露西在想，要是中间不休息，自己到底能不能爬上山顶。正想着呢，他们已经爬上了山顶。

山顶上平整开阔，绿意葱葱。向山下望去，目光所及之处，都是绵延不绝的森林，除了正前方。在正前方东边不远处，有什么东西闪闪发光，而且正在移动。“天哪！”彼得小声地对苏珊

something twinkling and moving. “By gum!” whispered Peter to Susan, “the sea!” In the very middle of this open hill-top was the Stone Table. It was a great grim slab of grey stone supported on four upright stones. It looked very old; and it was cut all over with strange lines and figures that might be the letters of an unknown language. They gave you a curious feeling when you looked at them. The next thing they saw was a pavilion pitched on one side of the open place. A wonderful pavilion it was and especially now when the light of the setting sun fell upon it with sides of what looked like yellow silk and cords of crimson and tent-pegs of ivory; and high above it on a pole a banner which bore a red rampant lion fluttering in the breeze which was blowing in their faces from the far-off sea. While they were looking at this they heard a sound of music on their right; and turning in that direction they saw what they had come to see.

Aslan stood in the centre of a crowd of creatures who had grouped themselves round him in the shape of a half-moon. There

说，“是大海！”在这片空地的正中央，有一块石台。四块笔直的石头撑着上面一块灰色的大石板。这块石板年代久远，上面刻满了奇怪的线条和符号，应该是一种人们不知道的语言。不过，当他们看着这些符号的时候，一种好奇的感觉油然而生。在空地的另一边立着一顶大帐篷。快要落山的夕阳照在帐篷上，发出黄色的绸缎般的光芒。帐篷上有着深红色的绳索，以及象牙色的帐篷桩。帐篷顶立着一杆旗，旗面上绣着一头跃起的红色雄狮。远处吹来的海风拂过脸庞，旗子也随风飘扬。这时，他们听见右边传来音乐声，随即他们看到了如下景象：

一群生灵围成了半圆形，把狮王阿斯兰围在中间。树神和水神（在我们的世界里，她们被称为森林女神和水中仙女）正在演

were Tree-Women there and Well-Women (Dryads and Naiads as they used to be called in our world) who had stringed instruments; it was they who had made the music. There were four great centaurs. The horse part of them was like huge English farm horses, and the man part was like stern but beautiful giants. There was also a unicorn, and a bull with the head of a man, and a pelican, and an eagle, and a great Dog. And next to Aslan stood two leopards of whom one carried his crown and the other his standard.

But as for Aslan himself, the Beavers and the children didn't know what to do or say when they saw him. People who have not been in Narnia sometimes think that a thing cannot be good and terrible at the same time. If the children had ever thought so, they were cured of it now. For when they tried to look at Aslan's face they just caught a glimpse of the golden mane and the great, royal, solemn, overwhelming eyes; and then they found they couldn't look at him and went all trembly.

"Go on," whispered Mr Beaver.

奏乐器，吹奏出美妙的乐曲。这里有四只半人马，马的那一部分很像英国农场里的大马，人的那一部分看上去像严肃而俊美的巨人。还有一只独角兽，一只牛身人头的生物，一只鹈鹕，一只苍鹰，还有一只大狗。阿斯兰的身边站着两头豹子，一头拿着它的王冠，一头举着阿斯兰的旗帜。

看到阿斯兰后，海狸夫妇和孩子们都不知道该怎么办、该对它说些什么。没去过纳尼亚的人们觉得，一个人不可能同时感到既高兴又害怕。而孩子们现在就怀着这样复杂的心情——当他们看向阿斯兰的脸，瞥到狮王那金色的鬃毛和高贵、庄严、摄人心魄的眼睛时，就不敢再看了，而且吓得有些发抖。

“快过去吧！”海狸先生小声地说。

"No," whispered Peter, "you first."

"No, Sons of Adam before animals," whispered Mr Beaver back again.

"Susan," whispered Peter, "What about you? Ladies first."

"No, you're the eldest," whispered Susan. And of course the longer they went on doing this the more awkward they felt. Then at last Peter realized that it was up to him. He drew his sword and raised it to the salute and hastily saying to the others "Come on. Pull yourselves together," he advanced to the Lion and said:

"We have come Aslan."

"Welcome, Peter, Son of Adam," said Aslan. "Welcome, Susan and Lucy, Daughters of Eve. Welcome He-Beaver and She-Beaver."

His voice was deep and rich and somehow took the fidgets out of them. They now felt glad and quiet and it didn't seem

"不，你先去。"彼得说。

"不，亚当之子要走在动物前面。"海狸先生悄悄地回了一句。

"苏珊，女士优先，要不你走前面？"彼得又小声地问苏珊。

"不，你最大，你先走。"苏珊说。他们这样推来推去会更尴尬，最后，彼得意识到，这事儿只能靠他。于是，他抽出那把剑，向狮王举剑致敬，随后有些犹豫地对大家说："来吧！大家勇敢点。"

然后，他第一个走向那头狮子，说："阿斯兰，我们来了。"

"欢迎你，彼得，亚当之子，"阿斯兰说，"欢迎你们，苏珊和露西，夏娃之女。欢迎你们，男海狸和女海狸。"

它的声音低沉而圆润，让孩子们感到不再害怕。他们觉得一股喜悦之情油然而生，内心很平静，即便站着不说话，也不会感

awkward to them to stand and say nothing.

"But where is the fourth?" asked Aslan.

"He has tried to betray them and joined the White Witch, O Aslan," said Mr Beaver. And then something made Peter say,

"That was partly my fault, Aslan. I was angry with him and I think that helped him to go wrong."

And Aslan said nothing either to excuse Peter or to blame him but merely stood looking at him with his great unchanging eyes. And it seemed to all of them that there was nothing to be said.

"Please Aslan," said Lucy, "can anything be done to save Edmund?"

"All shall be done," said Aslan. "But it may be harder than you think." And then he was silent again for some time. Up to that moment Lucy had been thinking how royal and strong and peaceful his face looked; now it suddenly came into her head

到尴尬。

“还有一个在哪里？”阿斯兰问。

“伟大的阿斯兰，他背叛了他们，去投靠了白女巫。”海狸先生说。

彼得听到这里，只好硬着头皮说：“这里面多少也有我的错。我对他发脾气了，可能导致他变坏了。”

阿斯兰既没有责备彼得，也没有原谅他。它站在那里，用大眼睛望着他。大家似乎也觉得没什么可说的。

“阿斯兰，请问，您能帮我们救救埃德蒙吗？”露西问。

“我会尽量想办法，”阿斯兰说，“可是，这件事比你们想象的要难办。”然后，它又沉默了一段时间。露西一直觉得，它的脸看上去是那么的高贵、坚毅和平静。可如今发觉，它的脸看上去也

that he looked sad as well. But next minute that expression was quite gone. The Lion shook his mane and clapped his paws together ("Terrible paws," thought Lucy, "if he didn't know how to velvet them!") and said,

"Meanwhile, let the feast be prepared. Ladies, take these Daughters of Eve to the pavilion and minister to them."

When the girls had gone Aslan laid his paw and though it was velveted it was very heavy on Peter's shoulder and said, "Come, Son of Adam, and I will show you a far-off sight of the castle where you are to be King."

And Peter with his sword still drawn in his hand went with the Lion to the eastern edge of the hilltop. There a beautiful sight met their eyes. The sun was setting behind their backs. That meant that the whole country below them lay in the evening light forest and hills and valleys and, winding away like a silver snake, the lower part of the great river. And beyond all this,

很悲伤，不过这种表情一闪而过。这头雄狮抖了抖鬃毛，拍了拍两只大爪子。"它的爪子好可怕，"露西心想，"幸亏它知道如何深藏不露。"

只听阿斯兰说道："现在，准备好宴席。女士们，麻烦你们把夏娃之女们带到帐篷里休息。"

女孩子们走了之后，阿斯兰把爪子搭在彼得的肩上。虽然它很轻柔，可是那只爪子还是很沉。它说："过来，亚当之子。你看，远处的那座城堡，那儿就是你要成为国王的地方。"

彼得手里握着剑，跟随阿斯兰来到东边的山崖处。在这里，纳尼亚的美景尽收眼底。太阳在他们身后缓缓落下，森林、山丘、还有那条似银蛇一样蜿蜒的大河，都笼罩在暮色当中。几英里远

miles away, was the sea, and beyond the sea the sky, full of clouds which were just turning rose colour with the reflection of the sunset. But just where the land of Narnia met the sea in fact, at the mouth of the great river there was something on a little hill, shining. It was shining because it was a castle and of course the sunlight was reflected from all the windows which looked towards Peter and the sunset; but to Peter it looked like a great star resting on the seashore.

"That, O Man," said Aslan, "is Cair Paravel of the four thrones, in one of which you must sit as King. I show it to you because you are the first-born and you will be High King over all the rest."

And once more Peter said nothing, for at that moment a strange noise woke the silence suddenly. It was like a bugle, but richer.

"It is your sister's horn," said Aslan to Peter in a low voice;

的地方就是大海，海天连成一片，落日将天上的云彩映得如同红红的玫瑰。在纳尼亚大陆与海洋的交界处，也就是大河的入海口处，有一座小山，上面有什么东西在闪闪发光。那是一座城堡，落日的余晖照在城堡的玻璃上，使得整座城堡都在发光。对于彼得来说，城堡就像是落在海边的一颗耀眼的星星。

“伟大的人类，那里就是凯尔·帕拉维尔城堡，里面有四个王座，你注定会坐在其中的一个王座上，成为国王。我指给你看，因为你是老大，你会成为高于他们的伟大之王。”

彼得还是没有说什么。正在这时，一声奇怪的声音划破寂静，听上好像号角，不过声音更加圆润。

“是你妹妹的号角声。”阿斯兰低声对彼得说。虽说狮王发出

so low as to be almost a purr, if it is not disrespectful to think of a Lion purring.

For a moment Peter did not understand. Then, when he saw all the other creatures start forward and heard Aslan say with a wave of his paw, "Back! Let the Prince win his spurs," he did understand, and set off running as hard as he could to the pavilion. And there he saw a dreadful sight.

The Naiads and Dryads were scattering in every direction. Lucy was running towards him as fast as her short legs would carry her and her face was as white as paper. Then he saw Susan make a dash for a tree, and swing herself up, followed by a huge grey beast. At first Peter thought it was a bear. Then he saw that it looked like an Alsatian, though it was far too big to be a dog. Then he realized that it was a wolf standing on its hind legs, with its front paws against the tree-trunk, snapping and snarling. All the hair on its back stood up on end. Susan had not been

像猫一样的呼噜声是很不敬的，但那声音低得确实很像是呼噜声。

一开始，彼得并不知道发生了什么。然后，他看见所有的生物都涌上前来。阿斯兰挥动爪子高声说道："后退！让王子立头功吧！"这时，彼得终于明白了。他以最快的速度跑向那顶帐篷。然后，他看到了可怕的一幕。

只见森林女神和水中仙女们吓得四散奔逃。露西撒开两条小短腿，以最快的速度跑向彼得，小脸吓得煞白。随即，他看到苏珊奔向了一棵树，奋力地往树上爬，她后面跟着一头灰色的野兽。一开始，彼得以为那是一头熊，再看一眼，觉得更像是一条德国大狼狗，可是又比狗大很多。最后，他意识到，那是一只狼！这只狼后腿站立，前面的两只爪子趴在树上，对着上面又咬又吼。它背上的毛根根竖起。这时，苏珊只爬到第二根大树杈上，没法

able to get higher than the second big branch. One of her legs hung down so that her foot was only an inch or two above the snapping teeth. Peter wondered why she did not get higher or at least take a better grip; then he realized that she was just going to faint and that if she fainted she would fall off.

Peter did not feel very brave; indeed, he felt he was going to be sick. But that made no difference to what he had to do. He rushed straight up to the monster and aimed a slash of his sword at its side. That stroke never reached the Wolf. Quick as lightning it turned round, its eyes flaming, and its mouth wide open in a howl of anger. If it had not been so angry that it simply had to howl it would have got him by the throat at once. As it was though all this happened too quickly for Peter to think at all he had just time to duck down and plunge his sword, as hard as he could, between the brute's forelegs into its heart. Then came a horrible, confused moment like something in a nightmare.

再爬得更高了。她一条腿吊在那里，脚离大灰狼龇出的獠牙只有一两英寸距离。彼得想，她为什么不爬得再高一点，或者抱紧树干？然后他发现，苏珊吓得都快晕过去了——她要是真晕过去，就会直接掉下来。

彼得并没有觉得自己有多勇敢，他现在甚至觉得有点恶心，但这并不影响他接下来的举动。他笔直地冲向那头野兽，对准巨狼的肋间刺了过去。但这一剑并没有刺中。那只巨狼像闪电一样转过身来，好似凶神恶煞一般，张着血盆大口冲着彼得怒吼。它要不是愤怒得大吼大叫，肯定会直接扑上去咬断彼得的喉咙。这一切发生得太快了，彼得根本没时间思考。他只来得及弯下身子，使出浑身力气，将手中的剑刺向狼的心脏。接下来，就像噩梦一样混乱而可怕。彼得用力地又拽又拉，那头野兽也不知是活着还

He was tugging and pulling and the Wolf seemed neither alive nor dead, and its bared teeth knocked against his forehead, and everything was blood and heat and hair. A moment later he found that the monster lay dead and he had drawn his sword out of it and was straightening his back and rubbing the sweat off his face and out of his eyes. He felt tired all over.

Then, after a bit, Susan came down the tree. She and Peter felt pretty shaky when they met and I won't say there wasn't kissing and crying on both sides. But in Narnia no one thinks any the worse of you for that.

"Quick! Quick!" shouted the voice of Aslan. "Centaurs! Eagles! I see another wolf in the thickets. There behind you. He has just darted away. After him, all of you. He will be going to his mistress. Now is your chance to find the Witch and rescue the fourth Son of Adam." And instantly with a thunder of hoofs and beating of wings a dozen or so of the swiftest creatures

是死了，可怕的獠牙磕在了彼得脑门上，到处都是鲜血、热气和毛发。过了一会儿，他发现，那头野兽已经倒在地上死去了。他拔出剑，挺直腰板，抹去脸上和眼睛上的汗水，觉得累死了。

不一会儿，苏珊从树上爬下来。两人面对面时都是浑身颤抖。他们哭着抱在一起，互相亲吻着对方。不过，在纳尼亚，没人会对这种行为有什么看法。

“快！快点！”阿斯兰喊道，“人马！苍鹰！我看见另一只狼跑进了灌木丛里，就在你们身后，它要逃跑，你们都去跟上它，它会回到它的女主人身边。这是救出第四名亚当之子的好机会。”话音刚落，四周就响起了雷鸣般的马蹄声和翅膀扑棱的声音。约有十几只动作迅捷的动物飞快地消失在夜色中。

彼得呼哧呼哧地喘着粗气，他一回头，看见阿斯兰来到他身

disappeared into the gathering darkness.

Peter, still out of breath, turned and saw Aslan close at hand. “You have forgotten to clean your sword,” said Aslan.

It was true. Peter blushed when he looked at the bright blade and saw it all smeared with the Wolf’s hair and blood. He stooped down and wiped it quite clean on the grass, and then wiped it quite dry on his coat.

“Hand it to me and kneel, Son of Adam,” said Aslan. And when Peter had done so he struck him with the flat of the blade and said, “Rise up, Sir Peter Wolf’s-Bane. And, whatever happens, never forget to wipe your sword.”

Now we must get back to Edmund. When he had been made to walk far further than he had ever known that anybody could walk, the Witch at last halted in a dark valley all overshadowed with fir trees and yew trees. Edmund simply sank down and lay on his face doing nothing at all and not even caring what was

边，对他说：“你忘了擦干净你的剑。”

这倒是真的。彼得看见光亮的剑身已经被狼毛和血弄污了，不由得脸一红。他蹲下来，把剑在草地上擦干净，又用自己的衣服擦了擦。

“把剑递给我，跪下，亚当之子。”阿斯兰说。彼得听令跪下以后，阿斯兰用剑脊轻触了他一下，然后说，“起来吧！我封你为屠狼勇士彼得。记住，以后不管发生什么事，不要忘了擦干净你的剑。”

现在，我们再来说说埃德蒙吧。他被迫走了好远好远，远到谁也走不了比这更远的路。最后，女巫终于在一片幽暗的山谷里停了下来。这里到处都是冷杉树和紫杉树。埃德蒙扑倒在地上，什么都不想干。如果他们允许他躺着一动不动，他也就毫不在乎接下来要发生什么事情——他累得都顾不上吃饭、喝水了。女巫

going to happen next provided they would let him lie still. He was too tired even to notice how hungry and thirsty he was. The Witch and the dwarf were talking close beside him in low tones.

"No," said the dwarf, "it is no use now, O Queen. They must have reached the Stone Table by now."

"Perhaps the Wolf will smell us out and bring us news," said the Witch.

"It cannot be good news if he does," said the dwarf.

"Four thrones in Cair Paravel," said the Witch. "How if only three were filled? That would not fulfil the prophecy."

"What difference would that make now that He is here?" said the dwarf. He did not dare, even now, to mention the name of Aslan to his mistress.

"He may not stay long. And then we would fall upon the three at Cair."

"Yet it might be better," said the dwarf, "to keep this one" (here he kicked Edmund) "for bargaining with."

和矮人在他身边窃窃私语。

“不，现在没用了，女王陛下。”小矮人说，“他们肯定已经赶到石台那里了。”

“或许，狼会闻见我们的行踪，给我们带回来口信。”女巫说。

“就算来了，也不一定是好消息。”矮人说。

“凯尔·帕拉维尔城堡有四个王座，”女王说，“要是只有三个人坐，预言就无法实现。”

“可是它既然来了，这又有什么关系呢？”矮人说。事到如今，他还是不敢在他的女主人面前提到阿斯兰这个名字。

“它可能并不会待很久。到时候，我们就可以抓住另外三个了。”

“不过，留着这个，还可以做交易。”说着，矮人踢了埃德蒙一脚。

CHAPTER THIRTEEN DEEP MAGIC FROM THE DAWN OF TIME

"Yes! and have him rescued," said the Witch scornfully.

"Then," said the dwarf, "we had better do what we have to do at once."

"I would like to have it done on the Stone Table itself," said the Witch. "That is the proper place. That is where it has always been done before."

"It will be a long time now before the Stone Table can again be put to its proper use," said the dwarf.

"True," said the Witch; and then, "Well, I will begin."

At that moment with a rush and a snarl a Wolf rushed up to them.

"I have seen them. They are all at the Stone Table, with Him. They have killed my captain, Maugrim. I was hidden in the thickets

第十三章 远古时期的深奥魔法

"对，先饶他一命。"女巫轻蔑地说。

"那么现在，"矮人说，"咱们该干正事了。"

"我希望在石台那里完成，"女巫说，"毕竟，那里才是合适的地点。以前，这种事情都是在那里进行的。"

"可咱们要好久才能走到那儿。"矮人说。

"你说得没错，"女巫说道，"那么，现在就开始吧。"

正说着，一只巨狼怒吼着急匆匆地朝他们跑来。

"我看见他们了，他们和它都在石桌那里。他们已经杀了毛戈林队长。我躲在灌木丛里，看得一清二楚，是一个亚当之子杀了它。快

and saw it all. One of the Sons of Adam killed him. Fly! Fly!"

"No," said the Witch. "There need be no flying. Go quickly. Summon all our people to meet me here as speedily as they can. Call out the giants and the werewolves and the spirits of those trees who are on our side. Call the Ghouls, and the Boggles, the Ogres and the Minotaurs. Call the Cruels, the Hags, the Spectres, and the people of the Toadstools. We will fight. What? Have I not still my wand? Will not their ranks turn into stone even as they come on? Be off quickly, I have a little thing to finish here while you are away."

The great brute bowed its head, turned, and galloped away.

"Now!" she said, "we have no table let me see. We had better put it against the trunk of a tree."

Edmund found himself being roughly forced to his feet. Then the dwarf set him with his back against a tree and bound him fast. He saw the Witch take off her outer mantle. Her arms

跑吧！快跑！"

"不，"女巫说，"没有逃跑的必要。快去，召集人马，速速来这里见我。去把巨人、狼人和站在我们这边的树精都找来。还要动员食尸鬼、妖怪、食人魔、牛头怪、獠牙怪、母夜叉、邪灵以及毒蕈族的所有人，把他们统统都找来。即便敌人找上来也没关系，我有魔杖，可以把他们都变成石头。快去，我这里还有一件小事要处理。"

那只巨兽鞠了一个躬，扭头飞快地跑走了。

"好了！"她说，"我们没有石台，让我想想，把他绑在树上。"

埃德蒙感觉到自己被人粗暴地从地上拽了起来。之后，矮人让他背靠着树，把他紧紧地绑在了树上。他看见白女巫脱掉身上

were bare underneath it and terribly white. Because they were so very white he could see them, but he could not see much else, it was so dark in this valley under the dark trees.

"Prepare the victim," said the Witch. And the dwarf undid Edmund's collar and folded back his shirt at the neck. Then he took Edmund's hair and pulled his head back so that he had to raise his chin. After that Edmund heard a strange noise whizz whizz whizz. For a moment he couldn't think what it was. Then he realized. It was the sound of a knife being sharpened.

At that very moment he heard loud shouts from every direction a drumming of hoofs and a beating of wings a scream from the Witch confusion all round him. And then he found he was being untied. Strong arms were round him and he heard big, kind voices saying things like -"Let him lie down give him some wine drink this steady now you'll be all right in a minute."

Then he heard the voices of people who were not talking to him but to one another. And they were saying things like "Who's

的斗篷，露出苍白的臂膀。在黑暗的山谷和树下阴影的衬托之下，她的胳膊惨白得吓人，白得埃德蒙只能看见那白惨惨的胳膊，其他的都看不见了。

“准备好祭品，”女巫说。矮人解开了埃德蒙的衣领，把领口往里掖了掖，露出他的脖子。然后，矮人又粗暴地抓着埃德蒙的头发，迫使他抬头露出下巴。紧接着，埃德蒙就听见一阵奇怪的“嗡嗡”声。开始，他并没反应过来那是什么声音。而后，他突然意识到——那是磨刀声。

就在这时，他听见四面八方喊声震天。周围一片混乱，马蹄声和翅膀声伴着女巫的一声尖叫。然后，埃德蒙被松绑了。他被抱在一只强有力的臂膀里，耳边传来洪亮的说话声：“让他躺下——给

got the Witch?" "I thought you had her." "I didn't see her after I knocked the knife out of her hand I was after the dwarf do you mean to say she's escaped?" "A chap can't mind everything at once what's that? Oh, sorry, it's only an old stump!" But just at this point Edmund went off in a dead faint.

Presently the centaurs and unicorns and deer and birds (they were of course the rescue party which Aslan had sent in the last chapter) all set off to go back to the Stone Table, carrying Edmund with them. But if they could have seen what happened in that valley after they had gone, I think they might have been surprised.

It was perfectly still and presently the moon grew bright; if you had been there you would have seen the moonlight shining on an old tree-stump and on a fairsized boulder. But if you had gone on looking you would gradually have begun to think there was something odd about both the stump and the boulder. And next you would have thought that the stump did look really

他点酒喝——喝这个——沉住气——你一会儿就没事了。"

然后，他听见很多人在说话，他们不是在对他说话，而是相互间交谈："女巫去哪了？""我以为你抓住她了。""我打掉她手上的刀之后，她就消失了。我在追矮人。什么叫她逃跑了？""谁也不能面面俱到。那是什么？哦，抱歉！看错了，就是个树桩。"听到这儿，埃德蒙就晕过去了。

不久，那些人马、独角兽、鹿和鸟，也就是此前阿斯兰派出的营救队伍，带着埃德蒙返回了石台那里。可是，如果他们知道在离开之后发生了什么，他们肯定会大吃一惊。

皎洁明亮的月光照着山谷，四处一片寂静。月光照在山谷中一节老树桩和一块不大不小的鹅卵石上。如果仔细看，就会发现，

remarkably like a little fat man crouching on the ground. And if you had watched long enough you would have seen the stump walk across to the boulder and the boulder sit up and begin talking to the stump; for in reality the stump and the boulder were simply the Witch and the dwarf. For it was part of her magic that she could make things look like what they aren't, and she had the presence of mind to do so at the very moment when the knife was knocked out of her hand. She had kept hold of her wand, so it had been kept safe, too.

When the other children woke up next morning (they had been sleeping on piles of cushions in the pavilion) the first thing they heard from Mrs Beaver was that their brother had been rescued and brought into camp late last night; and was at that moment with Aslan. As soon as they had breakfasted they all went out, and there they saw Aslan and Edmund walking together in the dewy grass, apart from the rest of the court. There

树桩和鹅卵石看上去都很奇怪。继续观察，你会觉得树桩看上去很像一个蹲在地上的小胖子。接着，你就会发现，树桩走到了鹅卵石旁边，而鹅卵石坐了起来，开始和树桩说话。实际上，树桩和鹅卵石就是女巫和矮人变的。原来，女巫手里的刀被打掉的那一刹那，她就不慌不忙地使用了变形的魔法。而她手里始终攥着魔杖，所以魔杖也完好无损。

孩子们昨晚就睡在了帐篷里的软垫子上。第二天一早，刚起床，他们就从海狸先生那里得知，他们的兄弟已经被救了出来，而且昨晚上就被带回了营地，现在正和阿斯兰在一起。孩子们吃完早饭，匆匆跑出帐篷，才发现阿斯兰和埃德蒙并没有和动物们在一起，一人一狮正在不远处湿漉漉的草地上散步。没人能听见

is no need to tell you (and no one ever heard) what Aslan was saying, but it was a conversation which Edmund never forgot. As the others drew nearer Aslan turned to meet them, bringing Edmund with him.

"Here is your brother," he said, "and there is no need to talk to him about what is past."

Edmund shook hands with each of the others and said to each of them in turn, "I'm sorry," and everyone said, "That's all right." And then everyone wanted very hard to say something which would make it quite clear that they were all friends with him again -something ordinary and natural -and of course no one could think of anything in the world to say. But before they had time to feel really awkward one of the leopards approached Aslan and said, "Sire, there is a messenger from the enemy who craves audience."

"Let him approach," said Aslan.

他们在说什么，大家也不需要知道。然而，对于埃德蒙来说，这段谈话令他终生难忘。三个孩子走了过去，阿斯兰和埃德蒙转身看见了他们。

“你们的兄弟平安无事，”阿斯兰说，“过去发生的种种，就让它们过去吧。”

埃德蒙和每个人都握手言和，并且依次说了对不起，大家都说没关系。彼得他们都再想说些什么——就是那种普通而且自然的话语——好让埃德蒙知道他们同他已经冰释前嫌了。可是，谁也不知道要怎么说。

好在，他们还没来得及感到尴尬，阿斯兰手下的一头美洲豹走上前说：“启禀陛下，敌人派来信使，说有事要禀告陛下。”

“带他过来。”阿斯兰说。

The leopard went away and soon returned leading the Witch's dwarf.

"What is your message, Son of Earth?" asked Aslan.

"The Queen of Narnia and Empress of the Lone Islands desires a safe conduct to come and speak with you,' said the dwarf, "on a matter which is as much to your advantage as to hers."

"Queen of Narnia, indeed!" said Mr Beaver. "Of all the cheek -"

"Peace, Beaver," said Aslan. "All names will soon be restored to their proper owners. In the meantime we will not dispute about them. Tell your mistress, Son of Earth, that I grant her safe conduct on condition that she leaves her wand behind her at that great oak."

This was agreed to and two leopards went back with the dwarf to see that the conditions were properly carried out. "But

那头豹子走开了，不一会儿，它带着女巫的矮人回来了。

"大地之子，你带来什么消息？"阿斯兰问。

"孤岛女皇——纳尼亚女王要你保证她的安全，才会前来会面。"矮人说，"她想和你谈一谈对双方都有利的事情。"

"她还好意思称自己是纳尼亚的女王，"海狸先生说，"脸皮可真厚！"

"安静，海狸！"阿斯兰说，"关于名号，自会对应其所有者，我不想现在讨论这个问题。大地之子，回去告诉你的女主人，只要她把魔杖留在那棵大橡树下，我会保证她的安全。"

双方达成一致，两只美洲豹跟着矮人回去，以保证女巫遵守条件。"万一她把两只豹子变成了石头该怎么办？"露西悄声地问

supposing she turns the two leopards into stone?" whispered Lucy to Peter. I think the same idea had occurred to the leopards themselves; at any rate, as they walked off their fur was all standing up on their backs and their tails were bristling like a cat's when it sees a strange dog.

"It'll be all right," whispered Peter in reply. "He wouldn't send them if it weren't."

A few minutes later the Witch herself walked out on to the top of the hill and came straight across and stood before Aslan. The three children who had not seen her before felt shudders running down their backs at the sight of her face; and there were low growls among all the animals present. Though it was bright sunshine everyone felt suddenly cold. The only two people present who seemed to be quite at their ease were Aslan and the Witch herself. It was the oddest thing to see those two faces the golden face and the dead-white face so close together. Not

彼得。我想，那两只美洲豹也会有这种担忧吧，它们走的时候，背上的毛都竖了起来，尾巴上的毛也炸着，就好像猫看见陌生的狗会炸毛一样。

“不会的，”彼得小声地回答，“要是真有事，它不会派他们去的。”

几分钟后，女巫来到了山顶上，径直走到阿斯兰面前。除了埃德蒙，其他三个孩子没见过她。现在看见女巫的样子，孩子们只觉得后背一阵发毛，所有的动物也都发出了低吼声。即便现在太阳高照，可大家还是觉得如堕冰窟。在场的所有人和动物里，只有阿斯兰和女巫保持着镇静。一张金色的脸，和一张惨白的脸凑得那么近，感觉实在是太古怪了。海狸太太尤其注意到，女巫

that the Witch looked Aslan exactly in his eyes; Mrs Beaver particularly noticed this.

"You have a traitor there, Aslan," said the Witch. Of course everyone present knew that she meant Edmund. But Edmund had got past thinking about himself after all he'd been through and after the talk he'd had that morning. He just went on looking at Aslan. It didn't seem to matter what the Witch said.

"Well," said Aslan. "His offence was not against you."

"Have you forgotten the Deep Magic?" asked the Witch.

"Let us say I have forgotten it," answered Aslan gravely. "Tell us of this Deep Magic."

"Tell you?" said the Witch, her voice growing suddenly shriller. "Tell you what is written on that very Table of Stone which stands beside us? Tell you what is written in letters deep as a spear is long on the firestones on the Secret Hill? Tell you what is engraved on the sceptre of the Emperor-beyond-the-Sea? You

竟敢直视阿斯兰的眼睛。

"阿斯兰，你这里有一个叛徒。"女巫说。当然，现在大家都知道，她指的是埃德蒙。不过，自从他经历过这些事，并且早上和阿斯兰聊过之后，他就不再只考虑自己了。无论女巫说了什么，他都只是看向阿斯兰。

"他也不是针对你。"阿斯兰说。

"难道你忘了远古时期的深奥魔法了吗？"女巫问。

"就当我忘了吧。"阿斯兰严肃地说，"跟我们讲讲这深奥的魔法吧。"

"给你讲？"女巫的声音突然尖锐起来，"给你讲这石台上写了什么吗？给你讲神秘之山上的火石上写着什么吗？给你讲海外

at least know the Magic which the Emperor put into Narnia at the very beginning. You know that every traitor belongs to me as my lawful prey and that for every treachery I have a right to a kill."

"Oh," said Mr Beaver. "So that's how you came to imagine yourself a queen because you were the Emperor's hangman. I see."

"Peace, Beaver," said Aslan, with a very low growl. "And so," continued the Witch, "that human creature is mine. His life is forfeit to me. His blood is my property."

"Come and take it then," said the Bull with the man's head in a great bellowing voice.

"Fool," said the Witch with a savage smile that was almost a snarl, "do you really think your master can rob me of my rights by mere force? He knows the Deep Magic better than that. He knows that unless I have blood as the Law says all Narnia will be overturned and perish in fire and water."

大君的权杖上刻着什么吗？你至少应该知道，大君起初在纳尼亚施的魔法吧！你也知道，每个叛徒都归我，并成为我的合法祭品，而且，我有权杀死每一个背叛我的人。"

"哦，原来你相当于大君的刽子手，怪不得自己称自己是女王呢！"海狸先生说。

"安静，海狸。"阿斯兰低吼道。

"所以，现在那个人类归我。"女巫接着说，"他的命归我了，他的血也是我的。"

"有种自己来拿！"一只人头牛身的动物愤怒地说。

"一群蠢货！"女巫狂傲地笑着，怒吼道，"你以为，你的主人可以单凭武力剥夺我的权利吗？它比谁都了解这深奥的魔法。要是我得不到本属于我的血，纳尼亚就会在烈火洪水中毁灭。"

"It is very true," said Aslan, "I do not deny it."

"Oh, Aslan!" whispered Susan in the Lion's ear, "can't we I mean, you won't, will you? Can't we do something about the Deep Magic? Isn't there something you can work against it?"

"Work against the Emperor's Magic?" said Aslan, turning to her with something like a frown on his face. And nobody ever made that suggestion to him again.

Edmund was on the other side of Aslan, looking all the time at Aslan's face. He felt a choking feeling and wondered if he ought to say something; but a moment later he felt that he was not expected to do anything except to wait, and do what he was told.

"Fall back, all of you," said Aslan, "and I will talk to the Witch alone."

They all obeyed. It was a terrible time this waiting and wondering while the Lion and the Witch talked earnestly together

"她说得没错，"阿斯兰说，"我不否认这一点。"

"天哪！阿斯兰！"苏珊对着阿斯兰的耳朵悄声说，"难道我们不能——我是说你不能阻止这一切发生吗？就没有什么可以破解这个深奥的魔法吗？你不能对付这个魔法吗？"

"对付大君的魔法？"它回过头来对着苏珊皱着眉头。于是没人再向它提这样的意见了。

埃德蒙站在阿斯兰的另一边，一直在看着它的脸。他总是有一种透不过气来的感觉，不知道自己是否应该说点什么。但过了一会儿，他觉得自己除了等待，以及按照别人吩咐的去做之外，什么都干不了。

"所有人，退后。"阿斯兰说，"我要和女巫单独谈谈。"

随即，大家都听令后退。狮王和女巫低声密谈着什么，其他

in low voices. Lucy said, "Oh, Edmund!" and began to cry. Peter stood with his back to the others looking out at the distant sea. The Beavers stood holding each other's paws with their heads bowed. The centaurs stamped uneasily with their hoofs. But everyone became perfectly still in the end, so that you noticed even small sounds like a bumble-bee flying past, or the birds in the forest down below them, or the wind rustling the leaves. And still the talk between Aslan and the White Witch went on.

At last they heard Aslan's voice, "You can all come back," he said. "I have settled the matter. She has renounced the claim on your brother's blood." And all over the hill there was a noise as if everyone had been holding their breath and had now begun breathing again, and then a murmur of talk.

The Witch was just turning away with a look of fierce joy on her face when she stopped and said, "But how do I know this

人只能耐心地等待，这段时间可真难熬。露西说了一声“哦，埃德蒙！”就开始哭起来。彼得背对着大家站着，望向远处的大海。海狸夫妇握紧彼此的爪子，低着头。人马们烦躁地跺着蹄子。但是，所有人都默不作声，周围安静得可以听到蜜蜂嗡嗡飞过的声音、鸟儿在山下林中的欢唱声，或者风吹树叶沙沙的声音。阿斯兰和白女巫还在不停地说着。

最后，只听见阿斯兰说：“大家可以回来了，我已经解决了此事。女巫宣布，放弃取你们兄弟的命了。”之前，大家一直屏息以待，听到这里，大伙大大地松了一口气，接着是一阵喃喃的议论声。

女巫的脸上露出一股狂喜的神情，正要转过身去，却一下子

promise will be kept?"

"Haa-a-arrh!" roared Aslan, half rising from his throne; and his great mouth opened wider and wider and the roar grew louder and louder, and the Witch, after staring for a moment with her lips wide apart, picked up her skirts and fairly ran for her life.

停了下来，说道："我怎么能确定，你会信守承诺？"

"嗷呜！"阿斯兰半身离开宝座怒吼了起来。它的嘴越张越大，怒吼声越来越高。女巫张着嘴，看了一会儿这头愤怒的狮子，拎起裙子灰溜溜地跑了。

CHAPTER FOURTEEN THE TRIUMPH OF THE WITCH

As soon as the Witch had gone Aslan said, "We must move from this place at once, it will be wanted for other purposes. We shall encamp tonight at the Fords of Beruna."

Of course everyone was dying to ask him how he had arranged matters with the witch; but his face was stern and everyone's ears were still ringing with the sound of his roar and so nobody dared.

After a meal, which was taken in the open air on the hill-top (for the sun had got strong by now and dried the grass), they were busy for a while taking the pavilion down and packing things up. Before two o'clock they were on the march and set off in a northeasterly direction, walking at an easy pace for they had not far to go.

第十四章 女巫的胜利

女巫走了以后，阿斯兰说："我们现在要马上离开这里。这个地方被征用了，我们今晚要在贝鲁娜浅滩扎营。"

每个人都非常想知道它和女巫到底谈了些什么。然而，它的表情非常严肃，加之刚刚的怒吼声还回荡在大家耳中，所以也没人敢问。

太阳升起后，湿漉漉的草地被晒干了。大伙在山顶的空地上吃了午饭。饭后，他们开始拆帐篷、打包，着实忙了一阵。下午两点之前，所有人便朝着东北方向行进。因为目的地离这儿不远，所以，大伙也就不紧不慢地走着。

During the first part of the journey'Aslan explained to Peter his plan of campaign. "As soon as she has finished her business in these parts," he said, "the Witch and her crew will almost certainly fall back to her House and prepare for a siege. You may or may not be able to cut her off and prevent her from reaching it." He then went on to outline two plans of battle one for fighting the Witch and her people in the wood and another for assaulting her castle. And all the time he was advising Peter how to conduct the operations, saying things like, "You must put your Centaurs in such and such a place" or "You must post scouts to see that she doesn't do so-and-so," till at last Peter said,

"But you will be there yourself, Aslan."

"I can give you no promise of that," answered the Lion. And he continued giving Peter his instructions.

For the last part of the journey it was Susan and Lucy who saw most of him. He did not talk very much and seemed to them

行程一开始，阿斯兰就跟彼得讲了它的计划："女巫在这里忙完了自己的事情，就会和同伙们一起回到她的城堡，准备对我们发起进攻。你或许可以在她回城堡的路上截住她，阻止她的进攻。当然，也有可能截不住。"

然后，阿斯兰提出了两种作战方案，一种是在树林里正面对抗，另一种是直接攻打她的城堡。在路上，它一直向彼得面授机宜，教他如何指挥战斗，比如，"你可以把人马安排在这里这里""你必须派出探子，以便时刻了解她的动向"，等等。直到彼得问它："阿斯兰，你不会在场亲自指挥吗？"

"这我可不敢向你保证。"狮王回答，又继续指导彼得该如何安排战斗。

行程的最后，苏珊和露西一直在观察阿斯兰。它基本上不说

to be sad.

It was still afternoon when they came down to a place where the river valley had widened out and the river was broad and shallow. This was the Fords of Beruna and Aslan gave orders to halt on this side of the water. But Peter said, “Wouldn’t it be better to camp on the far side for fear she should try a night attack or anything?”

Aslan, who seemed to have been thinking about something else, roused himself with a shake of his magnificent mane and said, “Eh? What’s that?” Peter said it all over again.

“No,” said Aslan in a dull voice, as if it didn’t matter. “No. She will not make an attack tonight.” And then he sighed deeply. But presently he added, “All the same it was well thought of. That is how a soldier ought to think. But it doesn’t really matter.” So they proceeded to pitch their camp.

Aslan’s mood affected everyone that evening. Peter was

话，看起来很悲伤。

傍晚时分，他们到达了目的地。这里河谷开阔，河面很宽，而且水也很浅。这就是贝鲁娜浅滩。阿斯兰下令，在河的一边扎营。但是，彼得提出了疑问：“为防止女巫半夜偷袭，咱们在河的另一边扎营岂不是更好？”

阿斯兰似乎在想着其他事，有些心不在焉的。它抖了抖鬃毛，回过神来问：“什么？你刚刚说什么？”彼得只好又说了一遍。

“不会的。”阿斯兰的声音听上去有些沉闷，似乎偷袭这件事并不重要，“她今晚不会偷袭。”说罢，它深深地叹了口气。

随后，阿斯兰接着说：“但是，你这样考虑周全是非常好的，一个士兵就应该这样想。不过现在倒是没关系。”然后，大家就开

feeling uncomfortable too at the idea of fighting the battle on his own; the news that Aslan might not be there had come as a great shock to him. Supper that evening was a quiet meal. Everyone felt how different it had been last night or even that morning. It was as if the good times, having just begun, were already drawing to their end.

This feeling affected Susan so much that she couldn't get to sleep when she went to bed. And after she had lain counting sheep and turning over and over she heard Lucy give a long sigh and turn over just beside her in the darkness.

"Can't you get to sleep either?" said Susan.

"No," said Lucy. "I thought you were asleep. I say, Susan!"

"What?"

"I've a most Horrible feeling as if something were hanging over us."

始支帐篷。当晚，阿斯兰的情绪影响了所有人。彼得想到这一仗全靠他自己，就有些坐立不安，尤其是得知阿斯兰不一定在场，更觉得自己受到了很大的打击。这顿晚餐大家吃得很安静，都感觉到这和昨晚甚至今早的感觉大不一样。就好像好日子才刚刚开始，却马上要结束了似的。

苏珊也受到这种情绪的影响，一时难以入睡。她躺在床上，翻来覆去地不停数羊。然后，就听见露西长长地叹了口气，在黑暗中翻到自己身边。

“你也睡不着吗？”苏珊问。

“嗯，睡不着。”露西说，“我以为你睡了呢。我说苏珊——”

“什么事？”

“我有种特别不好的预感，觉得有事情要发生。”

"Have you? Because, as a matter of fact, so have I."

"Something about Aslan," said Lucy. "Either some dreadful thing is going to happen to him, or something dreadful that he's going to do"

"There's been something wrong with him all afternoon," said Susan. "Lucy! What was that he said about not being with us at the battle? You don't think he could be stealing away and leaving us tonight, do you?"

"Where is he now?" said Lucy. "Is he here in the pavilion?"

"I don't think so."

"Susan! let's go outside and have a look round. We might see him."

"All right. Let's," said Susan; "we might just as well be doing that as lying awake here."

Very quietly the two girls groped their way among the other sleepers and crept out of the tent. The moonlight was bright

"是吗？说实话，我也有这种感觉。"

"是关于阿斯兰，"露西说，"要不就是它要出什么可怕的事，要不就是它要做什么可怕的事。"

"它整个一下午都不太对劲，"苏珊说，"露西，你还记得吗？它说，打仗的时候它可能不在现场？你觉得，它今晚会把我们抛下，一个人偷偷溜走吗？"

"它现在在哪儿？"露西问，"不在帐篷里吗？"

"我觉得它不在。"

"苏珊，咱们去外面转转，说不定会遇见它。"

"好，咱们走。"苏珊说，"不然躺在这儿也睡不着。"

姐妹俩摸索着穿过那些睡着的纳尼亚居民们，悄悄地爬出了

and everything was quite still except for the noise of the river chattering over the stones. Then Susan suddenly caught Lucy's arm and said, "Look!" On the far side of the camping ground, just where the trees began, they saw the Lion slowly walking away from them into the wood. Without a word they both followed him.

He led them up the steep slope out of the river valley and then slightly to the right apparently by the very same route which they had used that afternoon in coming from the Hill of the Stone Table. On and on he led them, into dark shadows and out into pale moonlight, getting their feet wet with the heavy dew. He looked somehow different from the Aslan they knew. His tail and his head hung low and he walked slowly as if he were very, very tired. Then, when they were crossing a wide open place where there where no shadows for them to hide in, he stopped and looked round. It was no good trying to run away so

帐篷。皎洁的月光洒在大地上，周围一片寂静，只能听见河水拍打石头的声音。苏珊突然拽住了露西的胳膊说："快看！"在营地的另一侧，树林的边上，她们看见狮子正缓缓地走进树林。她俩一句话也没说，默默地跟了上去。

她们跟着它爬上河谷的陡坡，朝着右边走去——这是他们下午从石台来到浅滩的那条路。它走啊走啊，从黑暗的阴影里走到苍白的月光下，走得她们鞋子都湿了。现在的它，看上去一点儿也不像她们认识的阿斯兰——它耷拉着脑袋和尾巴，缓慢地走着，好像非常劳累的样子。随后，狮王和孩子们走过一片空地，那里没有阴影可以躲藏了。阿斯兰停下脚步环望四周。这个时候逃跑也不太好，于是，姐妹俩走上前来。

they came towards him. When they were closer he said,

"Oh, children, children, why are you following me?"

"We couldn't sleep," said Lucy and then felt sure that she need say no more and that Aslan knew all they had been thinking.

"Please, may we come with you wherever you're going?" asked Susan.

"Well -" said Aslan, and seemed to be thinking. Then he said, "I should be glad of company tonight. Yes, you may come, if you will promise to stop when I tell you, and after that leave me to go on alone."

"Oh, thank you, thank you. And we will," said the two girls.

Forward they went again and one of the girls walked on each side of the Lion. But how slowly he walked! And his great, royal head drooped so that his nose nearly touched the grass. Presently he stumbled and gave a low moan.

阿斯兰问："哦！孩子们！你们跟着我干什么？"

"我们睡不着。"露西说。她觉得不需多说，阿斯兰始终都知道她们在想些什么。

"求求你，无论你去哪儿，让我们陪着你吧！"苏珊请求道。

阿斯兰想了想说："今晚有你们陪着，我很开心。你们可以跟过来，不过，你们要向我保证——当我要求你们停下时，你们就要停下，接下来的事情让我一个人去做。"

"我们保证！太谢谢你了。"两个女孩子说。

姐妹俩分别走在阿斯兰的两边。它走得可真慢啊！它低着庄严而高贵的头，鼻子都快碰到草地了。有一回，它还差点被绊倒，忍不住低吟了一声。

"Aslan! Dear Aslan!" said Lucy, "what is wrong? Can't you tell us?"

"Are you ill, dear Aslan?" asked Susan.

"No," said Aslan. "I am sad and lonely. Lay your hands on my mane so that I can feel you are there and let us walk like that."

And so the girls did what they would never have dared to do without his permission, but what they had longed to do ever since they first saw him buried their cold hands in the beautiful sea of fur and stroked it and, so doing, walked with him. And presently they saw that they were going with him up the slope of the hill on which the Stone Table stood. They went up at the side where the trees came furthest up, and when they got to the last tree (it was one that had some bushes about it) Aslan stopped and said, "Oh, children, children. Here you must stop. And whatever happens, do not let yourselves be seen. Farewell."

And both the girls cried bitterly (though they hardly knew

"阿斯兰！亲爱的阿斯兰！你怎么了？能告诉我们吗？"露西问。

"你生病了吗，亲爱的阿斯兰？"苏珊也问道。

"不，我没生病。"阿斯兰说，"我只是觉得很悲伤、很孤独。你们走路的时候，可以把手放在我的鬃毛上吗？我想感受到你们的存在。"

以前，没有它的允许，姐妹俩完全不敢这么做。现在，她们把冰凉的小手放在它美丽的鬃毛上，轻轻地抚摸着。不一会儿，她们就爬上了石台所在的那座山。她们走到树林的边缘，直到被灌木丛包围的那棵树下。这时，阿斯兰让她们停了下，对她们说："孩子们，你们必须停下来了。无论发生了什么，千万不要让别人看见你们。永别了，孩子们。"

why) and clung to the Lion and kissed his mane and his nose and his paws and his great, sad eyes. Then he turned from them and walked out on to the top of the hill. And Lucy and Susan, crouching in the bushes, looked after him, and this is what they saw.

A great crowd of people were standing all round the Stone Table and though the moon was shining many of them carried torches which burned with evil-looking red flames and black smoke. But such people! Ogres with monstrous teeth, and wolves, and bull-headed men; spirits of evil trees and poisonous plants; and other creatures whom I won't describe because if I did the grownups would probably not let you read this book Cruels and Hags and Incubuses, Wraiths, Horrors, Efreets, Sprites, Orknies, Wooses, and Ettins. In fact here were all those who were on the Witch's side and whom the Wolf had summoned at her command. And right in the middle, standing by the Table, was the Witch herself.

虽然不知道为什么，可两个女孩子开始抱着狮子放声痛哭，不停地亲吻它的鬃毛、鼻子、爪子和那双既庄严又悲伤的眼睛。然后，它转过头，孤身走向了山顶。露西和苏珊藏在灌木丛里目送它离开，随后看到了下面的情景：

石台四周围了一群人，尽管月光皎洁，可这群人都举着火把，火把燃烧时冒着邪恶的红色火焰和黑烟。这可明显不是一群好人啊！食人魔龇着獠牙，还有牛头怪、坏树精和毒植物精，恶魔、母夜叉和男妖，邪灵、鬼怪、火怪、地妖、石怪和双头巨人，等等。我要是再写下去，你们的父母都不会再让你们看下去了。事实上，那只恶狼传达了女巫的指令后，所有站在女巫那边的妖魔鬼怪、魑魅魍魉都来了。站在他们中间、靠着石桌的就是女巫本人。

A howl and a gibber of dismay went up from the creatures when they first saw the great Lion pacing towards them, and for a moment even the Witch seemed to be struck with fear. Then she recovered herself and gave a wild fierce laugh.

"The fool!" she cried. "The fool has come. Bind him fast."

Lucy and Susan held their breaths waiting for Aslan's roar and his spring upon his enemies. But it never came. Four Hags, grinning and leering, yet also (at first) hanging back and half afraid of what they had to do, had approached him. "Bind him, I say!" repeated the White Witch. The Hags made a dart at him and shrieked with triumph when they found that he made no resistance at all. Then others evil dwarfs and apes rushed in to help them, and between them they rolled the huge Lion over on his back and tied all his four paws together, shouting and cheering as if they had done something brave, though, had the Lion chosen, one of those paws could

看到这头伟大的狮子向他们走来时，所有的鬼怪都发出了惊慌的号叫，有那么一刹那，连女巫都有些害怕了。可是，不一会儿，她就镇定下来，发出粗野的狂笑。

“你这个蠢货！”她叫到，“这个蠢货自己送上门来了，把它捆起来！”

露西和苏珊都屏住呼吸，希望阿斯兰可以怒吼着跃起并击退敌人，但它并没有这么做。四个母夜叉龇牙咧嘴地斜眼看着阿斯兰，可走到一半，谁也不敢再往前走一步。“我说，把它捆上！”白女巫继续叫嚣着。母夜叉冲上去，发现它完全不抵抗时，发出了胜利的尖叫声。那些邪恶的矮人和猿猴也冲过来帮忙。他们把体形庞大的狮王掀翻在地，把它的四个爪子都绑了起来，不停地叫喊、欢呼，好像自己干了什么特别勇敢的事一样。可是，明明只要阿斯兰

have been the death of them all. But he made no noise, even when the enemies, straining and tugging, pulled the cords so tight that they cut into his flesh. Then they began to drag him towards the Stone Table.

"Stop!" said the Witch. "Let him first be shaved."

Another roar of mean laughter went up from her followers as an ogre with a pair of shears came forward and squatted down by Aslan's head. Snip-snip-snip went the shears and masses of curling gold began to fall to the ground. Then the ogre stood back and the children, watching from their hiding-place, could see the face of Aslan looking all small and different without its mane. The enemies also saw the difference.

"Why, he's only a great cat after all!" cried one.

"Is that what we were afraid of?" said another.

And they surged round Aslan, jeering at him, saying things like "Puss, Puss! Poor Pussy," and "How many mice have you

反抗就能一爪子拍死他们的。可它并不作声，任凭敌人紧紧地把它困住，绳子都勒到了肉里面。接着，暴徒们把它拽向石台。

“停！”女巫说，“先把它的毛剃了。”

一个食人魔拿着一把剪刀走过来，蹲在阿斯兰的脑袋边，女巫的爪牙们发出一阵恶毒的狂笑。剪刀“咔嚓咔嚓”地剪着，一缕缕金色的鬃毛掉在地上。之后，食人魔后退了一步，孩子们从藏身的地方看见了受虐的阿斯兰——没了鬃毛的它，脸显得那么小。敌人们也看到了这一差别。

“哈哈，原来不过是一只大猫啊！”一个妖怪叫道。

“咱们之前怕的是它吗？”另一只妖怪附和道。

它们围着阿斯兰，不停地嘲笑它，说什么“喵喵喵！可怜的小猫咪！”“臭猫，今天抓了几只老鼠啊？”或是“小猫咪，要不

caught today, Cat?" and "Would you like a saucer of milk, Pussums?"

"Oh, how can they?" said Lucy, tears streaming down her cheeks. "The brutes, the brutes!" for now that the first shock was over the shorn face of Aslan looked to her braver, and more beautiful, and more patient than ever.

"Muzzle him!" said the Witch. And even now, as they worked about his face putting on the muzzle, one bite from his jaws would have cost two or three of them their hands. But he never moved. And this seemed to enrage all that rabble. Everyone was at him now. Those who had been afraid to come near him even after he was bound began to find their courage, and for a few minutes the two girls could not even see him so thickly was he surrounded by the whole crowd of creatures kicking him, hitting him, spitting on him, jeering at him.

At last the rabble had had enough of this. They began to

要来一碟牛奶啊？"

"他们怎么可以这样？"露西说着，泪珠流过脸庞，"禽兽！畜生！"震惊过后，再看阿斯兰的那张脸，女孩们觉得它比以前更加勇敢、更加美丽也更加坚韧。

"把它的嘴给我堵上！"女巫说。爪牙们纷纷上去给阿斯兰戴嘴套。即便在这时，只要它张嘴咬下去，这些妖怪也会至少断掉几只手。可是，它仍旧一动不动。这似乎激怒了这些暴徒，他们纷纷把阿斯兰围起来。那些一开始时不敢接近它的妖怪，看着它被绑起来之后，也莫名地鼓起勇气围了上去。几分钟之后，两个女孩子就看不见它了。暴徒们将阿斯兰紧紧地围着，又踢又踹，还朝它吐口水，不停地嘲笑它。

最后，他们闹够了，就把五花大绑戴着嘴套的狮子拽到石台

drag the bound and muzzled Lion to the Stone Table, some pulling and some pushing. He was so huge that even when they got him there it took all their efforts to hoist him on to the surface of it. Then there was more tying and tightening of cords.

"The cowards! The cowards!" sobbed Susan. "Are they still afraid of him, even now?"

When once Aslan had been tied (and tied so that he was really a mass of cords) on the flat stone, a hush fell on the crowd. Four Hags, holding four torches, stood at the corners of the Table. The Witch bared her arms as she had bared them the previous night when it had been Edmund instead of Aslan. Then she began to whet her knife. It looked to the children, when the gleam of the torchlight fell on it, as if the knife were made of stone, not of steel, and it was of a strange and evil shape.

As last she drew near. She stood by Aslan's head. Her face was working and twitching with passion, but his looked up at

上。阿斯兰的体型巨大，妖怪们不得不使出全身的力气才把它吊到石台上。然后，又在它身上捆了好几道绳子。

"胆小鬼！胆小鬼！"苏珊呜咽道，"它都被绑成这样了，还需要怕它吗？"

最后，阿斯兰身上被捆了无数道绳子，无助地躺在石台的台面上。暴徒们安静了下来。四个母夜叉手举火把，站在石台的四角上。女巫脱下袍子，露出臂膀，就像那天晚上对付埃德蒙一样。她开始磨刀，借着火光，孩子们看到了那把刀，那似乎不像是钢做的，更像是一把石刀，形状丑陋无比。

最后，她走到阿斯兰脑袋边，表情扭曲而狰狞。但是，阿斯兰平静地望着天空，没有愤怒也没有害怕，只是显得有些悲伤。就在女巫举刀要砍下去的时候，她突然蹲下来，用颤抖的声音说：

the sky, still quiet, neither angry nor afraid, but a little sad. Then, just before she gave the blow, she stooped down and said in a quivering voice,

“And now, who has won? Fool, did you think that by all this you would save the human traitor? Now I will kill you instead of him as our pact was and so the Deep Magic will be appeased. But when you are dead what will prevent me from killing him as well? And who will take him out of my hand then? Understand that you have given me Narnia forever, you have lost your own life and you have not saved his. In that knowledge, despair and die.”

The children did not see the actual moment of the killing. They couldn’t bear to look and had covered their eyes.

“看看现在是谁赢了？你这个蠢货，真以为自己救得了那个人类的叛徒吗？你来替他死——这是我们之间的约定，也会平息深奥的魔法带来的灾难。可你死了，还有谁能阻止我杀了他？还有，有谁能从我手里把他救走？是你自己拱手永远地把纳尼亚给了我，你自己呢？不但丢了小命，也救不了那个人类。你现在知道已经太晚了，受死吧！”

刀砍下去的时候，两个孩子再也不忍心看了，她们蒙住了自己的眼睛。

CHAPTER FIFTEEN DEEPER MAGIC FROM BEFORE THE DAWN OF TIME

While the two girls still crouched in the bushes with their hands over their faces, they heard the voice of the Witch calling out, "Now! Follow me all and we will set about what remains of this war! It will not take us long to crush the human vermin and the traitors now that the great Fool, the great Cat, lies dead."

At this moment the children were for a few seconds in very great danger. For with wild cries and a noise of skirling pipes and shrill horns blowing, the whole of that vile rabble came sweeping off the hill-top and down the slope right past their hiding-place. They felt the Spectres go by them like a cold wind and they felt the ground shake beneath them under the galloping feet of the Minotaurs; and overhead there went a flurry of foul wings and a blackness of vultures and giant bats. At any other

第十五章　太古时期的高深魔法

两个女孩子藏在灌木丛中，双手掩面。这时，只听得女巫高喊："现在！大家跟着我，去收拾那些残兵败将！这只大蠢猫已经死了，那些人渣和叛徒已经不足为患了！"

姐妹俩现在的处境非常危险。只听野蛮的叫喊声、尖锐的风笛声和号角声响成一片。山上的暴徒们一哄而下，正好路过她们俩藏身的地方。她们只觉得恶灵像一阵阴风从身边掠过，牛头怪的蹄子踏得大地在震动。头上猛禽飞过，掠起一阵腥风，半空中黑压压的一片，全都是秃鹰和大蝙蝠。如果是以前，她们肯定已经吓得抖如筛糠了。可现在，阿斯兰的死让她们的心中充满着悲

time they would have trembled with fear; but now the sadness and shame and horror of Aslan's death so filled their minds that they hardly thought of it.

As soon as the wood was silent again Susan and Lucy crept out onto the open hill-top. The moon was getting low and thin clouds were passing across her, but still they could see the shape of the Lion lying dead in his bonds. And down they both knelt in the wet grass and kissed his cold face and stroked his beautiful fur what was left of it and cried till they could cry no more. And then they looked at each other and held each other's hands for mere loneliness and cried again; and then again were silent. At last Lucy said, "I can't bear to look at that horrible muzzle. I wonder could we take if off?"

So they tried. And after a lot of working at it (for their fingers were cold and it was now the darkest part of the night) they succeeded. And when they saw his face without it they burst

伤和愤恨，已经顾不得害怕了。

整个树林再次平静下来。苏珊和露西爬出灌木丛，来到山顶的空地处。一片薄云遮住了快要落下去的月亮，她们借着微弱的月光，看见死去的狮子仍然被绑在石台上。她们跪在湿漉漉的草地上，不停地亲吻着它冰凉的脸庞，抚摸着它所剩无几的美丽鬃毛，哭到眼泪都流干了。她们紧握双手，看着对方，这凄凉的情景让她们又大哭起来。一段沉默之后，露西说："我受不了看它戴着这个吓人的嘴套，我们帮它摘下来吧。"

这是黎明前最黑暗的时期，她们的手指都冻僵了，费了好大力气才把口套摘下来。当她们看见那张完整的脸，又忍不住哭了起来，不停地轻抚它的脸庞，尽可能地把阿斯兰脸上的污渍和血迹抹去——我都不知道要怎么才能形容孩子们当时那种孤单、绝

out crying again and kissed it and fondled it and wiped away the blood and the foam as well as they could. And it was all more lonely and hopeless and horrid than I know how to describe.

"I wonder could we untie him as well?" said Susan presently. But the enemies, out of pure spitefulness, had drawn the cords so tight that the girls could make nothing of the knots.

I hope no one who reads this book has been quite as miserable as Susan and Lucy were that night; but if you have been if you've been up all night and cried till you have no more tears left in you you will know that there comes in the end a sort of quietness. You feel as if nothing was ever going to happen again. At any rate that was how it felt to these two. Hours and hours seemed to go by in this dead calm, and they hardly noticed that they were getting colder and colder. But at last Lucy noticed two other things. One was that the sky on the east side of the hill was a little less dark than it had been an hour ago. The other was

望又恐惧的心情了。

"我们帮它把绳子解开吧。"苏珊说。由于敌人们怀恨在心，他们把阿斯兰捆得特别紧，她们俩完全没有办法把绳结解开。

我希望本书的读者没有一个人曾经历过苏珊和露西当时的绝望。如果你曾经有过这种经历——整晚不睡，哭到眼泪流干了为止——就会明白最后那种归于平静的心情，觉得无论再发生什么事，都无所谓了。姐妹俩现在就是这种心情。时间就这样在麻木的平静中过去了几个小时，她们甚至都没有意识到，自己的身体越来越冷。最后，露西总算注意到了两件事：一是山的东面，天空已经比一个小时之前亮了一点；另一件则是感觉到脚下的草地上有什么小东西在动。开始，她没有在意，这又不算什么。而且，现在来看，这还算是事儿吗？什么都不重要了！但是，后来，她

some tiny movement going on in the grass at her feet. At first she took no interest in this. What did it matter? Nothing mattered now! But at last she saw that whatever-it-was had begun to move up the upright stones of the Stone Table. And now whatever-they-were were moving about on Aslan's body. She peered closer. They were little grey things.

"Ugh!" said Susan from the other side of the Table. "How beastly! There are horrid little mice crawling over him. Go away, you little beasts." And she raised her hand to frighten them away.

"Wait!" said Lucy, who had been looking at them more closely still. "Can you see what they're doing?"

Both girls bent down and stared.

"I do believe -" said Susan. "But how queer! They're nibbling away at the cords!"

"That's what I thought," said Lucy. "I think they're friendly

看见，那些在草地上移动的东西又爬上了石台，爬到了阿斯兰的身体上。她凑近看了看，是一些灰色的小东西。

“啊！”苏珊的声音从石台的另一边传来，“多讨厌啊！好多讨厌的小老鼠爬到它身上啦！走开，你们这些小畜生。”她挥着手，试图把老鼠们赶走。

“等一下！”露西说。她凑近了些，仔细盯着它们看，“你快看，它们在做什么？”

两个孩子弯下腰，目不转睛地盯着。

“好奇怪！它们在啃绳子！”苏珊说。

“我也是这么想的，”露西说，“它们是善良的小老鼠。可怜的小家伙们，还没意识到它已经死了。或许，它们觉得，咬断绳子

mice. Poor little things they don't realize he's dead. They think it'll do some good untying him."

It was quite definitely lighter by now. Each of the girls noticed for the first time the white face of the other. They could see the mice nibbling away; dozens and dozens, even hundreds, of little field mice. And at last, one by one, the ropes were all gnawed through.

The sky in the east was whitish by now and the stars were getting fainter all except one very big one low down on the eastern horizon. They felt colder than they had been all night. The mice crept away again.

The girls cleared away the remains of the gnawed ropes. Aslan looked more like himself without them. Every moment his dead face looked nobler, as the light grew and they could see it better.

In the wood behind them a bird gave a chuckling sound. It

会让它好过一点儿。"

天空比之前更亮了一些。姐妹俩这才注意到彼此的脸是多么的苍白。然后，她们看见，成百上千只小老鼠在不停地咬着绳子。最后，绳子终于被咬断了。

此时，东方的天空已经泛白，星星渐渐隐没在天际，只有东方的地平线上还能看到一颗很大的星星。这时，她们觉得比晚上更冷了。这时，那些小老鼠也都爬走了。

姐妹俩把阿斯兰身上被咬断的绳子清理干净，它这时看上去好多了。天色越来越亮，她们也逐渐看清——即便那张脸上没有任何生气，看上去却更加高贵了。

她们身后的树林中，一声清脆的鸟叫划破了长久的寂静。孩

had been so still for hours and hours that it startled them. Then another bird answered it. Soon there were birds singing all over the place.

It was quite definitely early morning now, not late night.

"I'm so cold," said Lucy.

"So am I," said Susan. "Let's walk about a bit."

They walked to the eastern edge of the hill and looked down. The one big star had almost disappeared. The country all looked dark grey, but beyond, at the very end of the world, the sea showed pale. The sky began to turn red. They walked to ands fro more times than they could count between the dead Aslan and the eastern ridge, trying to keep warm; and oh, how tired their legs felt. Then at last, as they stood for a moment looking out towards they sea and Cair Paravel (which they could now just make out) the red turned to gold along the line where the sea and the sky met and very slowly up came the

子们吓了一跳。紧接着，另一只鸟也叫着，似乎是在回应什么。不一会儿，整个树林里都是鸟叫声。

虽然现在天色很早，可终究不是黑夜了。

露西说："我好冷啊。"

"我也是。"苏珊回答，"咱们四处走走，暖和一下吧。"

她们走到了山的东面，站在山崖边向下望去。东方地平线上的那颗明亮的星星已经快消失了，整个王国笼罩在一片灰暗之中，只有远处的大海一片苍白，天空开始逐渐泛红。为了取暖，她们在东边的山崖和石台之间来回走了好久，现在，姐妹俩的双腿已经累得好像灌了铅。最后，她们站在那里，望着远处的大海，以及刚刚能看清的凯尔·帕拉维尔城堡。海天相接的地平线处，一轮红日缓缓升起，把泛红的天空染成了金色。就在这时，她们听

edge of the sun. At that moment they heard from behind them a loud noise a great cracking, deafening noise as if a giant had broken a giant's plate.

"What's that?" said Lucy, clutching Susan's arm.

"I I feel afraid to turn round," said Susan; "something awful is happening."

"They're doing something worse to Him," said Lucy. "Come on!" And she turned, pulling Susan round with her.

The rising of the sun had made everything look so different all colours and shadows were changed that for a moment they didn't see the important thing. Then they did. The Stone Table was broken into two pieces by a great crack that ran down it from end to end; and there was no Aslan.

"Oh, oh, oh!" cried the two girls, rushing back to the Table.

"Oh, it's too bad," sobbed Lucy, "they might have left the body alone."

见身后传来了一声巨响，仿佛巨人的铠甲崩裂了一般。

“什么声音？”露西一把抓住了苏珊的胳膊。

“我……我害怕，不敢转过去看。”苏珊说，“我觉得发生了什么可怕的事。”

“他们肯定又对它下毒手了。”露西说，“快来！”说着，拉着苏珊转过身来。

太阳升起的那一刻，发出耀眼的光芒，周围的颜色和阴影看上去完全不同了。她们俩也没看见有什么大事发生。可不一会儿，她们就发现——石台完全裂成了两半，而阿斯兰不见了。

“哦！哦！哦！”两个孩子叫着跑向了石台。

“简直太糟糕了，”露西哽咽着说，“它们至少也要给它留个全尸啊。”

"Who's done it?" cried Susan. "What does it mean? Is it magic?"

"Yes!" said a great voice behind their backs. "It is more magic." They looked round. There, shining in the sunrise, larger than they had seen him before, shaking his mane (for it had apparently grown again) stood Aslan himself.

"Oh, Aslan!" cried both the children, staring up at him, almost as much frightened as they were glad.

"Aren't you dead then, dear Aslan?" said Lucy.

"Not now," said Aslan.

"You're not not a ?" asked Susan in a shaky voice. She couldn't bring herself to say the word ghost. Aslan stooped his golden head and licked her forehead. The warmth of his breath and a rich sort of smell that seemed to hang about his hair came all over her.

"Do I look it?" he said.

"这是谁干的？"苏珊叫道，"到底怎么回事？难道又是魔法？"

"没错！就是魔法。"一个洪亮的声音从她们身后传来。孩子们回过头，看见耀眼的阳光下，阿斯兰站在那里，身形比以前更高大了，它正抖着已经完全长回来的鬃毛。

"天哪！阿斯兰！"孩子们大叫着，目不转睛地看着它，既害怕又高兴。

"可你不是死了吗？"露西问。

"我还没死。"阿斯兰说。

"你、你该不会是——"苏珊颤抖着说——她不敢说出"鬼魂"这个字眼。阿斯兰俯下金灿灿的大脑袋，舔着苏珊的额头。它的气息暖暖的，从鬃毛里飘出的一阵香气笼罩着她。

"我像吗？"它说。

"Oh, you're real, you're real! Oh, Aslan!" cried Lucy, and both girls flung themselves upon him and covered him with kisses.

"But what does it all mean?" asked Susan when they were somewhat calmer.

"It means," said Aslan, "that though the Witch knew the Deep Magic, there is a magic deeper still which she did not know: Her knowledge goes back only to the dawn of time. But if she could have looked a little further back, into the stillness and the darkness before Time dawned, she would have read there a different incantation. She would have known that when a willing victim who had committed no treachery was killed in a traitor's stead, the Table would crack and Death itself would start working backwards. And now -"

"Oh yes. Now?" said Lucy, jumping up and clapping her hands."Oh, children," said the Lion, "I feel my strength coming

"哦！是真的！阿斯兰是真的！"露西叫着。两个孩子扑上去，把它亲了个遍。

"可这是怎么回事呢？"等大家的心情平静了一些，苏珊问道。

阿斯兰回答："虽然女巫知道深奥的魔法，可她却不知道，有一种更高深的魔法。她的魔法只能追溯到远古时期。可如果她再往前看，就会发现，在远古时期之前，即寂静和黑暗的太古时期，有另外一种咒语——如果祭品并没有背叛，却被当成叛徒处死，那么，石台就会崩裂，祭品就会死而复生。所以，现在——"

"太好了！就是现在吗？"露西拍着手蹦了起来。

"孩子们，"阿斯兰说，"我觉得我的力量完全恢复了。看看你们能不能抓住我！"它站在那里，眼睛闪闪发亮，不停地抖动四

back to me. Oh, children, catch me if you can!" He stood for a second, his eyes very bright, his limbs quivering, lashing himself with his tail. Then he made a leap high over their heads and landed on the other side of the Table. Laughing, though she didn't know why, Lucy scrambled over it to reach him. Aslan leaped again. A mad chase began. Round and round the hill-top he led them, now hopelessly out of their reach, now letting them almost catch his tail, now diving between them, now tossing them in the air with his huge and beautifully velveted paws and catching them again, and now stopping unexpectedly so that all three of them rolled over together in a happy laughing heap of fur and arms and legs. It was such a romp as no one has ever had except in Narnia; and whether it was more like playing with a thunderstorm or playing with a kitten Lucy could never make up her mind. And the funny thing was that when all three finally lay together panting in the sun the girls no longer felt in the least

肢，甩着尾巴。之后，它一跃而起，越过两个孩子的头顶，跳到了石台的另一边。露西大笑起来，虽然她不知道为什么会笑。她爬上石台去抓它，阿斯兰一蹦，随即躲开了。他们就这样在山顶上追逐着嬉戏起来。孩子们不停地追着它跑，它逗着孩子们，一会儿让她们够不着，一会儿又让她们差点抓住尾巴，一会儿从她们中间穿过，一会儿又把她们抛向空中，然后用柔软的大爪子稳稳地接住，一会儿又冷不丁地停下来。三个人嘻嘻哈哈地滚成一团——这样的嬉戏打闹，在纳尼亚可从来没有过。露西也说不好，这更像是和雷雨在玩呢，还是像和小猫咪在玩闹。有趣的是，最后，他们三个躺在太阳底下气喘吁吁的时候，孩子们既不饿又不渴，一点儿都不觉得累。

tired or hungry or thirsty.

"And now," said Aslan presently, "to business. I feel I am going to roar. You had better put your fingers in your ears."

And they did. And Aslan stood up and when he opened his mouth to roar his face became so terrible that they did not dare to look at it. And they saw all the trees in front of him bend before the blast of his roaring as grass bends in a meadow before the wind. Then he said, "We have a long journey to go. You must ride on me."

And he crouched down and the children climbed on to his warm, golden back, and Susan sat first, holding on tightly to his mane and Lucy sat behind holding on tightly to Susan. And with a great heave he rose underneath them and then shot off, faster than any horse could go, down hill and into the thick of the forest.

That ride was perhaps the most wonderful thing that happened to them in Narnia. Have you ever had a gallop on a

"好了，现在——"阿斯兰说，"咱们该干正事了。我要大吼了，你们最好把耳朵堵上。"

孩子们堵上了耳朵，之后，阿斯兰张开嘴大吼着——它的脸变得很恐怖，她们都不敢睁眼看它了。然后，只见它面前的树木在怒吼中全部弯下了腰，就像小草在风中被吹弯了腰一样。随后，它说："我们还有很长一段路要走。来吧，我来驮着你们。"

它蹲了下来，孩子们爬上它温暖的、金色的背。苏珊坐在前面，紧紧地抓住它的鬃毛，露西坐在她身后，紧紧地抱住她。它猛地一起身，站起来飞奔下山，朝着密林跑去，比任何骏马都要快。

这次骑狮子的经历，对于她们来说是在纳尼亚经历的最美妙

horse? Think of that; and then take away the heavy noise of the hoofs and the jingle of the bits and imagine instead the almost noiseless padding of the great paws. Then imagine instead of the black or grey or chestnut back of the horse the soft roughness of golden fur, and the mane flying back in the wind. And then imagine you are going about twice as fast as the fastest racehorse. But this is a mount that doesn't need to be guided and never grows tired. He rushes on and on, never missing his footing, never hesitating, threading his way with perfect skill between tree trunks, jumping over bush and briar and the smaller streams, wading the larger, swimming the largest of all. And you are riding not on a road nor in a park nor even on the downs, but right across Narnia, in spring, down solemn avenues of beech and across sunny glades of oak, through wild orchards of snow-white cherry trees, past roaring waterfalls and mossy rocks and echoing caverns, up windy slopes alight with gorse bushes, and

的事情了。你们骑过快马吗？想象一下，没有了沉重的马蹄声和鞍具的叮当声，取而代之的是悄无声息的奔跑。灰色、黑色或是栗色的马背变成了柔软的金色皮毛，美丽的鬃毛在风中飞舞，速度比赛马还要快两倍。而且，这次骑行既不需要带路，坐骑也不会累。它不停地跑啊跑啊，从来不会失蹄，也从来不会犹豫。它敏捷地穿过树桩，越过灌木丛、石南和小溪，游过大河。而且，这也不是在公园里或者大路上甚至是山丘上骑马，而是骑着狮子横跨整个纳尼亚！在春天里，走过布满山毛榉的林荫小路，穿过橡树中间的太阳地儿，穿过种有雪白樱花树的果园，路过水声轰鸣的瀑布、青苔覆盖的岩石、回声不断的山洞，爬上长满耀眼的金雀花的陡坡，越过石南丛生的山肩，沿着令人眩晕的山脊跑下

across the shoulders of heathery mountains and along giddy ridges and down, down, down again into wild valleys and out into acres of blue flowers.

It was nearly midday when they found themselves looking down a steep hillside at a castle a little toy castle it looked from where they stood which seemed to be all pointed towers. But the Lion was rushing down at such a speed that it grew larger every moment and before they had time even to ask themselves what it was they were already on a level with it. And now it no longer looked like a toy castle but rose frowning in front of them. No face looked over the battlements and the gates were fast shut. And Aslan, not at all slacking his pace, rushed straight as a bullet towards it.

"The Witch's home!" he cried. "Now, children, hold tight."

Next moment the whole world seemed to turn upside down, and the children felt as if they had left their insides behind them;

去，跑进了开阔的山谷，跑进了一片兰花地。

快到中午的时候，他们来到一个陡峭的山坡，俯瞰山下的一座城堡。从他们站的地方看去，城堡小得好像一个玩具，看上去全是尖尖的塔楼。雄狮俯冲下去，城堡在眼前越来越大。她们还来不及问这是那里，就来到了城堡跟前。此刻，城堡看起来已不再像玩具了，而是阴森森地耸立在她们面前。城垛上不见人影，城堡的大门紧紧地关闭着。阿斯兰并没有减速，而是像一颗子弹一样笔直地冲了过去。

“这就是女巫的城堡！”它叫道，“孩子们，抓紧了！”

下一刻，整个世界好像天翻地覆，孩子们只觉得五脏六腑都快翻出来了。阿斯兰使出全力纵身一跃——或者用“飞”来形容

for the Lion had gathered himself together for a greater leap than any he had yet made and jumped or you may call it flying rather than jumping right over the castle wall. The two girls, breathless but unhurt, found themselves tumbling off his back in the middle of a wide stone courtyard full of statues.

更为恰当——狮王飞过了城墙。孩子们没有受伤，却都觉得喘不上气来，她们颤颤悠悠地滑下狮背，站在一个宽阔的石头院子里，这里到处都是石像。

Chapter Sixteen What Happened about the Statues

"What an extraordinary place!" cried Lucy. "All those stone animals -and people too! It's -it's like a museum."

"Hush," said Susan, "Aslan's doing something."

He was indeed. He had bounded up to the stone lion and breathed on him. Then without waiting a moment he whisked round almost as if he had been a cat chasing its tail -and breathed also on the stone dwarf, which (as you remember) was standing a few feet from the lion with his back to it. Then he pounced on a tall stone dryad which stood beyond the dwarf, turned rapidly aside to deal with a stone rabbit on his right, and rushed on to two centaurs. But at that moment Lucy said,

"Oh, Susan! Look! Look at the lion."

I expect you've seen someone put a lighted match to a bit

第十六章 石像的变化

"这是什么地方啊！"露西叫到，"这里到处都是动物石像，还有人像，就像，就像一个博物馆。"

"嘘！"苏珊说，"阿斯兰好像在施魔法。"

它确实在施法。阿斯兰跳到石狮面前，对着石像吹了一口气。紧接着，它急转身，就像猫追着自己的尾巴，对着矮人石像也吹了一口气——如果大家还记得的话，就是那个离着石狮不远、背对着石狮的矮人。然后，阿斯兰又扑向矮人另一边一个高大的石头树精，迅速地转身吹了一下右边的石兔。接着，是两只人马……

这时，只听露西说："苏珊！快看！快看那只狮子。"

我想，大家一定见过用火柴点燃报纸的一角来点引燃整个火

of newspaper which is propped up in a grate against an unlit fire. And for a second nothing seems to have happened; and then you notice a tiny streak of flame creeping along the edge of the newspaper. It was like that now. For a second after Aslan had breathed upon him the stone lion looked just the same. Then a tiny streak of gold began to run along his white marble back then it spread then the colour seemed to lick all over him as the flame licks all over a bit of paper then, while his hindquarters were still obviously stone, the lion shook his mane and all the heavy, stone folds rippled into living hair. Then he opened a great red mouth, warm and living, and gave a prodigious yawn. And now his hind legs had come to life. He lifted one of them and scratched himself. Then, having caught sight of Aslan, he went bounding after him and frisking round him whimpering with delight and jumping up to lick his face.

Of course the children's eyes turned to follow the lion; but

堆的样子：开始的时候，什么都没发生，但紧接着，报纸边缘冒出一丝小小的火焰，逐渐蔓延、扩大。此时的情况正是如此。阿斯兰对着石狮吹了一口气，当时什么都没发生。之后，石狮那白色的大理石背上开始掠过一小缕金色，然后逐渐蔓延开来——就好像报纸被火焰烧起来一样，石狮瞬间变成了金色——尽管它的后腿还是石头。狮子抖了抖鬃毛，沉重的石头上竟然出现了褶皱，变成了栩栩如生的皮毛。然后它张开血盆大口，呼出温暖的气息，打了个大大的哈欠。这时，它的后腿也“活”了过来，它抬起一条后腿搔痒痒。然后，它看见了阿斯兰。这头活过来的石狮跳到阿斯兰身边，在它左右又蹦又跳的，高兴得呜咽起来，并且跳起来舔阿斯兰的脸。

孩子们的目光一直集中在那头狮子身上。然而，当她们看见

the sight they saw was so wonderful that they soon forgot about him. Everywhere the statues were coming to life. The courtyard looked no longer like a museum; it looked more like a zoo. Creatures were running after Aslan and dancing round him till he was almost hidden in the crowd. Instead of all that deadly white the courtyard was now a blaze of colours; glossy chestnut sides of centaurs, indigo horns of unicorns, dazzling plumage of birds, reddy-brown of foxes, dogs and satyrs, yellow stockings and crimson hoods of dwarfs; and the birch-girls in silver, and the beech-girls in fresh, transparent green, and the larch-girls in green so bright that it was almost yellow. And instead of the deadly silence the whole place rang with the sound of happy roarings, brayings, yelpings, barkings, squealings, cooings, neighings, stampings, shouts, hurrahs, songs and laughter.

"Oh!" said Susan in a different tone. "Look! I wonder I mean, is it safe?"

更多神奇的景象之后，很快就把它给忘了——这里的石像都活了过来，院子里看上去不再像是博物馆，而更像是动物园了。所有活过来的生灵都围着阿斯兰高兴地跳着舞，直到它被掩埋在其中。原来惨白的院子，一下子变得五彩缤纷：人马浑身栗色，独角兽的角是靛蓝色，披着绚烂羽毛的鸟儿，红棕色的狐狸，还有大狗和树精，小矮人穿着黄袜子，头戴猩红的帽子，还有一身银装的白桦树姑娘，晶莹碧绿的山毛榉姑娘，还有一身明亮的黄绿色的落叶松姑娘……原来死气沉沉的、一片寂静的院子，如今，到处回荡着欢乐的喧闹声：狮吼、驴叫、犬吠声、鸽子咕咕叫的声音、马儿的嘶鸣声，还有尖叫声、跺脚声、呐喊声、欢呼声、歌声和笑声。

"哦！"苏珊说话的声音都变了，"快看！我不知道——我想说，这安全吗？"

Lucy looked and saw that Aslan had just breathed on the feet of the stone giant.

"It's all right!" shouted Aslan joyously. "Once the feet are put right, all the rest of him will follow."

"That wasn't exactly what I meant," whispered Susan to Lucy. But it was too late to do anything about it now even if Aslan would have listened to her. The change was already creeping up the Giant's legs. Now he was moving his feet. A moment later he lifted his club off his shoulder, rubbed his eyes and said, "Bless me! I must have been asleep. Now! Where's that dratted little Witch that was running about on the ground. Somewhere just by my feet it was." But when everyone had shouted up to him to explain what had really happened, and when the Giant had put his hand to his ear and got them to repeat it all again so that at last he understood, then he bowed down till his head was no further off than the top of a haystack and

露西一看，原来阿斯兰正对着一个石头巨人的脚吹了口气。

"没事的！"阿斯兰兴冲冲地大喊道，"只要双脚恢复过来，身体其余的部分也会跟着好起来的。"

"我不是那个意思，"苏珊悄声对露西说。不过，即便阿斯兰听到她的话，现在说什么都晚了。巨人的双腿已经活了过来，他正在挪动着双脚。过了一会儿，他拿下扛在肩上的那根大棍子，揉了揉眼睛说："天哪！我一定是睡着了。嘿！那个到处跑来跑去的该死的小女巫哪儿去了？她刚才还在我脚边呢。"大伙儿抬头对他大喊着，解释着，告诉他所发生的一切。巨人把手放到耳边，让他们再说一遍。最后，他总算听明白了。接着，他低头深深地鞠了一躬，脑袋低到只有干草堆那么高，还一个劲儿地摸着

touched his cap repeatedly to Aslan, beaming all over his honest ugly face. (Giants of any sort are now so rare in England and so few giants are good-tempered that ten to one you have never seen a giant when his face is beaming. It's a sight well worth looking at.)

"Now for the inside of this house!" said Aslan. "Look alive, everyone. Up stairs and down stairs and in my lady's chamber! Leave no corner unsearched. You never know where some poor prisoner may be concealed."

And into the interior they all rushed and for several minutes the whole of that dark, horrible, fusty old castle echoed with the opening of windows and with everyone's voices crying out at once, "Don't forget the dungeons Give us a hand with this door! Here's another little winding stair Oh! I say. Here's a poor kangaroo. Call Aslan Phew! How it smells in here Look out for trap-doors Up here! There are a whole lot more on the landing!"

帽檐向阿斯兰致敬，笑容堆满了他那张诚实而丑陋的脸（无论哪一种巨人，如今，在英国都难得一见了，好脾气的巨人更是凤毛麟角——你们十有八九都没见过满面笑容的巨人——这情景倒是很值得一看）。

“现在，大家快进屋！”阿斯兰说，“赶快！楼上楼下，包括女巫的房间，每个角落都仔细地搜查。天知道她会把那些可怜的囚犯藏在哪里。”

于是，他们全都冲进了城堡。几分钟过后，整座黑暗、恐怖、发霉的旧城堡的窗户都被打开了，到处都能听见大家的叫喊声：“别忘了还有地牢——帮忙把这扇门打开！这里还有一个蜿蜒的楼梯——哦！这里有一只可怜的袋鼠。快叫阿斯兰过来——啧啧啧！

But the best of all was when Lucy came rushing upstairs shouting out, "Aslan! Aslan! I've found Mr Tumnus. Oh, do come quick."

A moment later Lucy and the little Faun were holding each other by both hands and dancing round and round for joy. The little chap was none the worse for having been a statue and was of course very interested in all she had to tell him.

But at last the ransacking of the Witch's fortress was ended. The whole castle stood empty with every door and window open and the light and the sweet spring air flooding into all the dark and evil places which needed them so badly. The whole crowd of liberated statues surged back into the courtyard. And it was then that someone (Tumnus, I think) first said,

"But how are we going to get out?" for Aslan had got in by a jump and the gates were still locked.

一股什么味儿呀——小心暗门——这里！楼梯的平台上面还有好多石像呢！”不过，这其中最好的发现要数露西了。她冲上楼梯大喊道：“阿斯兰！阿斯兰！我找到图姆努斯先生了！快来呀！”

不一会儿，露西和小羊怪手拉着手，高兴得手舞足蹈，转了一圈又一圈。这个小家伙只是被变成了石像，但没有受伤。他对露西告诉他的一切非常感兴趣。

最后，这场彻底的搜查终于结束了。整座城堡空空如也，所有的门窗都被打开，阳光照亮了所有黑暗和邪恶的地方，到处都可以闻到春天的气息——这个地方简直太需要阳光和新鲜的空气了。一大群重获新生的纳尼亚居民们回到了院子里。

这时，图姆努斯先生第一个开口说话：“可是我们怎么出去呀？”

"That'll be all right," said Aslan; and then, rising on his hind-legs, he bawled up at the Giant. "Hi! You up there," he roared. "What's your name?"

"Giant Rumblebuffin, if it please your honour," said the Giant, once more touching his cap.

"Well then, Giant Rumblebuffin," said Aslan, "just let us out of this, will you?"

"Certainly, your honour. It will be a pleasure," said Giant Rumblebuffin. "Stand well away from the gates, all you little 'uns." Then he strode to the gate himself and bang bang bang went his huge club. The gates creaked at the first blow, cracked at the second, and shivered at the third. Then he tackled the towers on each side of them and after a few minutes of crashing and thudding both the towers and a good bit of the wall on each side went thundering down in a mass of hopeless rubble; and when the dust cleared it was odd, standing in that dry, grim,

大门依旧紧锁着。之前阿斯兰是越过大门跳进来的。

"这个不必担心。"阿斯兰说。它直立后腿，对着巨人大声喊道，"嗨！对，就是你！你叫什么名字？"

"阁下，我是巨人伦波布芬。"巨人摸着帽檐，表示致敬。

"好的，巨人伦波布芬。"阿斯兰说，"你可以让我们从这里出去吗？"

"当然，阁下，乐意效劳。"巨人伦波布芬说，"你们这些小不点儿，都离大门远点儿！"他大步走向大门，抡起手中的大棍子，砰—砰—砰地砸了三下。第一下，大门吱吱作响；第二下，大门裂开了；第三下，大门被砸成了碎片。接着，他又对着大门两边的塔楼又捶又打。不一会儿，两边的塔楼和一部分高墙轰然倒塌，

stony yard, to see through the gap all the grass and waving trees and sparkling streams of the forest, and the blue hills beyond that and beyond them the sky.

"Blowed if I ain't all in a muck sweat," said the Giant, puffing like the largest railway engine. "Comes of being out of condition. I suppose neither of you young ladies has such a thing as a pocket-handkerchee about you?"

"Yes, I have," said Lucy, standing on tip-toes and holding her handkerchief up as far as she could reach.

"Thank you, Missie," said Giant Rumblebuffin, stooping down. Next moment Lucy got rather a fright for she found herself caught up in mid-air between the Giant's finger and thumb. But just as she was getting near his face he suddenly started and then put her gently back on the ground muttering, "Bless me! I've picked up the little girl instead. I beg your pardon, Missie, I thought you was the handkerchee!"

变成一堆碎砖烂瓦。尘土散尽后，站在这个光秃秃、阴森森的石头院子里，可以看见外面森林中的草地，随风摇曳的树木，波光粼粼的小溪，远处的青山和山巅蔚蓝的天空。

“我一身臭汗，脏兮兮的。”巨人说话的声音特别像轰鸣的火车，“这里的条件太差了，我在想，你们这些年轻的小姑娘都没有带手绢吧？”

“我有。”露西说着踮起脚尖，把手绢尽量高高地举起。

“谢谢你，小姑娘，”巨人伦波布芬说着，蹲了下来。接下来，露西被吓了一跳——她被巨人用两个指头捏住，提到了半空中。就在她凑近巨人的脸时，他一惊，赶紧把她轻轻地放在地上，嘴里喃喃道，“我的天哪！我怎么把人家小姑娘拎了起来。实在对不起，我以为你是那块手绢呢！”

"No, no," said Lucy laughing, "here it is!" This time he managed to get it but it was only about the same size to him that a saccharine tablet would be to you, so that when she saw him solemnly rubbing it to and fro across his great red face, she said, "I'm afraid it's not much use to you, Mr Rumblebuffin."

"Not at all. Not at all," said the giant politely. "Never met a nicer handkerchee. So fine, so handy. So I don't know how to describe it."

"What a nicc giant hc is!" said Lucy to Mr Tumnus.

"Oh yes," replied the Faun. "All the Buffins always were. One of the most respected of all the giant families in Narnia. Not very clever, perhaps (I never knew a giant that was), but an old family. With traditions, you know. If he'd been the other sort she'd never have turned him into stone."

"没关系啦，"露西笑着说，"手绢在这儿呢！"这次，他终于拿对了。可是手绢对他来说，就好像糖片对于我们一样——实在太小了。露西看着他一本正经地拿着手绢，在他那又大又红的脸上来回擦着，不由得说，"伦波布芬先生，这块手绢对你来说好像没什么用。"

"哪儿的话，哪儿的话，"巨人礼貌地说，"我从来没用过这么好的手绢，这么精致，这么方便，我都不知道怎么形容好了。"

"他真是个温柔的巨人！"露西对图姆努斯先生说。

"哦，当然了，"羊怪回答，"布芬家族的巨人都是这样的，他们是纳尼亚王国最受人尊敬的巨人家族。他们或许没那么聪明（我从来不知道还有比他们更聪明的巨人），但是，这个家族非常古老，有着自己的传统。他要不是个善良的巨人的话，女巫也不

At this point Aslan clapped his paws together and called for silence.

"Our day's work is not yet over," he said, "and if the Witch is to be finally defeated before bed-time we must find the battle at once."

"And join in, I hope, sir!" added the largest of the Centaurs.

"Of course," said Aslan. "And now! Those who can't keep up that is, children, dwarfs, and small animals must ride on the backs of those who can that is, lions, centaurs, unicorns, horses, giants and eagles. Those who are good with their noses must come in front with us lions to smell out where the battle is. Look lively and sort yourselves."

And with a great deal of bustle and cheering they did. The most pleased of the lot was the other lion who kept running about

会把他变成石头。"

这时，阿斯兰拍了拍爪子，让大家安静下来。

"我们的任务还没有完成。"它说，"现在，必须要找到女巫在哪里和另一队人马打仗，我们今晚就要消灭她。"

"阁下，打仗的话算我一个！"那头最高大的人马说。

"当然了，"阿斯兰说，"那么现在，那些跑得慢的，比如孩子们、矮人们和小动物们，你们要骑在那些跑得快的动物身上，比如狮子、人马、独角兽、骏马、巨人和雄鹰。那些鼻子灵敏的动物，务必要跟着我们狮子一起走在前面，去寻找战场。大家赶紧动起来分组吧。"

所有人欢欣雀跃地分了组。最开心的要数另一只狮子了，它

everywhere pretending to be very busy but really in order to say to everyone he met. "Did you hear what he said? Us Lions. That means him and me. Us Lions. That's what I like about Aslan. No side, no stand-off-ishness. Us Lions. That meant him and me." At least he went on saying this till Aslan had loaded him up with three dwarfs, one dryad, two rabbits, and a hedgehog. That steadied him a bit.

When all were ready (it was a big sheep-dog who actually helped Aslan most in getting them sorted into their proper order) they set out through the gap in the castle wall. At first the lions and dogs went nosing about in all dirctions. But then suddenly one great hound picked up the scent and gave a bay. There was no time lost after that. Soon all the dogs and lions and wolves and other hunting animals were going at full speed with their noses to the ground, and all the others, streaked out for about half a mile behind them, were following as fast as they could.

不停地到处跑来跑去，看上去好像很忙，而实际上，它到处跟别的动物说："你听到它说的了吗？我们狮子，那就是它和我呀！我们狮子！我就是喜欢阿斯兰这一点，从不端架子，也不盛气凌人。我们狮子，就是它和我呀！"它不停地重复这句话，直到阿斯兰把三个矮人、一个树精、两只兔子和一只刺猬放到它背上，它才安静了许多。

一只大牧羊犬帮着阿斯兰整理队伍，大家都准备好了之后，所有动物都冲出了城堡的缺口。开始时，狮子和大狗们四处闻着气味。突然间，一只大猎犬发现了女巫的踪迹，冲着他们叫了几声。不能再耽误时间了，所有的狗、狮子、狼还有那些以狩猎为生的动物们都把鼻子贴近地面闻着，然后全速朝着那个方向跑去。

The noise was like an English fox-hunt only better because every now and then with the music of the hounds was mixed the roar of the other lion and sometimes the far deeper and more awful roar of Aslan himself. Faster and faster they went as the scent became easier and easier to follow. And then, just as they came to the last curve in a narrow, winding valley, Lucy heard above all these noises another noise a different one, which gave her a queer feeling inside. It was a noise of shouts and shrieks and of the clashing of metal against metal.

Then they came out of the narrow valley and at once she saw the reason. There stood Peter and Edmund and all the rest of Aslan's army fighting desperately against the crowd of horrible creatures whom she had seen last night; only now, in the daylight, they looked even stranger and more evil and more deformed. There also seemed to be far more of them. Peter's army which had their backs to her looked terribly few. And

其他动物们在他们身后半英里远的地方紧紧跟着——这就好像是英国人在猎狐狸一样。不过，除了猎狗的叫声，现在还混合着狮子的咆哮，而最低沉、最有震慑力的咆哮声则是来自阿斯兰。气味越来越明显，他们跑得也越来越快。就在他们跑到一条狭长蜿蜒的山谷中最后一个转弯处时，露西听见了另外一种不同的声音——是一种高声的尖叫混合着金属碰撞的声音——这让她有种不好的感觉。

出了那条狭长的山谷，露西立即看见，彼得和埃德蒙正带着阿斯兰剩余的人马和昨晚看见的那群妖魔鬼怪奋战着。虽然现在是白天，可这群鬼怪看上去更加狰狞可怕，而且数量也更多了。而彼得的军队背对着露西，人数少得可怜。战场上到处都是石像，

there werestatues dotted all over the battlefield, so apparently the Witch had been using her wand. But she did not seem to be using it now. She was fighting with her stone knife. It was Peter she was fightin both of them going at it so hard that Lucy could hardly make out what was happening; she only saw the stone knife and Peter's sword flashing so quickly that they looked like three knives and three swords. That pair were in the centre. On each side the line stretched out. Horrible things were happening wherever she looked.

"Off my back, children," shouted Aslan. And they both tumbled off. Then with a roar that shook all Narnia from the western lamp-post to the shores of the eastern sea the great beast flung himself upon the White Witch. Lucy saw her face lifted towards him for one second with an expression of terror and amazement. Then Lion and Witch had rolled over together but with the Witch underneath; and at the same moment all war-like

很明显，这是女巫用魔杖干的好事。可是，她现在手里已经没有了魔杖，正拿着那把石刀和彼得打得难分上下，露西简直看不出来到底是怎么回事。她只能看得见那把石刀和彼得的剑在自己面前眼花缭乱地飞舞着，一时间刀光剑影，看上去好像有三把石刀和三把剑斗作一团。他们俩在战场中央厮杀着，战线向着两边延伸，无论哪一边，都可见无比可怕的情景。

"孩子们，快下来！"阿斯兰吼道。她们滑下狮背，紧接着阿斯兰一声怒吼，震撼了西起灯柱、东到海边的整片纳尼亚大陆，然后，它猛扑向了白女巫。露西看见，当女巫抬起头看着阿斯兰时，一瞬间脸上露出了恐惧混着惊讶的表情。接着，狮子和女巫滚作一团，女巫被压在了下面。此刻，阿斯兰从女巫城堡里带来

creatures whom Aslan had led from the Witch's house rushed madly on the enemy lines, dwarfs with their battleaxes, dogs with teeth, the Giant with his club (and his feet also crushed dozens of the foe), unicorns with their horns, centaurs with swords and hoofs. And Peter's tired army cheered, and the newcomers roared, and the enemy squealed and gibbered till the wood re-echoed with the din of that onset.

的所有动物也同时怒吼着加入了战斗。矮人举起了斧子，猎犬龇出獠牙，巨人抡起了棍子，还用脚踩死了好多敌人，独角兽刺出尖角，人马亮出宝剑和马蹄。彼得率领的那支累得不行的军队瞬间士气大振。新加入战斗的动物们怒吼着冲向叽里呱啦乱叫的敌人，一时间，树林里杀声震天。

CHAPTER SEVENTEEN THE HUNTING OF THE WHITE STAG

The battle was all over a few minutes after their arrival. Most of the enemy had been killed in the first charge of Aslan and his companions; and when those who were still living saw that the Witch was dead they either gave themselves up or took to flight. The next thing that Lucy knew was that Peter and Aslan were shaking hands. It was strange to her to see Peter looking as he looked now his face was so pale and stern and he seemed so much older.

"It was all Edmund's doing, Aslan," Peter was saying. "We'd have been beaten if it hadn't been for him. The Witch was turning our troops into stone right and left. But nothing would stop him. He fought his way through three ogres to where she was just turning one of your leopards into a statue. And when

第十七章 追逐白鹿

随着他们的到来，这场战斗片刻间就结束了。实际上，在阿斯兰和它的队伍发起第一次冲锋时，大部分的敌人就已经被消灭掉了。而活着的那些在看见白女巫死了之后，不是投降了就是逃跑了。之后，露西注意到，彼得和阿斯兰在握手。她觉得这时的彼得看上去很怪，他的脸色苍白，神情坚毅，感觉成熟了很多。

"这都是埃德蒙的功劳，阿斯兰。"彼得说，"要不是他，我们早就被打垮了。女巫把我们的军队都变成了石头，可什么也挡不住她。就在女巫把你的一只美洲豹变成石头时，埃德蒙一路打倒了三个食人魔来到她面前，他很理智，并没有直接向她进攻，而

he reached her he had sense to bring his sword smashing down on her wand instead of trying to go for her directly and simply getting made a statue himself for his pains. That was the mistake all the rest were making. Once her wand was broken we began to have some chance if we hadn't lost so many already. He was terribly wounded. We must go and see him."

They found Edmund in charge of Mrs Beaver a little way back from the fighting line. He was covered with blood, his mouth was open, and his face a nasty green colour.

"Quick, Lucy," said Aslan.

And then, almost for the first time, Lucy remembered the precious cordial that had been given her for a Christmas present. Her hands trembled so much that she could hardly undo the stopper, but she managed it in the end and poured a few drops into her brother's mouth.

"There are other people wounded," said Aslan while she

是用剑一下子打断了女巫的魔杖，这样一来，她就再也没法施展把人变成石头的魔法了，其他所有人正是犯了这个错误。要不然我们不会损失这么惨重。她的魔杖一断，局势立刻就有转机了。可是埃德蒙伤得很严重，我们必须去看看他。"

埃德蒙就在离战场不远的后方，海狸太太正在照顾他。他浑身上下都是血，张着嘴，脸上泛着可怕的绿光。

"露西，快！"阿斯兰说。

露西这才想起自己得到的那个神奇的圣诞礼物——那瓶灵丹妙药。她颤抖着双手，试图打开瓶塞。最后，她终于打开了，在她哥哥嘴里滴了几滴药。

"我们还有很多其他的伤员，"阿斯兰说。可露西还是一脸焦

was still looking eagerly into Edmund's pale face and wondering if the cordial would have any result.

"Yes, I know," said Lucy crossly. "Wait a minute."

"Daughter of Eve," said Aslan in a graver voice, "others also are at the point of death. Must more people die for Edmund?"

"I'm sorry, Aslan," said Lucy, getting up and going with him. And for the next half-hour they were busy she attending to the wounded while he restored those who had been turned into stone. When at last she was free to come back to Edmund she found him standing on his feet and not only healed of his wounds but looking better than she had seen him look oh, for ages; in fact ever since his first term at that horrid school which was where he had begun to go wrong. He had become his real old self again and could look you in the face. And there on the field of battle Aslan made him a knight.

急地看着埃德蒙那张苍白的脸，也不知道这个药管不管用。

"我知道，"露西不耐烦地说，"等一下。"

"夏娃之女，"阿斯兰的声音一下子严肃起来，"其他伤员也处在生死关头。你想让更多人因为埃德蒙而丧命吗？"

"阿斯兰，实在抱歉。"露西说着，起身跟着它离开。在接下来的半个小时里，他们忙得不可开交。露西忙着照顾伤员，阿斯兰忙着把变成石像的动物再变回原样。最后，她终于有空抽身回到埃德蒙那里，发现他站在那里，不但伤口痊愈了，整个人看上去也更精神了。实际上，自从上了那个讨厌的学校，他从第一个学期就变坏了。可如今，他又恢复了本来面貌，敢直视别人的双眼了。于是，就在战场上，阿斯兰封他为骑士。

"Does he know," whispered Lucy to Susan, "what Aslan did for him? Does he know what the arrangement with the Witch really was?"

"Hush! No. Of course not," said Susan.

"Oughtn't he to be told?" said Lucy.

"Oh, surely not," said Susan. "It would be too awful for him. Think how you'd feel if you were he."

"All the same I think he ought to know," said Lucy. But at that moment they were interrupted.

That night they slept where they were. How Aslan provided food for them all I don't know; but somehow or other they found themselves all sitting down on the grass to a fine high tea at about eight o'clock. Next day they began marching eastward down the side of the great river. And the next day after that, at about teatime, they actually reached the mouth. The castle of Cair Paravel on its little hill towered up above them; before them

"他知道吗？"露西小声对苏珊说，"他知道阿斯兰为他做了什么吗？他知道阿斯兰和女巫之间的真正交易吗？"

"嘘！他当然不知道。"苏珊说。

"难道不应该告诉他吗？"露西问。

"千万不要，"苏珊说，"那样对他来说实在太可怕了。想一想，如果你是他，你会怎么想？"

"尽管如此，我觉得还是要告诉他。"露西说。可就在这时，她们之间的对话被打断了。

当晚，他们就地扎营。我也不知道阿斯兰从哪里找来的食物，不过，晚上八点的时候，大家都坐在草地上，美美地吃了一顿茶点。第二天，他们沿着那条大河朝着东边行进。第三天，快到下

were the sands, with rocks and little pools of salt water, and seaweed, and the smell of the sea and long miles of bluish-green waves breaking for ever and ever on the beach. And oh, the cry of the sea-gulls! Have you heard it? Can you remember?

That evening after tea the four children all managed to get down to the beach again and get their shoes and stockings off and feel the sand between their toes. But next day was more solemn. For then, in the Great Hall of Cair Paravel that wonderful hall with the ivory roof and the west wall hung with peacock's feathers and the eastern door which looks towards the sea, in the presence of all their friends and to the sound of trumpets, Aslan solemnly crowned them and led them to the four thrones amid deafening shouts of, "Long Live King Peter! Long Live Queen Susan! Long Live King Edmund! Long Live Queen Lucy!"

午茶的时候，他们到达了入海口。凯尔·帕拉维尔城堡高高地矗立在面前的小山上。他们的前方是沙滩、岩石、小小的咸水坑，迎面可以闻到海草和大海的气息。青绿色的海水不断地拍打着岸边。听！还有海鸥的叫声！你们听过海鸥的叫声吗？还记得吗？

那天傍晚，喝过茶之后，四个孩子再次来到海边，脱掉鞋袜，光着脚在海边玩耍。不过，到了第二天，大家就严肃了许多。凯尔·帕拉维尔城堡的大厅上方镶嵌着精美的象牙屋顶，西面的墙上插满了孔雀的羽毛，东面的那扇门直通大海。在这个华美的大厅里，号角声齐鸣，阿斯兰当着所有朋友的面，庄严地为孩子们加冕，带着他们走上了四个王座。在它的带领下，所有人大喊着："彼得国王万岁！苏珊女王万岁！埃德蒙国王万岁！露西女王万岁！"

"Once a king or queen in Narnia, always a king or queen. Bear it well, Sons of Adam! Bear it well, Daughters of Eve!" said Aslan.

And through the eastern door, which was wide open, came the voices of the mermen and the mermaids swimming close to the shore and singing in honour of their new Kings and Queens.

So the children sat on their thrones and sceptres were put into their hands and they gave rewards and honours to all their friends, to Tumnus the Faun, and to the Beavers, and Giant Rumblebuffin, to the leopards, and the good centaurs, and the good dwarfs, and to the lion. And that night there was a great feast in Cair Paravel, and revelry and dancing, and gold flashed and wine flowed, and answering to the music inside, but stranger, sweeter, and more piercing, came the music of the sea people.

But amidst all these rejoicings Aslan himself quietly slipped

"在纳尼亚，一朝为王，终身为王。亚当之子，夏娃之女，请谨记！"阿斯兰说。

与此同时，从敞开的东边大门外，传来了雄性人鱼和雌性人鱼美妙的歌声。他们缓缓游向岸边，放声歌唱，向纳尼亚的新国王和女王致敬。

孩子们坐在王座上，手持权杖，为所有人犒赏庆功，包括羊怪图姆努斯、海狸夫妇、巨人伦波布芬、美洲豹、善良的人马、矮人以及狮子。那晚，城堡里举行了盛大的宴会，大家纵情狂欢，到处都是金光闪闪，美酒汩汩，与城堡里的音乐相呼应的是海上传来的更奇妙、更甜美、更动人心弦的仙乐。

可是，在欢庆中，阿斯兰悄悄溜走了。两个国王和两个女王

away. And when the Kings and Queens noticed that he wasn't there they said nothing about it. For Mr Beaver had warned them, "He'll be coming and going," he had said. "One day you'll see him and another you won't. He doesn't like being tied down and of course he has other countries to attend to. It's quite all right. He'll often drop in. Only you mustn't press him. He's wild, you know. Not like a tame lion."

And now, as you see, this story is nearly (but not quite) at an end. These two Kings and two Queens governed Narnia well, and long and happy was their reign. At first much of their time was spent in seeking out the remnants of the White Witch's army and destroying them, and indeed for a long time there would be news of evil things lurking in the wilder parts of the forest a haunting here and a killing there, a glimpse of a werewolf one month and a rumour of a hag the next. But in the end all that foul brood was stamped out. And they made good laws and kept the

注意到了，却也没说什么。因为海狸先生曾对他们说过："它来去自由。今天你看见了它，明天它却消失了。它不喜欢束缚，而且，它还有其他的王国需要操心。没关系的，它会常常来。只是你们不能逼它。你们知道，它不是一头被驯化的狮子，而是一头真正的野兽。"

故事讲到这里，也就快结束了。两个国王和两个女王就这样开始治理纳尼亚。在他们的统治下，在这里生活的子民们生活得很快乐。当然，最开始的时候，他们把大部分时间都花在搜寻白女巫残余的手下并消灭他们上。确实，长时间以来，一直有作恶多端的坏蛋游荡在森林的偏僻地带，到处扰乱治安，滥杀无辜。这个月有人看见一只狼人，下个月又有传闻说母夜叉出现了。不

peace and saved good trees from being unnecessarily cut down, and liberated young dwarfs and young satyrs from being sent to school, and generally stopped busybodies and interferers and encouraged ordinary people who wanted to live and let live. And they drove back the fierce giants (quite a different sort from Giant Rumblebuffin) on the north of Narnia when these ventured across the frontier. And they entered into friendship and alliance with countries beyond the sea and paid them visits of state and received visits of state from them. And they themselves grew and changed as the years passed over them. And Peter became a tall and deep-chested man and a great warrior, and he was called King Peter the Magnificent. And Susan grew into a tall and gracious woman with black hair that fell almost to her feet and the kings of the countries beyond the sea began to send ambassadors asking for her hand in marriage. And she was called Susan the Gentle. Edmund was a graver and quieter man than Peter, and great in council and

过到头来，所有的祸害都被消灭殆尽了。此外，他们还制定法律，维护治安，保护那些善良的树木不会被滥砍滥伐，不让年幼的矮人和树精被迫上学，严禁乱传谣言，鼓励愿意安居乐业的普通子民安定下来。他们还击退了进犯纳尼亚北部边境的凶猛巨人——当然，这些是坏巨人，和伦波布芬可不一样。同时，他们还和海外的一些国家结成友好联盟，时不时地去其他国家访问，同时也接待对方的回访。随着时间的流逝，孩子们都长大成人了。彼得长成了一个身材高大，胸脯厚实的男子。他是一名英勇的战士，大家都称他为“彼得大帝”；苏珊长成了一名身材颀长，举止文雅的女子，一头乌黑亮丽的头发垂到脚踝——海那边的很多国家都纷纷派来大使，希望可以和她联姻，大家都称她为“温柔女王苏

judgement. He was called King Edmund the Just. But as for Lucy, she was always gay and golden-haired, and all princes in those parts desired her to be their Queen, and her own people called her Queen Lucy the Valiant.

So they lived in great joy and if ever they remembered their life in this world it was only as one remembers a dream. And one year it fell out that Tumnus (who was a middle-aged Faun by now and beginning to be stout) came down river and brought them news that the White Stag had once more appeared in his parts the White Stag who would give you wishes if you caught him. So thcsc two Kings and two Queens with the principal members of their court, rode a-hunting with horns and hounds in the Western Woods to follow the White Stag. And they had not hunted long before they had a sight of him. And he led them a great pace over rough and smooth and through thick and thin, till the horses of all the courtiers were tired out and these four

珊”；埃德蒙和彼得比起来，更加的严肃和沉默，非常善于主持会议和审判，大家都叫他“公正之王埃德蒙”；至于露西，她长着满头金发，一直过得无忧无虑，那一带的王子们都想娶她为王后，大家都叫她“英勇女王露西”。

于是，他们就这样开开心心地生活着，曾经在人类世界的记忆，对于他们来说就像一场梦。很多年过去了，图姆努斯先生已经变成了一只胖胖的中年羊怪。有一年，羊怪顺河而下，给他们带来口信说，白鹿又在这一带出现了——只要你抓住了白鹿，它就可以实现你的愿望。随即，两位国王和两位女王偕同大臣们，带着号角和猎犬，骑着马往西边的树林里去追逐白鹿。刚进树林不久，他们就发现了白鹿的身影。白鹿带着他们飞快地越过崇山峻岭，穿过时

were still following. And they saw the stag enter into a thicket where their horses could not follow. Then said King Peter (for they talked in quite a different style now, having been Kings and Queens for so long), “Fair Consorts, let us now alight from our horses and follow this beast into the thicket; for in all my days I never hunted a nobler quarry.”

“Sir,” said the others, “even so let us do.”

So they alighted and tied their horses to trees and went on into the thick wood on foot. And as soon as they had entered it Queen Susan said,

“Fair friends, here is a great marvel, for I seem to see a tree of iron.”

“Madam,” said,King Edmund, “if you look well upon it you shall see it is a pillar of iron with a lantern set on the top thereof.”

“By the Lion’s Mane, a strange device,” said King Peter, “to

而浓密、时而稀疏的树林，到最后，所有大臣的坐骑都累得跑不动了，可他们四个还是穷追不舍。最后，他们看见白鹿钻进了一片灌木丛，骑着马根本进不去。这时，国王彼得说：“各位皇弟皇妹，咱们下马，随那只白鹿进入灌木丛。我还从来没猎过这么高贵的猎物。”他们在朝执政已经多年，说话的方式全都变了。

“皇兄，”其他人说，“既然如此，我们走吧。”

他们飞身下马，把马拴在树上，徒步向密林走去。他们刚刚走进树林，苏珊女王说：“陛下们，我好像看见了一颗神奇的铁树。”

“皇姐，”国王埃德蒙说，“如果你仔细看，会发现那是一根铁柱，它的上面还有一盏灯。”

“哦！阿斯兰保佑，这真是个神奇的物件。”国王彼得说，“周围树木这么密集，在这里竖起一盏灯，还放得那么高，怎么能照

set a lantern here where the trees cluster so thick about it and so high above it that if it were lit it should give light to no man!"

"Sir," said Queen Lucy. "By likelihood when this post and this lamp were set here there were smaller trees in the place, or fewer, or none. For this is a young wood and the iron post is old." And they stood looking upon it. Then said King Edmund,

"I know not how it is, but this lamp on the post worketh upon me strangely. It runs in my mind that I have seen the like before; as it were in a dream, or in the dream of a dream."

"Sir," answered they all, "it is even so with us also."

"And more," said Queen Lucy, "for it will not go out of my mind that if we pass this post and lantern either we shall find strange adventures or else some great change of our fortunes."

"Madam," said King Edmund, "the like foreboding stirreth in my heart also."

见人呢！”

“皇兄，”露西女王说，“很有可能，这盏灯和这根铁柱立在这里的时候，周围都是小树苗，或者基本没有树。毕竟，这里的树木很新，而这根铁柱很旧。”于是，他们都站在那里看着铁柱。

这时，国王埃德蒙说：“虽然我不知道是怎么回事，可是，铁柱上的这盏灯让我觉得很奇怪。似乎记忆当中我在哪里见过，或者是在梦里见过。”

“陛下，我们也有同样的感觉。”其他人说。

“而且，还有，”露西女王说，“我脑中一直有一种挥之不去的想法，如果我们越过这个柱子和这盏灯，就会有奇遇发生。甚至，我们的命运会发生非常大的变化。”

“皇妹，”国王埃德蒙说，“我心中也有类似的预感。”

"And in mine, fair brother," said King Peter.

"And in mine too," said Queen Susan. "Wherefore by my counsel we shall lightly return to our horses and follow this White Stag no further."

"Madam," said King Peter, "therein I pray thee to have me excused. For never since we four were Kings and Queens in Narnia have we set our hands to any high matter, as battles, quests, feats of arms, acts of justice, and the like, and then given over; but always what we have taken in hand, the same we have achieved."

"Sister," said Queen Lucy, "my royal brother speaks rightly. And it seems to me we should be shamed if for any fearing or foreboding we turned back from following so noble a beast as now we have in chase."

"And so say I," said King Edmund. "And I have such desire to find the signification of this thing that I would not by my good will turn back for the richest jewel in all Narnia and all the islands."

"Then in the name of Aslan," said Queen Susan, "if ye will all have it so, let us go on and take the adventure that shall

"皇弟皇妹，我也一样。"国王彼得说。

"我也是，"苏珊女王说，"依我所见，我们还是回到拴马的地方，不要再继续追逐白鹿了。"

"皇妹，"国王彼得说，"请你原谅，自从我们在纳尼亚登基以来，无论何种大事，诸如战争、审判、比武、执法，从来不会半途而废。我们向来都是一旦着手，就会完成。"

"皇姐，"露西女王说，"皇兄说得很对。在我看来，如果是出于恐惧或预感就不再追逐那头高贵的野兽，未免有些丢脸。"

"我很同意，"国王埃德蒙说，"我非常想找到这只珍奇的野兽，哪怕用纳尼亚最珍贵的珠宝和所有的岛屿来交换，我也绝不回头。"

"以阿斯兰的名义，"苏珊女王说，"如果你们都这么认为，那我们就去探险吧——无论遇到什么，都要坦然面对。"

fall to us."

So these Kings and Queens entered the thicket, and before they had gone a score of paces they all remembered that the thing they had seen was called a lamp-post, and before they had gone twenty more they noticed that they were. making their way not through branches but through coats. And next moment they all came tumbling out of a wardrobe door into the empty room, and They were no longer Kings and Queens in their hunting array but just Peter, Susan, Edmund and Lucy in their old clothes. It was the same day and the same hour of the day on which they had all gone into the wardrobe to hide. Mrs Macready and the visitors were still talking in the passage; but luckily they never came into the empty room and so the children weren't caught.

And that would have been the very end of the story if it hadn't been that they felt they really must explain to the Professor why four of the coats out of his wardrobe were missing. And the Professor, who was a very remarkable man, didn't tell them not to be silly or not to tell lies, but believed the

两个国王和两个女王走进了灌木丛。刚走几步，他们都想起来，刚才看到的那根柱子叫灯柱。再走了不到二十步，他们发现，自己不是在树枝之间往前走，而是在大衣堆里找路。下一刻，他们全都从衣橱里滚到了那间空屋子里，而且，他们不再是穿着一身狩猎装的国王和女王们，而是穿着过去的衣服的彼得、苏珊、埃德蒙和露西。时间还是那一天——也就是他们躲进衣橱的那个时刻——麦克雷迪太太正在过道里和游客们说话。幸运的是，他们没进这间空屋子，孩子们没被他们发现。

要不是他们觉得必须要和教授解释一下，为什么衣橱里少了四件大衣，故事到这里本该结束了。而教授呢，也是个非常了不起的人。他并没有教训他们不要胡言乱语，不要说谎，而是相信了整个故事。"不，"他说，"不要再通过衣橱回到纳尼亚拿回那几

whole story. "No," he said, "I don't think it will be any good trying to go back through the wardrobe door to get the coats. You won't get into Narnia again by that route. Nor would the coats be much use by now if you did! Eh? What's that? Yes, of course you'll get back to Narnia again some day. Once a King in Narnia, always a King in Narnia. But don't go trying to use the same route twice.Indeed, don't try to get there at all. It'll happen when you're not looking for it. And don't talk too much about it even among yourselves. And don't mention it to anyone else unless you find that they've had adventures of the same sort themselves. What's that? How will you know? Oh, you'll know all right. Odd things they say even their looks will let the secret out. Keep your eyes open. Bless me, what do they teach them at these schools?"

And that is the very end of the adventure of the wardrobe. But if the Professor was right it was only the beginning of the adventures of Narnia.

件衣服了，这对你们没什么好处。你们也不要再从原路返回纳尼亚了。再说，把那几件大衣拿回来也没什么用。当然了，总有一天，你们会回到纳尼亚。因为‘一朝为王，终身为王’。不过，你们不要再走同一条路了。说真的，不要想方设法地去那儿了。你们不去找它，它自然就会出现。而且，即便是你们之间也不要过多地谈论此事，更不要和别人讲起，除非那个人之前也经历过。什么？你们怎么会知道？哦，你们到时候准会知道。碰上这样的怪事，他们的话语，甚至是神情都会露出马脚。你们只要留心就好。我的天哪，现在的学校都教些什么呀？”

好了，衣橱中的探险就这样结束了。不过，如果教授说的都是真的，那么，纳尼亚的探险才刚刚开始。